PRAISE FOR

MW01242467

"*Letters in Time* is like a wonderful meal with a delicious balance of engaging characters (both sweet and bitter), a fascinating peek at history, a captivating community, and a slow-burning romance for dessert."

— Donna K. Weaver, *USA TODAY* Best-Selling Author

"Once more, one of my favorite authors, Susan Reiss, has crafted a story that keeps the reader guessing. *Letters in Time* reflects the author's creativity and ability to write 'outside the box'. She writes about enduring love. She delves into old mysteries that affect the present. Can't wait to read the next book!"

— Amazon Review

"It has a perfect way to draw you into the story, then adds mysterious twists and turns, then pulls at your heartstrings and leaves you with satisfaction in two important ways, yet leaves a couple stones unturned to follow in the book of Letters #2. This story includes some history of the Civil War which intertwines with the wonderful 'Emma' story that's so well written. There's not a ghost of a chance that you won't love this first memorable book of the series, it's the best I have read from this author."

— Goodreads Review

"The ending is perfect - not what you might want at first, but something that leaves you with hope and could not have been improved in any way. Wonderful."

— Amazon Review

"A new-to-me author and the blurb drew me in to give this book a chance and boy, am I glad I did."

"This book was a joy ride. It included a romantic fictional plot, some supernatural elements, and a reasonable mystery to boot. Ms. Reiss kept me away from the mindless TV drivel for almost three days since I found the book difficult to put down."

"Enjoyable story with some supernatural overtones. This is the first book in a new series. If you enjoy historical fiction with mystery and a bit of the supernatural, this book would be a great choice. Well written, the story flows nicely. Characters are developed. Recommended."

Enchanting mystery that blends historical fiction with modern day mystery. I could not put this book down and am so excited to see that this will be an ongoing series. Purchase this and put aside a couple of hours to yourself. You will not be sorry. I loved this book!

Delightfully different! This book was different than the mysteries I tend to usually read. It very cleverly blends a current day story with a historical paranormal twist that was quite touching.

PRAISE FOR ST. MICHAELS SILVER MYSTERYSERIES

"Susan Reiss captures the magic, mystery, and charm of that quintessential Eastern Shore town – St. Michaels. Secrets lay hidden for generations among the stunningly beautiful estates along the Miles River. Can't wait for her next book!"

— Kathy Harig, Proprietor
Mystery Loves Company Bookstore
Oxford, Maryland

"Susan Reiss will transport you to the Eastern Shore of Maryland but will remind you of whatever town has a special place in your heart. It leaves me wondering what other secrets this quaint little Eastern Shore town is hiding and I'm waiting for Susan to tell us."

— Barbara Viniar, Retired President
Chesapeake College, Maryland

"This is a series that captures the local flavor of our town of St. Michaels, including the history, food, and the quirky characters who live here. The descriptions of all the real places make me feel like I'm there. The mysteries keep me turning the page. This is a series I recommend to my library patrons... and to you."

— Shauna Beulah, Branch Manager, St. Michaels Library

"Loved how the book (*Tarnished* Silver) ended in an uplifting way, and I can't wait to see what happens to the characters next as the author made me care about them. A truly enjoyable read and I will happily read any future books in this series."

— Goodreads Review

"A diabolical mystery, which could easily be a made-for-TV movie."

"Reading Susan Reiss's fourth installation to her Silver Mystery series, *Hammered Silver*, was a thrill. It has been on my "gotta read list" for the past year. Greatly enjoyed Susan's first three books. Love character Abby Strickland's sterling silver tidbits as well as her curiosities in solving mysteries. And yes, I look forward to reading *Foiled Silver*, her fifth book! Keep 'em coming!"

"(In *Painted Silver*), I thoroughly enjoyed learning about the intricacies of what the artists are looking for, and how important, as well fleeting, the light is. Now I'd like to go to such a festival to see it for myself."

Reading Susan Reiss's fourth installation to her Silver Mystery series, *HAMMERED SILVER*, was a thrill.

[*Deathly Silver*] Great quick read! Loved the characters and the story was fast-paced with plenty of twists to keep me guessing. A welcome addition to the series, though it can be read as a stand-alone.

BOOKS BY SUSAN REISS

IN TIME SERIES

Letters in Time
Diaries in Time

ST. MICHAELS SILVER MYSTERIES

Tarnished Silver
Sacred Silver
Painted Silver
Hammered Silver
Foiled Silver
Deathly Silver, Novella

HISTORICAL FICTION

The Dream Dies

The Butler's Guide to Fine Silver
with Mr. Hollister

Diaries
IN TIME

BOOK TWO

SUSAN REISS

INK & IMAGINATION PRESS
an imprint of Blue Lily Publishers

ISBN: 978-1-949876-60-4

Cover and Interior Design by Rachael Ritchey, RR Publishing

Website: www.SusanReiss.com
Instagram: SusanReissAuthor
Twitter: @SusanReiss
Bookbub: Susn Reiss
Goodreads: SusanReiss, Goodreads Author
Facebook: Susan Reiss Author

Dedicated to
Christina Jones

A woman with an energetic
outlook on life, filled with happiness,
excitement, and
a love of things with a history
that is contagious!
Thank you for all your work and inspiration, Chris!

CHAPTER ONE

"The dark clouds of trials and sorrows are over our beloved country, and who can escape the shadow, even if sheltered from the bursting storm?"

— From *Godey's Lady's Book* 1862

A low growl of thunder like an angry beast sent a warning into the night. I looked out a window and saw the edges of dense clouds galloping across the sky overhead, pulling a veil to obscure the starlight. But there was little to fear. Usually, when a storm moved from the west, the Chesapeake Bay would break it apart or fling it to the north. The Bay kept it away from the Eastern Shore, making it a sanctuary for boats and people. To me, it meant safety, discovery, and adventure since I was a little girl.

But tonight, the storm's deep rumble was building, adding layer upon layer of sound, giving voice to its fury. This storm had overwhelmed the forces of the largest bay of salty water in the hemisphere. And it was getting closer. This storm was coming to Waterwood Plantation, the Cottage, and me.

White-hot bolts of energy crackled through the night sky. The explosions they triggered sent jarring vibrations through my body, reminding me of Civil War cannons firing into the night. And that brought up thoughts of Daniel and Emma and the cabin where his desk now stood.

In the lightning flashes, I could see the wind had torn a tree limb off its trunk. A splintered lightning fork stabbed the earth. The Cottage shook. The lights flickered and went out. That strike was close. I'd have to check the cabin in the morning.

Then the rain came in a furious downpour that pelted the glass. Driven back from the window, I inched my way across the floor in the dark. The last thing I needed was to trip over something. My leg, mangled in an accident months earlier, was better, but, in my mind, I couldn't chance even a stubbed toe.

Keeerrrack! Boom! The storm's symphony went on and on. I'd had enough. I wanted it to stop. Lightning flashed white hot, and its sound slammed like a fist coming down on the Cottage. I ran, launched myself into the bed, and pulled the covers over my head. I knew I was being foolish. The Cottage had weathered storms for more than a hundred years!

Yes, but I'll never get to sleep with all this racket. I'll never get to sleep. I'll never...

Rays of sunlight warmed my face. It was morning. The storm was over.

The storm! The lightning strike! The cabin!

Quickly, I scrambled out of bed and into a pair of clean sweats and a hoodie. At the top of the stairs, I forced myself to hold the banister and step carefully. *Easy does it.* A fall would ruin everything.

Safely on the main floor, I slipped my feet into my rubber moccasins, went outside, and skidded to a stop. After the nighttime uproar and fireworks, Mother Nature had created a breathtaking morning. The tall pines sparkled with diamond raindrops in the sunlight. Birds greeted me with a lively symphony of song. Not just one bird, but a forestful of those who had not yet flown south. There were Blue Jay squawks and Chickadee chirps plus the voices of those who had come for the winter: robin trills, crow caws, and Canada goose honks. And over it all was the cloudless sky of an achingly gorgeous blue. But it was the air that impressed me the most. Scrubbed clean by the storm, the air was as Mother Nature had intended it to be in the beginning.

You don't get clean air like this in the big city, I thought as I drew in a deep breath and then scurried down the path toward the cabin. But the thick mud and deep puddles made it slow-going, giving my brain plenty of time to concoct all kinds of nightmares for the cabin. I half-expected the wind gust had carried away the roof, or the lightning strike had left only a burned-out shell. Or…

I came around a bend in the path and saw the cabin was safe, nestled in a grove of crepe myrtle and wild grasses, as it had always been. Relieved, I took the key from its hidey place and opened the door.

From the outside, all appeared intact, but inside, a tempest had struck. I looked to the old plantation desk. Daniel's desk. Thankfully, it was not damaged, but sheets of white paper I'd left on its writing surface were strewn everywhere, as if someone had thrown an almighty tantrum. It was a sight I'd hoped never to see.

Months earlier, on the day I arrived at the Cottage, the antique desk was discovered in the garage. I had the movers set it up in the den and an extraordinary adventure began. A letter addressed to Emma by a man named Daniel appeared on the desk. I thought it was written to me until I looked at it carefully.

His letter was dated 1862 and this was the 21st century. Daniel wasn't writing to me. He wanted to contact his true love, Emma. Our only connection was that we shared the same name. In a moment of silliness or boredom, I'd responded. It launched our correspondence. Daniel's desperation and loneliness made me want to help. I figured anything was possible since I was corresponding with a ghost.

We went through many harrowing moments complicated by a murder. Two, actually. Then, thinking that Daniel had reunited with his Emma, this cabin was built to shelter the desk. If all was well, I assumed he would never leave another letter on the desk.

Now this! Papers scattered everywhere, as if flung into the air in a fit of rage. Had Emma failed to join him? Was this another betrayal in his life, one that had finally broken his heart and ignited eternal grief and fury? Would an angry ghost now haunt the Cottage? I jumped when I heard footsteps.

"There you are." The deep male voice sounded relieved. It was TJ, the tall, muscular local farmer in his thirties who was hired to watch over the Cottage and me. Dressed in clean jeans and a pale green shirt that brought out his eyes, he walked into the cabin with a large yellow lab at his feet that was so light he looked white. That was why he'd named the dog Ghost.

"I thought the cabin... whoa!" Looking around and seeing the mess, he realized what it probably meant. "Did Daniel...?"

I turned away, fighting tears of disappointment. "I'm sorry," I murmured as he put his arms around me.

He didn't say a word. What could he say? The evidence was all around us. We'd failed to reunite the lovers of old. After all the research I'd done to uncover their true connection... and discovering the identity of the man who'd torn them apart. After learning of a rich treasure rumored to be life-changing...and the terrifying confrontation at the Lone Oak. After TJ rebuilt the cabin ... we were left with disappointment and rage.

"I'm sorry," I mumbled as I turned and looked up at TJ.

"It's okay." He pulled out a cloth handkerchief from the back pocket of his jeans. "Time to dry your tears and let me see what happened here."

"Isn't it obvious? I-I-I failed them," I sputtered.

"Sh-h-h, we don't know that yet." He went around the small cabin interior, collecting the papers flung everywhere. "Didn't you say that if our efforts to reunite Emma and Daniel failed, he would write a scathing letter about betrayal and being abandoned?"

I nodded.

TJ held up a fistful of white sheets to me. "Emma, every one of these pages is blank."

I took the papers and inspected them. It was true. "Maybe his words have already faded?"

"You have been checking the cabin several times a day over these past weeks. There hasn't been a hint of a problem."

I was surprised. "How did you know..."

"Because you're not the only one who wants them to be happy. I've been anxious to know if we succeeded. I haven't found any evidence of correspondence from Daniel either. I don't think Daniel did this. He isn't a vengeful ghost, thank goodness. If we were going to have a ghostly encounter, we were lucky it wasn't with a creepy, vindictive spirit."

He gestured to one of the cubbyholes of the massive desk. "If Daniel wanted to send you a message, he probably would have shredded the butterfly you made."

I followed his gaze to the origami crimson butterfly I'd folded for the lovers to symbolize a soul set free and a bond of love meant to last forever. It sat untouched where I'd left it.

"Stop worrying, please. I think we succeeded," TJ said softly. "I don't think Daniel made this mess. I think the storm..." He paused, his hazel-green eyes slowly inspecting the ceiling, the door, the ... "There's your culprit." He pointed to a broken pane in the window overlooking the creek and the Lone Oak tree. He looked outside. "Yes, there's a branch on the ground out there. Probably broke off and hit the window in the storm."

TJ was ever optimistic, and I decided to follow his lead. It was much better than the alternative. I folded his handkerchief and stuck it in my pocket. "I'll put this through the wash."

"OH! I almost forgot." He reached into his shirt pocket. "I wanted to check on the cabin and to show these to you, two letters I found last night in the box of family history my Aunt Louisa put together." He handed me the small envelopes, discolored with age. The heavily canceled one-cent stamps dated in the 1860s. "They're addressed to Emma Collins, Daniel's Emma after her marriage, right?"

"Yes," I said, all disappointment gone. "This is exciting."

He pointed to one of the envelopes. "You need to look at that one."

I eagerly took out the letter and unfolded it.

"See the notation there?" He pointed to the bottom of a page. "Do you think Emma wrote it?"

The words that looked as if written by a different person were squeezed into the only blank space left on the paper. It read:

Which is worse ~ to live without the man you love as I do or to live with your beloved, a man who many revile and despise.

I tapped my index finger against my lips, thinking. "Yes, I think Emma might have written those extra words since the letter was addressed to her, but what did she mean?"

TJ smiled. "I suspect you have a new research project, and you'll find out."

CHAPTER TWO

"Come, and whisper in my ear which of your sisters you
love the best."

— From *Godey's Lady's Book*, 1863 v. 66

I now believed we'd laid Daniel to rest, so to speak, since no
new letters had appeared on the plantation desk. I guessed
Emma would remain a mystery. I guessed wrong.

Since TJ's discovery of these old letters, Emma's presence
had risen in my mind as vividly as if she were standing in front
of me.

"I'll see what I can find out," I told TJ. "If you'll take me to
the Talbot County Free Library's Maryland Room." I resisted
the temptation to bat my eyelashes. "Please."

"I can take you tomorrow after your physical therapy
appointment in Easton." His kindness made me smile, a
considerate man with a confident, self-assured manner.

"Thank you!" I said, meaning it.

The plan was perfect. I'd have time to photograph the letters, transcribe them, and do a little online research now that I had internet service at Uncle Jack's Cottage.

I should probably stop thinking of my home here as Uncle Jack's Cottage. I'd spent almost every summer here since the time I was knee-high to a blue heron, as Uncle Jack liked to say. After I graduated from college and settled in Philadelphia, I should have come down to see him more often, but there was always something else to do. After the divorce, I threw myself into my work as a kindergarten teacher and earned a master's degree. Then a truck jumped the highway divider and smashed into my car. Everyone said it was a miracle I'd survived the accident. Somehow, I'd found the courage to endure the surgeries and months in a rehabilitation facility.

Uncle Jack came to visit me once when my spirits needed lifting. He gave me the courage to keep fighting. I didn't notice how frail he'd become. Whenever I see lilies now, I think of him and the last bouquet he placed beside my bed. It wasn't long after that he quietly passed away. Only my mother was surprised that he'd left the Cottage to me. He knew Mom would have sold it, but I would cherish the place of my summer memories. I chose to move to his Cottage, under the supervision of doctors and physical therapists here on the Shore, instead of Philadelphia.

Thinking of my upcoming visit with the librarian, I sat in Uncle Jack's recliner that evening and pulled the reading lamp closer. I slipped one of the antique letters from its envelope. The ink had faded from a strong India black to a rusty brown. The handwriting was ornate but if I read slowly, I could find my way through the loops and flourishes and antiquated language.

The letter was written to Emma—Daniel's love—our Emma, who had been the daughter and mistress of Waterwood Plantation. She'd lived her entire life at Waterwood House, now owned and occupied by her descendant, Thomas Jefferson Wood, known as TJ. It was amazing that the house was still in the family after more than 160 years. Though chunks of land had been sold off, it was still an impressive property.

The letter began:

Miles Bend House
December 4, 1861

Dear Emma,

I hope you are faring well. I find this brutal winter weather intolerable. The ferocious wind drives the icy temperatures through my heaviest wool clothes like a knife. You might think I am exaggerating, but I feel the cold most keenly. It is surprising that this is the case for I assure you the quality of the material I wear is of the highest quality. I have had to order a new wool cloak to protect me. I believe the expenditure is valid for it would not be to anyone's advantage for me to fall ill or worse. My only fear is that it will be so heavy, I will sink into the snow not to be seen again until spring.

But I write not to exchange complaints about the weather. I beg for your help. I fear Lottie, my dear sister, has lost her mind. Does she not realize that her support of the Union endangers her own prosperity and way of life? I am gratified that her husband resigned from the federal military, but must he continue to work on its behalf? Can she not reason with him? Her actions are causing great consternation and animosity within our family. Tensions are running high.

I beg you to write to her. Perhaps she will listen to you. She holds you in high regard. Remind her that her loyalty is to our family.

In gratitude, your dear friend,
Minnie

History talks of the Civil War causing fractures within families. I was holding evidence of it. It would be fascinating to identify this *Minnie* and find out more about her. She must have been Emma's close friend to write such a heartfelt letter. I remembered the notation that Emma had added to the other letter and took it out to reread. Maybe there was a clue in the letter itself. I began to read.

Safe Harbor House
January 4, 1862

Dear Emma,

I hope this letter finds you well after the Christmas & New Year's celebrations. I cannot believe the weather we have had to endure these last several weeks. I must say that the brutal wind drives the icy temperatures inside my bones. I do not want to leave the confines of the kitchen and the comfort of the fire. It has been a godsend to have dear Henry here to help shoulder the responsibilities of the estate in these challenging times.

I am not certain which is the most difficult: the challenges from Mother Nature or the shortages and worry caused by the war. There are also the silent or obscure slights that are whispered about my dear Henry.

After serving in the United States Army with distinction for so many years, this War Between the States, as they call it, is pulling families apart, destroying lifelong friendships, and breaking down ways we used to depend upon to feed our families and maintain our land holdings.

It breaks my heart to see the toll it is taken on my dear husband. The way he was reviled at the family gathering for Christmas dinner was troubling. There was no direct confrontation, but the atmosphere was noxious. Don't they understand his heart is broken by this conflict that pits brother against brother? He retired because he could not find the resolve to raise a gun against our neighbors and friends who side with the South. It is a most disheartening and frightening situation. Why can't the family understand and respect Henry's beliefs?

What will happen to our social connections with friends and family? Whatever will happen to our way of life?

I did not intend for this letter to fall into the depths of despair. Please write to me of your holiday time and I shall share with you recent events and chatter.

Your Loving and Most Loyal Friend

Lottie

Oh, why didn't these women sign their last names? It would have made my life so much easier. I looked at the cryptic comment we believe was written by Emma.

Which is worse ~ to live without the man you love as I do or to live with your beloved, a man who many revile and despise.

The next day, after my physical therapy session, TJ dropped me off at the library in Easton. It felt strange to walk into the Maryland Room, home of so much Talbot County history. Strange, because the library intern Stephani who had helped me learn about Daniel and Waterwood was now in jail awaiting trial on all kinds of charges. I was a naïve idiot to trust her. I'd been lucky to get away with my life.

Now, I could work with the true research librarian, Charles Tompkins. As I entered, I had plenty of time to observe the man standing at the desk at the far end of this rare book room. He was a little on the short side and achingly thin, as if he lived off knowledge, not food. Hearing my footsteps in the quiet, he stood and walked toward me. I noticed a small white towel hanging from his belt that reminded me of one used by many quarterbacks to wipe their hands before they handled the ball. I had to hide my smile at the thought of Charles *quarterbacking* the research done here.

When I introduced myself, he scowled. I was sure he'd heard the story involving his library intern and how my request for research information had led to dangerous events and revelations. He hesitated as if he didn't want to involve himself with me, but after a long moment, he gestured for me to sit at one of the library tables in the center of the room. "And how may I help you today?"

"Two letters have come to my attention." I reached into my tote, took out the letters each nestled safely inside a baggie, and held them out to him. "I'd like to see if we can trace the letter writers and any other information connected with them."

He wiped his fingers on the white towel, took the plastic bags, and examined everything he could see through the plastic. Then he reached into his pockets for the tools of his trade. From the back pocket of his dress pants came a pair of white cotton gloves and, from his shirt pocket, he pulled a pair of long tweezers. When he was ready, he pulled the envelope from one baggie then extracted one of the letters from its envelope as carefully as a surgeon. I sat quietly, afraid to move. Afraid to ask any of the dozen questions roaring in my head. Afraid any interruption might break his concentration.

After what felt like an hour, he put the letter down on the library table and looked at me. "This letter is quite interesting because it mentions tensions at family gatherings."

"I tried to read it and made some guesses when the handwriting wasn't legible." I shook my head. "Shouldn't the writer have written clearly to be sure the recipient could read it?"

Charles settled back. "They had to consider several factors. There was the availability of paper, for example. It wasn't as…"

Charles' words melted into the background as I thought back to the first from Daniel. He was apologizing. He'd had no paper.

I refocused on what Charles was saying. "…and having a stamp was a challenge sometimes. In truth, these letters are easy to read once you understand how they were written. Many people wrote in the margins and even across words they'd already written. To make it easier to read, they wrote in a different direction, say perpendicular to their first words."

"We're fortunate that much of our communicating uses technology today," I said.

"That is an advantage, but if your letter writer had access to technology in the 19th century," he held up the letter. "We might not have this today. May I ask how you came into possession of these documents?"

"They belong to a friend who wants to learn about the sender and recipient who had a connection to his family," I explained. "His roots are here in Talbot County."

"I see," he said, nodding slowly. "That is quite interesting." He began to fold the letter to return it to its envelope.

I reached out to stop him. "Would you look at one more thing and give me your opinion?"

He lowered his head a bit. "Of course, if I can."

Now that I'd observed his precautions and gentle way he handled the letter, I didn't want to touch it with my bare fingers again. "Would you look at the notation on that one side? It stands out from the rest of the writing and begins with the words, *Which is worse*."

He located the notation on the paper crammed with writing and read it. "Yes, it strikes me as introspective and melancholic. What is your question?"

"Do you think the person who made that notation also wrote the letter?" I asked, then held my breath.

"It would be most unusual for the letter writer to make such a notation separately, one that is not part of the body of the letter." He looked closer. "No, I don't think the same person wrote that comment. Notice the slant of the letters and the differences in the coils and twists around the capitalized letters." He leaned back in the wooden chair. "In my humble opinion, and I'm no expert, this notation was not written by the letter writer, but perhaps by this Mrs. Joshua Collins, the addressee."

He was talking about Emma.

I glanced quickly around the empty reference room. "If you have another moment, could you help identify the women who wrote these letters? They only wrote their first names."

His forehead tightened and his eyes narrowed in intense concentration. "That, I'm afraid, is going to be a challenge. I'm afraid the closing signature of *Your Loving and Loyal Friend* tells us almost nothing. We have a number of letters captured on microfilm from that period that I could arrange for you to see for comparison." His face filled with hope. "Of course, it might make it infinitely easier if your friend has other letters we could compare. It's entirely possible that the *loving and loyal* friend wrote more often to this Emma Collins. Another letter might have a name and we could compare the handwriting and the quality of the letter paper and…" His voice and enthusiasm trailed off as I slowly shook my head.

"These are the only letters my friend has been able to find."

The librarian heaved a deep sigh. "May I suggest that your friend keep looking, because, without additional documentation or clues, I'm afraid that it will be difficult to identify the letter writer."

I expected him to fold the letter and put it back in the envelope, but he looked at the first page again. His lips moved silently. Something had caught his eye that may have opened another pathway to identity of the writer. I was bursting to ask what he was thinking, but I forced myself to stay quiet. Finally, he put the letter down on the library table and rose from his chair.

"Maybe," he murmured to himself. "Just maybe…"

CHAPTER THREE

"As Christmas Eve dawned, a storm from the northwest pushed out the mild weather of the week before. Ladies in crinolines headed through the blustery cold in wraps and capes."

             – *Baltimore Sun Newspaper*, Christmas, 1861

Charles, the research librarian, retreated through the doorway leading to the Staff-Only stacks. It must have been his private world of research materials.

While I waited patiently, I glanced around the room and noticed a young woman sitting at a desk in an alcove. She was small. No, delicately petite. Except for her wild head of shiny coal-black curls. She raised her chin and our eyes met.

"I'm so sorry," I said. "I hope our talking hasn't disturbed you. I didn't even know you were there."

She shook her head and her curls danced. "Oh no, you're fine," she insisted. "I can usually block out distractions, except out there." She pointed through the glass to the main library area outside the Maryland Room. "I just can't deal with all the commotion out there."

I looked and was impressed how quiet it seemed out there with people hunched over their keyboards or quietly turning pages of a book or magazine. Oh well, each to his… or her own.

"I've seen you in here before," she mused. "You were working with that intern, right?"

A shudder ran through me as I thought of Stephani. A woman I trusted. A woman who betrayed me. A woman who almost killed me. I took a deep breath, forcing away the memory. "Yes, but now I'm working with Charles and it's much better."

"Everyone was shocked about what happened. She always looked so put-together. Perfect hair, perfect nails. And her clothes… I wish I had the time and money to put together a wardrobe like hers."

I was eager to change the subject. "What keeps you busy?"

Her shoulders slumped as she put her hand on a thick open book. "I'm in real estate."

"Oh, you're an agent?"

"Not an agent," she corrected me. "Not yet. My name is Catherine, but my friends call me Cookie. I'm here studying for the state real estate exam."

"Oh, are you taking it soon?"

Cookie shook her head. "I already took it, but I'm sure I failed. I'm starting the review now so I'm better prepared when I have to take the test again."

How well I knew that sinking feeling of failure after taking an important test. I was always sure I'd fallen short. Then, my soon-to-be husband was always sure I'd exceeded professors' expectations. He was right. I was the only one surprised that I graduated from college with honors. I was wrong not only about my success, but about him. I failed to see what a rat he'd turn out to be.

"Speaking from experience, Cookie," I said with a wink. "You should wait until you get the results before you react. You strike me as the type of person who is committed to success." I looked around the lonely study area. "Not everybody would plant themselves in these spartan surroundings to study. I bet you did just fine. When do you find out?"

"Anytime now." She straightened up in her chair. "I know this is what I want to do. I've seen the business up close. I work as an assistant to a very successful agent here in town."

"Oh, then you must know …" As I mentally scrambled for the name of Ms. Real Estate in the county, I noticed that the young woman took in a quick breath and held it.

"Do you know Belle?" Her voice was pitched high from strain.

I shook my head, wondering why she was panicking.

"If you see her, please don't say that you met me or that I'm studying for my license!" she squeaked. "Please, you have to promise."

I held up my hands to calm her. "It's okay, I'm not going to tell anybody anything."

Her body sagged with relief. She swallowed and spoke again in a more normal voice. "Thank you. I want it to be a surprise. She is so talented, really knows what she's doing. I've been lucky to work for her for almost two years. I've learned so much. I know she can teach me how to be a really successful agent." She twisted the small diamond ring on her left hand. "And that's really important because Billy and I are getting married soon.

"That's wonderful. Congratulations."

In a small voice, she thanked me. "Yes, it's very exciting. We have plans, big plans. We wanted to have a nice wedding, but my dad's gone and my mom doesn't have a lot of resources so we're paying for the wedding ourselves."

I frowned a little, wanting to sympathize. "Oh dear, that could be a financial drain."

"It could be, but we're being careful." She continued in a small voice. "If Belle finds out I took the test already, I don't know what she'd do." Her face tensed, realizing what she'd just said was not complimentary. "Don't get me wrong. She's taught me so much about being a professional woman and a successful agent. I want to work *with* her rather than *for* her. And speaking of work, I need to go." She stood and gathered up her things.

"That's a worthy goal," I said with a broad smile. "Your secret is safe with me."

As Charles walked back from the stacks, my new friend mouthed the words *thank you* and headed out the door of the Maryland Room. I was about to turn my attention to Charles when something caught my eye about the young woman. It was her shoes. The heels were very high. She probably picked them because she was short and wanted to appear taller. The other thing that caught my eye were the soles on the bottom of the shoes. They were bright red, the signature of a big-time fashion designer.

But this was not the time to dwell on shoes. Charles was motioning me to a file cabinet with very narrow drawers. I hustled over and he handed me one long file folder, then another.

"It's often worthwhile to wander through these files for information." He opened one, then with a gentle shake of his head, returned it to its place in the drawer. "But today, we're looking for something specific." He opened another file, shook his head again, returned the folder and closed the drawer.

I was worried that his efforts had led to a dead-end, but he hadn't given up yet. He went to his desk and pulled a thick binder from a row of others and began to flip through sections, then pages. It boggled my mind to think of how much work was done to get so organized. He ran a finger down one list and stopped. A smile of triumph spread across his face. "It may be nothing. Or something. At the top of the letter, above the date, she wrote Safe Harbor House, correct?"

"Yes, that's right," I confirmed. "Is that a place in the area?"

"I think it is. It was traditional to name the houses and estates rather than try to use house numbers and street names like they do in cities. The name Safe Harbor is fairly innocuous, but it is on my list. Let's see what we can find."

He scurried, as much as a reference librarian might, from his desk back to the room marked *Staff Only*. I tried to be patient, but soon found myself pacing. Would he find the house? Was it here on the Shore? Was the letter written by the owner of the house or a visitor? So many questions. So close to the truth that could slip into disappointment.

After what felt like ages, Charles emerged from the inner sanctum, his thin, wispy black hair with some graying strands floated around his head like an ethereal crown. "I found something, but I'm not sure..." His words dwindled as he moved to a nearby library table. "We can only look at what we have and hope that it leads us to the answers we want."

I was heartened by his use of the pronoun, *we,* and felt confident that this librarian didn't have a hidden agenda linked to treasure.

"Yes, here it is," he announced with exuberance. "Safe Harbor House. Owned by Henry Graham." Then his face fell. "I'm afraid that's all we have, at least in this file."

I reached for the single piece of paper and saw he was right. The information rated its own folder, but the single line on the page gave me almost nothing to go on. "Do you have anything—"

"Charles." A woman spoke from behind me, her voice was like nails dragging across a chalkboard. "You haven't forgotten our appointment, have you?"

I turned to see what I could only describe as an old biddy. Her hair was dyed the color of wet brown mud though it should be gray to go with the many lines etched on her face. She gave me a smile that was so cold I felt the chill from across the room. With a sigh, I realized that my research session had ended.

"Thank you so much, Charles, for your help," I said quickly. "I'll try to follow the breadcrumbs you've unearthed." I took off the cotton gloves he'd given me to use and handed them back.

He held up his hand. "No, no, you keep them. I suspect you'll continue the search. When you come across more letters and things, you should wear them to protect any items you find."

"Thank you so much." I tucked the gloves into my tote.

"You will be back, won't you?" He asked me.

"Yes, and soon. Thank you again for your help."

"Thank you," he said with emphasis, "For the puzzle. I love looking into mysteries."

I grabbed my things and sped by the woman who watched me leave, her head held high with disapproval. I failed to hide my smirk.

CHAPTER FOUR

"Children of the same family, the same blood, with the same first associations and habits, have some means of enjoyment in their power, which no subsequent connections can supply."

– Jane Austen

As TJ drove us down the road toward home, I rattled on and on about what little I'd found out about the antique letters. Knowing the letter was addressed to Emma—our Emma—was important and intriguing. The fact that it was written at the Safe Harbor House on January 4, 1862, was an important clue. But I was no closer to identifying the writer or her relationship to Emma.

"Charles, the reference librarian, said you need to look for more letters. They might hold valuable clues." Seeing him roll his eyes, I hurried on. "TJ, this is important. Look, I know you're busy. I know you're still harvesting and—"

Ghost, stretched out on the back seat, groaned as TJ ran down his work list. "Like billing for the custom farming services, bringing the books up to date, setting the schedule for the rest of the month and into the next…"

"And making repairs to Waterwood," I added

The interruption snagged his attention. "Yes, that's right. I have a lot of repairs to make to my house. At least I'm getting some help there. But just because it's fall—"

"I get it," I said with gentle kindness. "You don't have time to look for some old, dusty letters. But I can help you." I touched the sleeve of his Oxford-cloth shirt. He was never one to wear a T-shirt like many other farmers. "I have oodles of time. I could go through the materials your aunt put together, maybe even find a trunk of Emma's things in the attic and—"

"Whoa!" He held his hands off the steering wheel for a moment. "I thought we were talking about a few letters, not all of Aunt Louisa's finds."

"I meant to ask you about her name." Early on, he'd explained how named babies after famous, accomplished people to inspire them to do something with their lives. His name, TJ, was short for Thomas Jefferson. "Who was Aunt Louisa named after?"

"Okay, if you really want to know. She was named after Louisa May Alcott," he said.

"The author of *Little Women* and other beloved books?" It gave me a warm feeling that she was named after a woman who was so attuned to the feelings of girls and women.

"That's right." TJ cocked his head and smiled. "The author was also a nurse during the Civil War, probably why Aunt Louisa has always had an active interest in Waterwood. She is like the family historian."

"I'd love to see what she's collected." Mentally, I kept my fingers crossed that he wouldn't turn me down.

"There is a box where she keeps everything she's found of Emma's so far."

I tried to hide my excitement. "You mean, she has collected other things?"

He sighed. "There are some things. She kept saying she was coming back to continue the hunt, but she can't come right now."

"So, I can help you *and* her ... if you'll let me in the house to look." The thought of Emma's letters, maybe even a diary, lying in a 19th century dresser drawer or an antique trunk was so electrifying that I wanted to race up to Waterwood House at that moment.

"Emma, you know I'm working on the house. It's a mess right now. I have repairs to do and ... When it's in better shape, you'll be the first person I invite—"

"That could be ages." I was whining. How embarrassing. But I really wanted access. I took a deep breath and began again without so much emotion. "I don't care what the house looks like, I mean I do..." I was getting tongue-tied.

"I don't think this is a good idea right now," TJ concluded.

"But you're letting other people in the house," I countered.

"Come on, Emma. They're contractors. They repair things. They're supposed to see the place at its worst."

I sat back in my seat, put my hands primly in my lap, and modulated my voice so there was no trace of impatience. "It's sweet that you care what I think. I appreciate that, but this is really all your fault." His head whipped around, a look of surprise on his face. "TJ, you're the one who gave me this new research project."

Realizing I was right, he bent his head back and mumbled, "Me and my..."

"No, you did a good thing," I insisted, as I turned toward him in my seat as far as the seat belt would allow. "You triggered my imagination and got me interested in something other than my healing body and utter boredom. It's all good. Please, may I do this?"

He grabbed a quick glance at me. "Okay, but only if you promise we can go slow. I mean, I value things that are part of my family's history, but it's overwhelming and —"

I nodded quickly. "We can move slowly. I won't do anything without your okay. You're in charge, I promise."

His face relaxed. "Okay, I'm going to trust you."

As I settled back in my seat, it occurred to me that he was quick to ask me to trust him, but slow to put his trust in others. I wondered why, but now I was on the quest for lost items. "You said there is a box of things? When can I come and look at it?"

He took a deep breath and sat up with his shoulders back. His energy was flowing again. "Yes, there is a box. You can come tomorrow, but—" He held up an index finger like he was about to lecture an errant student. "You have to promise you will only go where I tell you. No wandering all over the house."

I held up three fingers in salute. "I promise." I hoped I hadn't mentioned I flunked out of Girl Scouts with poor cookie sales. I knew that where there was two letters, there may be more. Maybe even a diary!

When we pulled up to the Cottage, I jumped out of the truck so he couldn't change his mind. The growl of tires on our main gravel road caught my attention. A huge black SUV roared up the driveway to the Cottage. As it moved past the fields of cornstalks, it reminded me of a yacht cruising on the nearby Miles River.

"Who is that?" I asked TJ.

"I'm not sure," he said slowly. When the vehicle pulled up and the driver's side window buzzed down, a groan escaped his lips.

"Hey, you two!' A pert strawberry blonde called out as she opened the door, slipped out of the driver's seat, and hung suspended in mid-air for a second as her feet felt for the ground. The SUV was obviously too big for her petite body, but something in her attitude suggested she wouldn't even consider a smaller vehicle. I glimpsed a little crystal angel swinging wildly from her rearview mirror, sending out rainbows of light. "I'm glad I caught you both. You must be Emma, the new owner of this adorable cottage."

She walked right up to me, flashing a 10,000-watt smile, and stuck out a navy-blue business card. "I'm Belle Howard, award-winning agent with *The* Realty Company."

I was almost tongue-tied. "How do you know--?"

"Oh, you'd be surprised what I know." She tapped her index finger against her nose then pointed at me. Her smile became a know-it-all grin.

Did she know about Daniel? I gave myself a mental shake. Of course, she didn't know about him unless… I glanced at TJ who was in the process of taking off his ball cap and smoothing his hair down with his other hand. It was a nervous habit he showed when he felt awkward. And I could see why. This attractive woman had turned on the charm and kicked into flirt mode without missing a beat.

"I want to talk to you both, …" Belle continued with a little pout. "But every time I've come by, you haven't been home." Her eyes drilled into me, as if it was my fault.

TJ jumped in to defuse the tension. "What brought you here today, Belle?"

"To find out if she's ready to sell, of course." She turned on her electrifying smile again.

I shouldn't have been surprised. Interest in property close to Washington, D.C., Baltimore, and Philadelphia was skyrocketing. Now that staff and employers had learned they could work remotely and be productive, there was a move to leave the cities and their long commutes behind. People wanted small communities where people knew their neighbors.

I could understand the attraction, but a kindergarten teacher had to be with her class. Soon, my rehabilitation would be done, and I would be discharged to go back to work in a classroom, back to my normal life. Or I could stay here on the Shore. Soon, I'd have to make a decision. Soon, but not yet. I wasn't ready to make a choice.

I announced, "I can tell you I'm not selling and probably will hold on to this property for many years to come." I mentally brushed away this woman and turned to go inside when her next words stopped me.

"TJ, are you getting ready to sell?" Belle had pinned him. "My sister tells me you're doing some work on that big, beautiful house of yours."

I retraced my steps. I wasn't going anywhere until I knew what he intended to do. Was he thinking of selling Waterwood, his family's plantation home that dated back to well before the Civil War? Was he giving up the acres that he loved to farm? He hadn't breathed a word of this to me. Was this the reason he was so reluctant to have me look for letters at Waterwood House?

Belle meowed like a kitten. "You wouldn't do that without contacting me for the listing, would you, TJ?"

The real estate agent prattled on while I locked my eyes on TJ. The question must have been scrawled all over my face because he looked at me and frowned with an unspoken question of his own. *What?*

The agent caught our silent exchange and said in dismay, "Wait? Oh, no!" She brought her hands over her heart. "TJ, you didn't!"

"Didn't what?" TJ said, fumbling to catch up.

Belle put her hands on her hips. "Collaborate with your neighbor here to list your property with another agent!" Belle stamped her high-heeled shoe on the ground. "TJ, how could you?"

He took a step back and held up his hands in self-defense. "Whoa there, lady. You should know better than to think I'd sell Waterwood."

I turned away so they couldn't see my eyes gazing heavenward in gratitude and relief.

Belle heaved a dramatic sigh. "Well, I am certainly pleased to hear that you're not working with someone else." Then she turned indignant, as if chastising a child. "I'd hate to think you could betray me." But then a slow smile spread over her lips. "But TJ, what about letting go of some of your acreage? I could get you a nice price so you could really fix up the house."

"Nope, land is more important than the house. He touched the brim of his hat. "And now, I have to go. Nice seeing you, Belle. Miss Emma." He escaped to his truck.

I wasn't so lucky. She wasn't done with me. "Emma, I need *you* to solve a puzzle for me. Let me get the papers out of my car. Won't take a minute."

She touched a button on her key fob and the hatch of her SUV rose with great solemnity as if granting access to the Inner Sanctum. She returned with a rolled-up chart. "Could we talk inside?"

"I'm sorry, Belle. I'm in the middle of something and only have a few minutes," I lied.

A little perturbed, she took the rubber band off the rolled-up chart and spread it across the hood of her car. "Hold down those corners," she instructed. "Be careful, it might be a little hot."

I looked closer and realized the chart was a land map of Waterwood. She was serious about trying to sell TJ's land.

She began her pitch. "This area is perfect for a new development, so I pulled the land records."

"Maybe you should have this conversation with TJ. I—"

"Oh no, my question is for you. Look here." She pointed to a spot on the map but pulled her finger back for a close inspection of her nail. "Hmm, the polish is cracking already. It's not supposed to do that." She looked up at me. "Ignore my manicure. I'll get it fixed later." She pointed back to the Waterwood Plantation boundaries using her perfectly manicured middle finger. "This is Waterwood." Then she moved her finger. "This little piece of land is your cottage."

"It's tiny in comparison to Waterwood," I said.

"Yes, but, look closely. Your land isn't very big, but it is symmetrical and completely surrounded by Waterwood, as if it was carved out on purpose. It has its own deed, as you know." Her finger stabbed the paper. "Why would someone do that? Do you know? You can tell me. I'm very good at keeping secrets."

"No," I began. "I don't know why it's separate like that." *And if I did, I don't think I'd tell you.* I lifted my head and looked out at the cornfields beyond the towering pine trees that I'd grown to love and wanted to protect. I looked at the real estate plat again. The creek on the other side of the Cottage formed the fourth boundary of my property. The land on the other side of the creek where the Lone Oak grew belonged to Waterwood and TJ.

"It does seem odd. I'm sorry, Belle. I have no idea why it was split off and deeded separately." I shrugged my shoulders, hoping to hide how much the question intrigued me. "I guess you can check your land records or something."

"I'll have to dig deeper to satisfy my curiosity." That little smile danced at the corners of her mouth again. "Maybe I'll talk to TJ about it." She began folding up the large map. "He must know since it was cut out of his family's land-holding. It's probably part of his family's lore." She raised her eyes to meet mine. "Maybe you don't know because he didn't want to tell *you.*"

I suspected that by emphasizing the word *you,* she was trying to drive a wedge between TJ and me. I froze my expression. I wasn't going to let her know that her little ploy had hit the mark.

I turned toward the Cottage. "Well, if you find out, let me know."

And that was the last time I talked to Belle, but not the last I saw her alive.

CHAPTER FIVE

"...we're twins, and so we love each other more than other people..."

— Louisa May Alcott, *Little Men*

I worried all night. Was Belle really encouraging TJ to sell Waterwood, even part of it? TJ could do whatever he wanted, but no buyer would want to leave the small parcel known as the Cottage in someone else's hands. I'd said I wouldn't sell. My little slice was mine. If I didn't want to sell, I didn't have to. I shook off my concern and went to sleep.

The next morning, excitement woke me very early. TJ had agreed that I could see the contents of Aunt Louisa's box at ten o'clock. The dusty work ahead called for jeans and a sweatshirt. And I needed time to walk up to the main house. Even if I had a car at the Cottage, I had no intention of sliding behind a steering wheel, not now, maybe not ever. I knew that probably wasn't a rational plan, but I was holding tight to it for now. Driving meant freedom, of course. But after the near-fatal accident with the truck and using a Jeep Wrangler as a battering ram on a starlit night, I'd had my fill of driving for a long time, thank you.

Before leaving for Waterwood House, I poked my nose outside and quickly closed the door again. It was typical on the Shore that the incoming season did not slam us with cold temperatures all at once. It teased us. One day, it was Indian Summer with mildly warm temperatures and the next, the growing autumn chill reminded us that winter was coming.

I rummaged through the coat closet by the door and found one of Uncle Jack's old oilskin jackets. It had a warm lining to keep out the nip in the air. The waterproofed fabric would protect me if those gray clouds overhead dropped any precipitation. Slipping it on, I felt engulfed by the material, but enfolded by Uncle Jack. He hadn't been an especially large man, but he was always a tower of strength and an oasis of calm for me especially when life got choppy. Though I missed him terribly, I'd found some comfort that I was here in the Cottage now.

Okay, I ordered myself. *No time for tears. You wanted a treasure hunt. TJ agreed. You'd better get going.*

I pulled my blonde hair back in a ponytail and ruffled my bangs so they laid down as they should. I set off to face the elements and look for clues to the mystery.

I soon spied a stand of stately maples that must have turned overnight from lush green to a blaze of ruby and scarlet colors. The leaves fluttered on the branches until they released their grip and exploded into a cascade of reds to cover the rich brown earth below. There were always amazing sights – big and small – to see here on the Shore if one just took the time to notice.

After a fifteen-minute walk, I arrived at the front door of Waterwood House, which faced the water, and raised the door knocker. It was a black cast iron ring with enough detail and form to give it character. My knocks on the door competed with the bongs of the grandfather clock in the foyer chiming the hour. The front door swung open with a creak. TJ hadn't taken the oil can to the hinges yet. He'd been too busy taking care of the countless things that demanded his attention when caring for an old house and a growing farm business.

"Hi," I said too brightly. I had to act calm, as if what I was about to do was not a big deal.

"And right on time," he said as the clock finished its announcement of the hour.

"I came around to the front door as you requested." I held out my arms, swamped by Uncle Jack's coat. "See, I'm willing to cooperate."

He didn't say a word. He just looked at me. His forehead formed deep furrows and his eyes squinted in disapproval.

Don't send me away. Please don't send me away.

"Where in the world did you find that coat? Is that the latest style in Philadelphia?" He barely smothered a laugh.

I thought of all the attractive jackets, raincoats, coats, ponchos, and capes I'd packed away at my condo to make room for my renter's things when I sublet it. I normally took pride in what I wore. I didn't want to sound defensive now. With an embarrassed giggle, I said, "It's Shore style, perfect for the sudden changes in the weather." As if on cue, the heavy gray clouds pulled the plug and released their load.

He grabbed my arm. "You'd better come inside."

TJ closed the front door of Waterwood House with me inside. It was the main entry used by many generations of TJ's family. The foyer was as I remembered it. The large room was lit by a huge crystal chandelier and several wall sconces. Large oil paintings in heavy gilt frames lined the walls of the wide staircase leading to the next level.

"I'll be right back. Stay there," TJ said and headed off to the interior of the house.

"I promise, I'll stay right here." I turned to the portrait of Emma, the daughter and later mistress of Waterwood from the mid to late 1800s. She wore a soft blush-pink gown, its sleeves full at the shoulder then gathered tightly at the elbow. Her eyes were the color of the deep blue waters of the Chesapeake on a sunny day. Her flaxen hair was drawn up softly under a straw hat that gave her flawless pale complexion some protection from the sun. The hint of a soft smile on her lips suggested she had found contentment and peace.

This portrait of a glowing Emma was remarkable for it was in stark contrast to a family portrait that included her husband and young children painted earlier, when she was locked in an unhappy marriage to Joshua. Its toll showed on her worn face and listless posture. She must have ached over the difference between her marriage and the true love she'd shared with Daniel. If only I could hear the story from her point of view. Somehow, I'd felt a connection with her from the first moment I realized that we shared first names.

"Hey there." The words were as smooth as honey, spoken in a warm female voice.

I turned and saw her — *Belle* — coming down the grand stairway, taking each step with the confidence of someone who feels like she owns the place.

As I watched her glide to the bottom step then walk over to me, so many thoughts crashed through my brain: What was *she* doing here? Why did *she* have free run of the house? Was TJ having a relationship behind my back, not that I had any claim on him? How shocking to see Belle in cutoff jeans! When I first met her, she was wearing a tailored, professional, color-coordinated outfit. Now, she had a tool belt around her waist. When had she stopped worrying about her precious manicure?

The woman looked me up and down, but in a friendly way. "You don't look like any contractor I know so y'all must be a good friend of TJ's or he would never have let you through that door. I'm Dee." She held out her hand to me, her eyes dancing with amusement. My response was automatic. I reached out and we shook hands.

The woman, Dee, laughed softly. "I can tell by the look on your face that you don't know. It's always a shocker for new people here. I'm Belle's twin. We're alike in looks, but little else. Almost total opposites."

I'd always been curious about twins. Unanswered questions flew through my mind: What was it like seeing yourself walk down the street or sitting across the table at dinner? Could you read each other's minds? Was it fun playing pranks on people? Could your parents tell you apart? It all seemed weird, but fascinating.

"What's it like being a twin?" The question popped out without thinking. How embarrassing. My tongue tied itself into a knot as I struggled to say something to hide my awkwardness. As usual, TJ saved the day.

"I see you two have met." He must have seen the surprise still lingering on my face. He looked to Dee. "She didn't know, did she?"

Dee tossed her long strawberry blonde hair pulled back in a ponytail over her shoulder. "Nope, just another newbie amazed out of her socks." She gave me a smile that said she was teasing. "I don't mean no harm. It's a joke with everybody we know." Then she turned to TJ. "I checked some of the electrical connections upstairs." She bit her lower lip and shook her head. "I'm afraid there's a lot of wiring we should change out, so you're not barbecued in your bed. I'm afraid this is no piddling job."

He frowned. "Ouch, that sounds expensive. Is there any work I can do?"

She huffed a little laugh. "Work you'll do in all your spare time? She glanced around at the cracks in the plaster walls, rich wood floors that deserved to be refinished, and the heavy dust coating on the crystal chandelier above our heads. "Why don't you let me handle the electric? After all, you said it wasn't your strongest skill."

TJ's body slumped.

"It will be okay. I changed things out in the areas we talked about, so the house shouldn't burn down tonight, but I'd go easy on using electricity upstairs until I can get back and finish checking things out."

"Thanks so much." He dropped his eyes, almost shy about accepting help.

"No problem. If friends don't watch out for friends, where would we be?" she said.

TJ's phone rang. He looked at the screen. "Gotta take this. Thanks again, Dee. I'll be back, Emma. Stay right there."

As we watched him disappear down the hallway, questions about the condition of the Cottage rose. *Was it ready for winter? Was the heating system ready? Was there enough insulation so the pipes wouldn't freeze? What about the roof?*

I figured if TJ trusted Dee with Waterwood House, she must be good, and I could follow his lead. "Can I ask you a question?"

Dee shrugged her shoulders. "Sure, what is it? Something about the Cottage? I've always been drawn to that sweet little property. I hope nothing is upside down there."

"I don't think so, but there are a few things here and there that need a little TLC." I cleared my throat, feeling a little embarrassed. TJ might not have strong skills, but I didn't have any. "I'm a little worried with winter coming and all. I'd ask TJ, but he's so busy right now. Do you think you could come and take a look?

"I'd be happy to," she said with a genuine smile. "I wish I could do it now, but I have an appointment. Can I text you?"

We exchanged contact information. TJ came back in time to watch Dee stow her things and climb into her truck with a built-in toolbox in the back. Dee handled her tools, the tailgate, everything like they were feathers. I suspected she developed her strength from the work she did rather than spending hours in the gym.

"You have the right kind of friends," I said.

"Yes, we're able to swap or barter our services. Helps us both," he said with satisfaction.

I turned to him. "Ready? I can't wait any longer to see the things your aunt collected."

CHAPTER SIX

Godey's Lady's Book, known as a fashion magazine, was launched by Louis Godey in 1830. By the American Civil War, it was the most popular American periodical with over 150,000 subscribers. Known for its hand-tinted fashion plates, each issue included a mix of fashion, nonfiction articles, fiction and poetry plus features on cooking and needlework.

I was eager to see Emma's things that had survived from the mid-19th century and hoped those things might reveal something about the woman.

"I have you set up in here," TJ said, as he headed through a door off the foyer. As I passed Emma's portrait, I winked at it.

TJ led me into the dining room and began an apology. "I haven't used this room…"

He kept talking but my attention was drawn to the magnificent antique furniture there. I could only imagine the fine parties held in this space. I looked up to take in the two bronze chandeliers, each decorated with figures of cherubs and lions and glass globes etched with figures of Roman warriors and chariots.

I'd always been fascinated by lighting fixtures. They could add so much to a room, whether it was modern or antique. It showed the owner had given thought to the atmosphere of a room and what would happen there. Here, at Waterwood House, this room would have been the scene of lavish dinners, celebrations, and maybe intimate conversations in times of stress or sadness. I could only imagine…

TJ noticed my preoccupation with the lighting and misunderstood. "Like I was saying, I haven't had a chance to clean the chandeliers. It will probably take a week to get the dust and grime off all those little crystal parts. There must be more than a hundred of them."

"I could help," I said in a small voice. This room was truly special.

TJ frowned a little. "I don't get it. Why are you so interested in my ancestors?" He didn't ask in a suspicious way. Merely curious.

"I don't have a long family history like you do … not one that is tied to something long-lasting like the land. There's no Lone Oak in my life like the one across from the Cottage where your ancestors laughed and loved and cried. There is no grand home where my several-greats grandmother learned to climb steps, sew a sampler, or taught her own babies how to walk."

I looked around the dining room and thought of all that had happened here. "Everybody wants to know about their family, to get a hint of why they are who they are. It's a luxury to see what was important to the family before they were born. The condo where I lived my teenage years holds nothing for me. Strangers live there now. I can only hope my sister has retained a box of what family mementoes survived."

I held my arms out as if to embrace all of Waterwood House. "Here, you can see the past, your past, just by looking around. All the clues are here. It's fun and I think important to unearth them. And if I can help do that for you, I'm happy. You've helped me. Now, it's my turn."

TJ looked at me for a long moment, considering what I'd said. "I tend to live in the present and to plan for the future. That's what a farmer does."

"That makes sense, but you need to look at how well a field or crop did in the past, don't you? Learning about who has gone before is important and fascinating, too. After all, what are you afraid of? Do you think I might find a pirate or murderer among the skeletons in your closet?" With a little giggle, I concluded, "Really TJ, I think you're safe."

"Okay, you've made your point. I appreciate your offer to help clean up, but you're just getting back on your feet. I don't want you climbing ladders and all," TJ insisted. "Promise?"

Reluctantly, I agreed. "But I can give you some advice, like there might be a pulley system to lower and raise the chandeliers." TJ looked confused so I explained. "My grandmother's friend lived in a house with very high ceilings. Each of her chandeliers had a pulley system. She explained that someone had devised an easy way to move the chandeliers up and down in fine houses and palaces. Didn't you ever wonder how they lit and snuffed out the candles or replenished the oil or just cleaned them when they were suspended so many feet above the floor?"

"Frankly, no, but now that you mention it…"

I glanced around the room. "Look around for a pulley or rod system. I bet you'll find it tucked away somewhere."

"Okay, I will," he said. "For now, I want you to know that I did run the vacuum cleaner on the floor and wiped a cloth over the furniture so you shouldn't be overcome by dust."

I beamed. "Thank you. That was considerate."

A ghost of a smile crossed his lips. "And Aunt Louisa's genealogical treasure trove is in the box at the end of the table."

"That's it?" The words slipped out before I realized what I was saying. "I mean, is this all she found?"

"Yes, Aunt Louisa was meticulous about putting Emma's things in the box… I mean the other Emma," he said.

We still hadn't figured out how to differentiate between the two Emma's—TJ's ancestor named Emma from the Civil War era and me. In a way, I felt that my last name in this situation was fitting: Chase. I'd spent quite a bit of time *chasing* after Emma and Daniel who lived in the 19th century.

TJ stepped up to the box and pointed. "Look, you can see that Aunt Louisa marked it 1850-1900 so the time span is right. The only earlier mention she found was the recording of Emma's birth in the family Bible. And look here." We both leaned in closer to read the handwriting where he pointed to Aunt Louisa's notes. It read, *Emma Elizabeth Ross Collins.*

"That's our girl," I said triumphantly.

TJ reached out to adjust the position of the box on the table a smidge. "Aunt Louisa was meticulous to a fault. If there is anything that she found around the house that might have belonged to Emma or was associated with her time as mistress, it's in this box. At least, that's what she said."

It was obvious that TJ was nervous, but I had no idea why. I hoped he'd tell me when he was ready. "I'm so glad you found the painted miniature Emma wore in the portrait. It gave us a peek at what Daniel looked like. Was it in this box?"

"Yes, I found the miniature on the chain carefully stored in a little velvet pouch in this box," he said.

"That was so great. It's amazing that you thought to bring out the box and look inside." My comments were making him blush, so I backed off.

I took the lid off the box and was dismayed to see that it was barely half full. "TJ?"

"I know, I know," he said in a way that meant he understood. "There isn't much there. I didn't look at everything. Maybe if you dig down to the bottom, you'll find something interesting." He was trying to sound upbeat, but he didn't really believe what he was saying. "Maybe you'll find more letters. If you do, you can put them together with materials from the Maryland Room and solve the mysterious note you think Emma left on the letter." He gave me a look filled with hope, but it drained away quickly.

I felt terrible. He was trying so hard. "That's OK. I'll look. As you said, we'll never know what we'll find unless we look."

His phone rang.

"I need to take this call." He left me in the beautiful room with the little bits we had left of Emma.

The sun came out from behind a cloud and light streamed through the tall windows overlooking the river. Two massive pieces called sideboards were pushed to the walls, their faceted glass drawer knobs glinting in the light. The table was spectacular. I ran my hand lightly over its satiny wood. In a few places, there was a random scratch or dent, evidence of use over the past century and more. Overall, the table was in miraculous condition. I peered closer. The wood grain created a special effect that I'd seen before. It was called *flame mahogany,* dramatic markings of deepest brown, red and light orange in the wood. As I walked around the table, the colors seemed to take on a life of their own, moving like the flames of a fire. Thus, the name: *flame mahogany.*

All right, I lectured myself, *you'd better dive into that box before TJ changes his mind and takes it away. I wish I could figure out what is making him so uncomfortable.*

I pulled out the host's chair at the head of the table and was rewarded with a surprise. The seat was covered with a hand-worked needlepoint canvas, like the ones my mother once made. She thought if we worked on needlepoint canvases together, it would give us a chance to bond, but my stitches were uneven no matter what I tried to do. Finally, she gave up and sent me outside with my books. I couldn't stitch the canvas, but I could appreciate the work and concentration it took to make them so beautiful. The floral design in the center was set off by a rich gold background. I was tempted to run around the table to look at all the other chairs but made myself stay in place to do what I had come to do.

I positioned the box in the sunlight, showing every crinkle and bend of the old cardboard carton. Inside was a mishmash of things. The only way to make any sense of it was to take each thing out separately. I could use the table to organize everything since it was open to accommodate twelve people.

On the top of the accumulation in the box was a pair of fine tortoiseshell hair combs that looked nothing like the machine-made plastic ones of today. Any woman would have prized these combs to dress her long hair swept up into the styles of the period, from plain to elaborate.

Next, there was a hair ribbon in a shade of blush pink. Thinking that I had seen it before, I held it in my hand for a moment. With a spark of excitement, I scooted out to the foyer and held the ribbon up to Emma's portrait. The gown she wore in the painting had darkened a little with age, but the color was close. Feeling a little zing of excitement in making a connection, I hurried back to the dining room, eager to make more.

Next, there were some pieces of paper that looked so fragile, I was afraid they would crumble in my fingers. They were handwritten recipes: One for Ginger Beer with a list of ingredients and a note that it would *sparkle like champagne in two weeks;* One for Crab Sauce that called for cayenne, allspice, an anchovy, which seemed a little curious, and enough cream to give someone a heart attack by just reading the amount. The recipe for George Washington Cake had a note to make it on his February 22nd birthday. Underneath were envelopes with letters inside. I left everything on the table until I could put them in baggies to help preserve them.

Next, I found a triangular kerchief. Oh, what was it called? A lady would wear it to protect the back of her neck from a draft. She could use the ends to fill in a low-cut neckline for modesty or a little warmth. While my brain searched for the name, I inspected the once lovely lace, now yellowed and stained where it had come in contact with her skin. Many stitches were torn or split by wear. It might have been an everyday piece from Emma's wardrobe. The name finally emerged from the fog. A fichu! I had to remember my French class to pronounce it correctly: *FEE-shoo*. A lace fichu, once part of Emma's everyday life.

Next, I found a pair of leather gloves, the color of a robin's egg, now stiffened with age. They were so small and delicate in my hand, I wondered if they had belonged to a child. I could barely slip a finger inside. Then I remembered the women in the 1860s were much smaller, often five feet or less, tiny in comparison to my 5'7" height. A small place at the tip of the index finger of the right glove had been expertly repaired. Emma's work? She had touched them and now, so had I.

Next, there was a small basket, about nine inches square, lined with soft white linen. Inside were a printed paper pattern and a straight piece of lace about eight inches long and two inches wide. Had Emma transformed simple white thread into these fine stitches? There was a small box with a painted top nestled at the bottom of the basket. Inside were various sewing tools, many of them silver suggesting they were used by the lady of the house, not a servant. The tools included a pincushion, a silver thimble, a cloth tape measure in a silver holder, and a silver needle case. Again, I felt the connection to Emma when I picked up the pair of ornate embroidery scissors made for smaller hands than mine.

The items were spread out on the table. Had I found everything? I looked again. Tucked in the corner of the box was a hefty iron skeleton key with a tiny brass one tied to it by a pink ribbon. How curious! What locks did they open?

CHAPTER SEVEN

"The humblest tasks get beautified if loving hands do them."

— Louisa May Alcott, *Little Women*

TJ walked into the dining room and stopped when he saw
the contents of the box spread all over the massive dining
room table. "Whoa! That's a lot of things!"

"Not as many as I'd hoped, but it's special to touch the
things that Emma had touched. And made!" I reached over and
held up the delicate but worn fichu.

His face scrunched up in confusion. "A lace scarf?"

"It's called a fichu," His forehead scrunched up in
confusion. "You're right, a kind of lace scarf."

He relaxed until I held up the iron skeleton key with the little
brass one tied to it. "Any idea what these open?"

He inspected them then shook his head. "Your guess is as
good as mine."

"There are lots of things to look at. Do you mind if I take them to the Cottage... so I'll be out of your way?" I added quickly to head off his objection. "I promise to keep everything together and return them in the box."

He mulled over the idea as he scanned the things on the table.

"I could make notes about what I find. You could send them to Aunt Louisa if you'd like," I suggested.

He raised his eyes to my face and peered at me. I felt like I was being inspected.

Really, TJ? After everything we've been through? But I held my tongue.

Finally, he closed his eyes and let out a small sigh. "That would be good, really good." I don't know if Aunt Louisa is still interested. She is in a good assisted-living environment, so they can watch over her. So, I guess it's fallen to me to preserve our family history now." He grabbed the box and began to load the things inside. It was surprising that this farmer, used to wrestling big equipment and bags of supplies, handled these heirlooms with such delicacy and care.

In a flash, I understood why he was so hesitant to have me in the house pawing through this box. TJ was proud and protective of his heritage. With Aunt Louisa, the family historian, getting up in years, the responsibility of keeping their history intact had fallen to him. It was a heavy responsibility because he cared so much.

"I'll make notes, so you have the information tucked away now and for the future."

TJ looked at me again, but the sharp, inspecting eyes had softened and his face glowed. "That would be great. Thanks," he said.

We hustled out to his truck before the darkening skies could deliver more rain and headed down to the Cottage. Ghost panted at the back window, fogging it up with his doggie breath. I wrestled the box inside on my own and headed to my dining room. With the box safely on the table, my eyes fell on one of the letters TJ had found earlier. A wave of frustration came over me. Sure, I was finding things connected to Emma, but she was elusive. If I'd wanted information about Daniel and his life, I asked. In comparison, it was easy dealing with him, once I'd gotten over the uneasy feeling of corresponding with a ghost.

"This is so hard," I complained aloud. "Why didn't people mark keys so others would know what they opened? And why didn't they sign their letters?"

What am I doing? If anyone overhears me, they'll think I'm crazy. I need a dog like TJ's, then I wouldn't feel so creepy talking to myself.

Complaining wasn't getting me anywhere, so I went into the kitchen, made a cup of coffee to keep my hands warm, and went outside to the patio hoping the fresh air would help clear my thinking. Questions about the letters kept ricocheting around in my mind. Who was the original letter writer? What made Emma make the notation on it. I felt sure those were Emma's words. Reading them, I could feel the emotion rolling off the page. I wanted to know what she meant.

I resolved that there was only one way to find out. I threw the leftover coffee into the rose bed. Somewhere I'd read that coffee was good for roses. Or was it tea leaves? Oh well, another question to look up. But now, I needed to go to the cabin.

I found the key TJ and I had hidden away and unlocked the door. Before my resolve could falter, I took a blank piece of paper from the stack on the desk, opened the inkwell, and dipped the pen.

Dear Emma,

I am writing to you from the desk used by Daniel's father. I hope we may be able to correspond. Before you decide, I hope you will first read this letter.

I am here at Waterwood, your beautiful home on the Eastern Shore. I now own the Cottage on the small piece of ground carved out of your father's plantation. I have had the honor to learn about your life and to love this place. You must be a remarkable woman to have captured Daniel's heart and earned his loyalty so completely.

I admire you. I wish we'd had the opportunity to meet. Perhaps we have the next best thing. I have a few questions and it would mean a great deal to me if we could establish a correspondence.

People on your family tree have gathered a few of your things and shared them with me. Among them are some letters written to you. One is from Minnie. The other was written by Lottie. There are no last names, but they must have been close friends of yours.

If it is not asking too much, would you tell me who these women were. I found it interesting that you made a notation on the letter from Lottie:

Which is worse ~ to live without the man you love as I do or to live with your beloved, a man who many revile and despise...

I want you to know that I respect your privacy and if you choose not to respond, I understand.

Yours very truly,
Emma

Would Emma use the gateway Daniel had opened through the desk? Would she open her heart and respond to my letter? Before I could change my mind, I closed the lid on the inkwell, did a quick job of cleaning the pen with a tissue from my pocket, and placed the letter in the center of the writing surface of the desk. I was out the door, up the path back to the Cottage, and leaning over the kitchen counter almost hyperventilating in moments. What had I just done? I had chosen to begin a correspondence with another ghost. When I first wrote to Daniel, I was simply responding to his letter.

Now, I was the one trying to start the correspondence. I didn't know Daniel's Emma. I had no idea how she would respond, if she did. I remembered TJ's concern about a vengeful ghost. I closed my eyes and dropped my head down to my chest. I was torn. I wanted to know about Emma. I wanted to know what was behind the notation on that antique letter. But I didn't want to create problems.

No, this is a bad idea.

I stood up straight, burst through the kitchen door, and raced back to the cabin. When I got the door opened, I found my letter to Emma had already disappeared.

CHAPTER EIGHT

"I keep turning over new leaves, and spoiling them, as I used to spoil my copybooks; and I make so many beginnings there never will be an end."

— Louisa May Alcott, *Little Women*

Slowly, I retraced my steps back to the Cottage and considered I might be spending too much time thinking about the past. Was I forgetting to live in the present? Months ago, my days were filled with exercises, painful visits to physical therapy, and pills. Finally, I graduated from all that. I could begin to live a normal life again. The doc said I wasn't ready for a full-term teaching commitment, but I could do some substitute teaching in the spring. Now, was the perfect time to work on a lifelong dream: writing a book.

I'd done a college minor in English with that goal in mind. After I graduated with my teaching degree, my time was filled with learning the things they didn't teach me in class and taking care of my new husband who was in medical school. When his infidelities came to light, I concentrated on my students to avoid the pain of the divorce. I told myself I didn't have the time to write, but, deep down, I knew a good writer had to open up, not hide from herself. I wasn't ready to do that then, but now...

The time had come. I had to move my laptop to the dining room table until I found a new desk. With a legal pad and pen to one side of the keyboard and a steaming mug on the other, I sat down and opened a new folder labelled "My Book." Twenty minutes later, I was still staring at a blank page on the screen. When there were sounds at the front door, I jumped up, thankful for the interruption and tried to help Maria with an profusion of grocery bags as she maneuvered through the door.

"Don't you touch them!" she ordered as she headed to the kitchen. "The day you can manage grocery bags, I'm out of a job and I need this job so, I have work to do that I need to get done." Maria was in fine form with her run-on sentences. "You just go ahead and do whatever you were doing, because the doing is what is important."

But I didn't want to face that flashing cursor on the screen. It felt like the word processor was drumming its digital fingers, saying *Well? Type already.* I could avoid the stress and guilt by staying in the kitchen, watching Maria put away the groceries. After all, it was my kitchen.

"What's new," I asked weakly.

Maria was frazzled. "I would have been here earlier, but traffic was backed up. Big farming equipment was blocking the road. I have no idea what those things do. They look so threatening with those massive wheels and spikes sticking out everywhere."

When she finally took a breath, I squeezed in a comment. "Why are they still on the roads? I thought the farming activity had stopped for the winter."

Maria shook her head. "You're asking the wrong person. Ask your farmer friend about it. I have no idea what they do in the fields and I really don't care, as long as I can get the things I want at the grocery store ... but when they bring their equipment out of the fields and on to the roads, I—I—I –" She was so flummoxed, I wasn't sure she was going to get the rest of the sentence out, but I should have feared not. Maria was never short on words. "I don't know why they can't make them go as fast as their noisy pickup trucks, because I wasn't sure I would get here before the ice cream melted and I picked up some Butter Pecan for you. That's for later. Now, you run along," Maria directed.

"But I want to stay," I complained, sounding like one of the little girls in my class.

"This is where *I* work. Your work is in the dining room. I have things to do. Off you go." She shooed me out of her kitchen. Maria didn't like an audience when she was cooking.

I felt like my head was hanging down to my knees as I dragged myself back to the dining room and the impatient cursor on my laptop. I had to pick a subject and get serious or give up this idea about writing a book.

People said, *write what you know.* I knew children as my teaching experience and graduate degree showed, but I wasn't an illustrator or ready for a collaboration. People also said to write about something that has captured your attention. The story of Daniel and Emma had captured mine. Set against the backdrop of the Civil War on the Eastern Shore, that would be a book I'd read. At my first meeting of local writers, Maureen offered to help me get started. I called to invite her for coffee sometime soon, and it turned out she was free and not too far away. Before I closed my laptop, I sneered at the flashing cursor. *You're not going to get the best of me. The cavalry is coming.*

It wasn't long before Maureen was pulled up in a sporty red Porsche SUV. I went out to meet her and offered to help with a stack of books she was juggling.

"Don't fuss, but you can take them. I brought them for you."

"For me?" I said while trying not to drop any of them.

"If you're going to write a good story, you have to learn your craft or you'll make every mistake possible." She shook her head hard. "And that's not what you want to do."

After we made coffee and settled down in front of the fire, she jumped right in. "Do you have an idea for your book?"

"I think so. I've been doing some research for TJ. His family has owned this land since the early 1800s," I explained. "I'm intrigued with a story about one of his ancestors and a man she loved."

"Oh, a love story," she exclaimed. "What fun."

"Yes, and I can add lots of historical information. So many possibilities." A surge of excitement began to grow.

Maureen's face took on a serious expression. "Let's put this together. Boy meets Girl."

"Um, make that Girl grows up with Boy," I corrected.

Maureen shrugged. "Then Girl loses Boy."

"Um, not exactly," I held up a finger. "Boy goes off to war with her father."

"Girl loses Boy," Maureen repeated. "Then...?"

"Boy comes home." I liked this game.

"Girl gets Boy?"

"Yes," I said with enthusiasm. "They marry and have an interesting life here on her plantation. That's where the historical detail comes in." I paused. "Maureen, did you just groan?"

"Oh, you heard that. Sorry." She sounded contrite. "Emma, where is the conflict?"

"Why does there have to be conflict?" I countered. "Isn't real life hard enough? Why can't this be a happy book with history woven through?"

Maureen disconnected from me and gazed out a window. "So, you're writing a textbook."

"A TEXTBOOK? NO!" We sat in silence for long minutes while I cast around for something to say. "Okay, what if they report Boy dead, but he didn't die and shows up one day very much alive."

"With only one arm," she added gleefully. "That should create some problems. Your book can be a true romance. You need to—"

"Um, no. I don't read romance novels. How can I write one?" I hoped she didn't throw up her hands and give up on me. What she did next confused me more than ever.

She smiled as she said, "At least you understand *that* part of being an author. You should write what you like to read."

"Okay," feeling more confident, I declared, "I want to write a book of women's fiction to show the lost love and plight of women in the 1860s."

"That's progress, but I must ask again... where is the conflict?"

"The war?" But that didn't feel right either. I peered into my mug of cold coffee. I hadn't put a single word on paper, and I was tempted to give up. "I don't know," I finally admitted. Where would you put it?"

"One possibility is that Boy is reported dead. Girl marries Brute. Boy reappears." She continued. "You could have poignant scenes of What If. They could conspire to meet in secret. They could conspire to kill the Brute."

"WHOA!" I interrupted. "That's over the top."

Maureen laughed. "Okay, now you see there are possibilities. Read the books I've brought. Learn the rules and get to work."

"Rules?" I said, feeling indignant. "I don't want to—"

"Read those books" she repeated. "Learn the rules for your genre, then you can break them. But you need conflict and that means a bad guy!"

I was grateful for Maureen's time but, when she left, my head was spinning. I looked at the stack of books and my body drooped. Instead of diving in, I opted for another cup of coffee.

CHAPTER NINE

"Age adds glory to the homestead in the eyes of the family, and this is reason enough for building something for all time."

– *Farmer's Almanac* 1863

I kept thinking about TJ and this land. If Belle was enticing him to sell with the promise of a big payout, maybe strengthening his connection to Emma might help. I sounded like a manipulating woman, the kind I hated. But TJ would be the one to benefit from any information I uncovered. I needed to know if Emma could help. It was time to find out if there was a reply to my letter.

I wanted to skip down the path, but it's a good thing I didn't. TJ was coming from the other direction. Ghost, his huge dog and ever-present companion, jogged along next to him. Sometimes, he'd stop to sniff a leaf or patch of vines, but he was never far from TJ's side.

"Good morning," he said. "You're up early."

I plastered a big smile on my face. "Well, you set a good example. If I get up, I have more time to get more done."

He narrowed his eyes as if he suspected something was up. "Really?"

I heaved a deep sigh. "I guess it's time for me to confess. I'm on my way to the cabin to see if there is a letter."

"That's not a confession. We've been checking the desk for weeks now. So far, there's been nothing from Daniel."

I bit my lip.

"Emma?" When he said my name, starting low and going right up the scale, that made me feel like a little girl who'd been caught stealing cookies. "What have you done?"

Losing my nerve, my eyes strayed to a nutshell in the middle of the path, probably left by a squirrel. "What kind of a nut is this?"

"Don't try to change the subject," he snapped. "It's a black walnut. They're all over the place. Now, tell me what you've done."

"I'm not looking for a letter from Daniel." I took another quick breath and braced myself. "I wrote to Emma."

"YOU DID WHAT?"

I didn't know a man's eyes could get so large or his face so red. He bellowed. "Couldn't you leave well enough alone?" Ghost barked, upset by the angry words.

I reached out my hands to grab his arms to what...? Calm him? Take control? But he took a step back, away from me. "Let me explain," I said as coolly as I could.

"Explain? There is nothing to explain. The first letter from Daniel arrived without warning. You didn't initiate the correspondence. The connection with Daniel wasn't your making. Don't you remember how hard it was for you, for both of us, to understand what was happening? Think about all the effort it took to find a solution." He laughed, but there was no humor in the sound. He restated his greatest fear when we were dealing with Daniel. "And it could have gone very wrong. You could've ended up with an angry, vengeful ghost haunting your cozy Cottage." He huffed. "If you believe in such things."

"I do," I shot back. "And so do you, now."

TJ leaned toward me and lowered his voice. "Maybe, but we dodged a bullet. I believe Emma and Daniel are reunited and happy for all eternity. Now is the time for us to go on with *our* lives." He stepped back and threw his arms up to the sky, beseeching the powers that be, and called out, "But what does she do? She stirs the pot and writes to another ghost!" He dropped his hands to his sides, his palms making a slapping sound against his denim jeans.

"Let me explain," I pleaded.

"Oh, please do." He folded his arms across his broad chest. "And it better be good."

"First, you're right. It took a lot of effort to reunite the spirits of Daniel and Emma. And yes, I think you're right, they are together."

"Then why—" he challenged.

"I've always had a feeling that something was bothering Emma, something that kept her spirit unsettled."

"Of course, she was waiting for Daniel to come home," TJ declared.

"Yes, but I have a feeling there's something more. When you were so kind to show me the box that Aunt Louisa put together of Emma's things, I was disappointed."

He took a step back and raised his shoulders to shrug me off. "Well, I'm sorry if—"

"No, don't misunderstand. There was a random pair of gloves, some lace, a sewing kit,,, random things that might have been left around the house. Nothing treasured."

He tilted his head to one side. "What do you mean, treasured?"

"Baby clothes, a diary, a wedding gown. Oh, a wedding photo."

He frowned a little. "I found the miniature of Daniel in that box," he said, as if that fact shot down my theory.

"Probably because she wore it every day."

He quickly asked another question. "Did they take wedding photos during the Civil War in a rural area like this, away from the big cities?"

"They weren't photographs as we know them today. They were called tintypes or daguerreotypes. Photographers captured the romantic moments of weddings and, if they were brave enough, the horrors of the war. There were everyday things, not treasured ones in the box."

TJ raised his shoulders in a dramatic shrug. "I don't know why there were so few things or treasures as you call them. Aunt Louisa was diligent about gathering family possessions she found. She didn't sell anything to some antique dealer or…"

"No, no, I think those items were more valuable to her than any money they would bring at a sale. That is what she found, but there aren't enough of Emma's things in the box. She was a woman who'd spent her entire life here at Waterwood. There must be more." I took a step closer to TJ. "Those items should be found and preserved for your family, TJ. The letters you found are part of that collection. Don't you want to know about the notation she made? How are we going to accomplish all that?"

"I don't know." His neck stiffened and he raised his chin. "But you do. You decided on your own to write to a ghost, 'Hey Emma, where did you stash your stuff so I can learn all your secrets.' Clever, and dangerous."

I was surprised by his reaction. He'd been so supportive in finding a way to reunite Daniel and Emma. Now, his sarcasm seemed out of place. Had acknowledging the existence and interacting with ghosts unnerved him more than I had realized?

I tried to appear contrite. "I'm sorry. I guess we should've talked before I wrote the letter."

"You think?" he shot back. "Who knows what or who could come through that channel Daniel opened in the desk?"

"You're right," I conceded. "But it's done. My letter has already disappeared, so either there is nothing there now or her response is waiting for me. Do you want to come with me to find out?"

He took a step away from me. "No, no. I've had enough of ghosts to last me quite a while, thank you. I have things to do that are important in *this* world. Now, if you'll excuse me." He brushed past me and headed up the path.

"TJ?" I called out.

He paused but did not turn around.

"I may need access to your attic at Waterwood," I said, glad he couldn't see the earnest plea or the fear of rejection I felt.

He threw his hands up in the air and let them fall in frustration. "Fine. Whatever. You're going to do what you want anyway." He sighed deeply. "Let me know when you want to come to the house. I've got a lot going on, so please don't just show up." And he walked away.

I was sorry that he was upset. I must have expected this would be his reaction or I probably would have told him I was going to write the letter. I didn't want him to stop me. This felt like a quest. Not just for information. There were books and letters and the Maryland Room for that. It was something more. It felt like Emma had been hiding something, something important to her... and now to me. I took a step forward and then another and soon I was at the door to the cabin where answers might lay inside.

When I'd left the letter on the desk, the place smelled a little musty so, I left the door open now. Before the breeze could freshen the air, I caught a whiff of a scent, but it was so fleeting, I couldn't put my finger on what it was. Or maybe it was my imagination. I walked over to the desk.

There, in the middle of the writing surface, was a page of bright white printer paper taken from the stack I'd left there. On it, was the smooth, flowing handwriting of another time.

Emma had answered my letter.

CHAPTER TEN

"You don't need scores of suitors. You need only one... if he's the right one."

— Louisa May Alcott, *Little Women*

I grabbed Emma's response from the desk, as if afraid she could call it back. I reached into my pocket for my phone only to find I'd left it on the kitchen table. After locking the cabin door, I scurried up the path to the Cottage to capture her words before they could fade away.

Safe in my kitchen, I photographed the letter. In a few minutes, I would transcribe her words into a computer file as I had with all Daniel's letters, because after a bit of time the words faded away. I never knew why, but it happened. But first, I had to read what she had written.

My Dear Emma,

It feels strange to write those words. I feel like I am writing to myself. Nevertheless, I was glad to receive your communication. You seem to be a thoughtful and considerate woman. Allow me to be forthright with you. Daniel showed me the letters he received from Emma. From you. Your good heart shines through the words that you sent him. Through your kindness and effort, we are now united.

Of course, I did not write those letters. He does not know that and never will. He is new to this concept of the world hereafter. Thankfully, his delight in our reunion has blocked out any questions that may confuse him.

After Daniel left Waterwood with my father, I never knew the details of his fate. Unlike Daniel, I knew when I died and that was when I began my search for him. I cannot fathom how he could remain at his father's desk, waiting for his Emma. Thankfully, you made contact and found a way for us to be together. For that, I will be eternally grateful.

In the spirit of mutual cooperation and appreciation, I will answer any questions about my past that I can to indulge your curiosity.

I received many letters. My friends and I wrote often. It was the only way to trade news, offer support and solace, and to maintain contact with family and friends. Though we did not live many miles apart, the weight of our responsibilities and personal activities precluded frequent travel between our houses.

Regarding the letters you found, I believe you are referring to Charlotte Graham, the mistress of Safe Harbor House. She was the daughter of a prominent family whose fortunes benefitted from the labor of their many slaves. Her sister Mary—we called her Minnie—lived nearby at Miles Bend House and also owned slaves. We all did.

Here on the Shore, slavery was the key to our prosperity. Our way of life was more closely linked to the South than to the rest of the state of Maryland. That was the heart of the trouble. Charlotte was married to Henry, an officer of the Federal Army. She lived with him at Safe Harbor House and suffered deeply during the War Between the States because she loved him.

Many of us suffered because of those we chose to love. Our disagreements almost destroyed our attachments. The war even came between sisters. Minnie and Lottie were always so loving. At times, I would have given anything to have been sisters as they were, to share the burdens of life. Then the war happened, and their relationship was torn apart like a piece of fine cloth, rent, frayed, unraveling. But now, all is resolved.

May I repeat my gratitude to you for bringing us together again? Though we have not been properly introduced, I think of you as a friend.

Most fondly,
Emma

It worked. The connection through the desk to the past was still open and my letter had found a cooperative and friendly soul on the other end.

I hated fighting with TJ. He was so kind and compassionate and... lovable. But lovable wasn't in my plans. I replaced the thought with the word, fun. Once I told him about my correspondence with Daniel, his excitement and support were amazing. Now, I felt like I was on my own. Maybe knowing about Emma's warm response would help calm his worries about corresponding with a dreadful ghost.

After transcribing Emma's letter, I needed to write a response. I thought of the old dip pen and ink in the cabin and realized I didn't need them. Emma knew she was dead and that I was writing from a future time. I didn't have to pretend to be someone else the way I did with Daniel. I found the pen Uncle Jack had given me when I graduated from college. It was a present that might have been a cliché to someone else, but he had taught me to appreciate a fine writing instrument. He said it was an excellent way to honor my own thoughts and words. Now, more than ever, I needed to select the right words and express them in just the right way. With pen and paper in hand and the resolution to find a new desk in the back of my mind, I went to work in the dining room.

I wanted to be clear and gentle about the things to know. To do that, I prepared the dining table with an old, but clean sheet spread over the wood as the first line of protection. With Aunt Louisa's carton open, I carefully placed Emma's things on the end of the table away from my computer. The dining room was turning into an office. It wasn't my first choice, but I was grateful to have the space.

I set the hair combs and pink ribbon in a small box so they couldn't get lost, slipped each handwritten recipe into its own baggie, and set aside the lady's gloves. Remembering my mother's warnings about the effects of sunlight on fabric and paint, I grabbed some old cotton pillowcases, laid the lace fichu flat, and covered it. And, of course, there were the keys.

Now, with everything spread out, I could begin to frame my questions. First, there was the iron skeleton key. I had spent a lot of time fantasizing what it might open: A trunk? A garden gate? A secret room in the basement? And there was the tiny key tied to it. I needed Emma's help with these things.

I also wanted to know if she had crafted the fine stitches of the lace. Why was the lace pattern cut out of a publication so important? I knew that Victorian women loved the Godey's Lady's Book. My mother had framed illustrations with breathtaking detail hanging on a wall in her sewing room. They probably published patterns for everything from lace to formal gowns. Did Emma cut out this lace pattern to master it? Perhaps her practice piece was the straight length of lace I'd found in the box.

I looked over the collection again to be sure I wasn't missing anything. If Emma told me about the keys and the lace, I would be happy. I was ready to write the letter.

My Dear Emma,

Thank you for your kind response. I am so pleased that you call me your friend. It was my honor to play a part in your reunion with Daniel. I too am mystified how it happened. The important thing is that it did.

She hadn't addressed my question about what she'd written in the margin of that letter. It could have been an oversight, but I didn't think so. Should I ask again? There was always the chance it was too personal and she might cut off all correspondence. I could only hope its significance would become clear over time. I continued with safer topics.

Waterwood House is now owned by one of your descendants, a fine young man who respects its history and yours. He has shown me a few things he believes belonged to you. I find it surprising that so few things remain from a life spent entirely at Waterwood.

I do not mean to pry, but I'm interested in learning more about your life here and how the War Between the States affected you.

If I may, I would like to ask you two questions. Were you a lacemaker? There were two beautiful pieces of lace in the collection of things believed to be yours along with a lace pattern and delicate sewing tools. It is beautiful work, and I would love to find out more.

My second question is about a large iron skeleton key and a small brass key tied to it. I don't know where it was found but it was in the collection of your possessions. Would you tell me what they open?

I eagerly await your reply.

With great fondness,

Emma

CHAPTER ELEVEN

"If you dear little girls would only learn what real beauty is, and not pinch and starve and bleach yourselves out so, you'd save an immense deal of time and money and pain. A happy soul in a healthy body makes the best sort of beauty for man or woman."

— Louisa May Alcott, *Eight Cousins*

I decided I needed to go to the library to do more research into the original letter TJ found. That effort would keep my mind off the answers Emma would send back in response to my questions, *if* she responded. I couldn't worry about that now. I had done all I could.

TJ and I agreed on a time in the early morning when I could ride along with him and work at the library while he did some business at a farm outside of Easton, the county seat and the largest town in the area. He hadn't asked about the letter from Emma. The fact that he was willing to take me to the library showed he had declared a truce. I would keep the details contained in the letter until he was ready.

When I entered the Maryland Room, Charles sprinted across the reading area to me. The excitement rolling off this quiet, composed man was a little shocking.

"I'm so glad you're here," he said in a squeezed whisper though there was no one else around. "I have something for you." He set some folders on a table and we sat down.

"I found that Henry Graham retired from the U.S. Army. I guess he didn't want to get caught between the two factions—North and South—here on the Shore. Plantations were big business and slavery was part of life here for many families. But there were pockets like St. Michaels that supported the Union and abolition of slavery. There were plantation owners who wanted to find a way to preserve the Union while keeping slaves at least until an alternative form of labor could be found. Frankly, it was a terrible situation. You could call it a powder keg."

An older couple walked in with notebooks, probably genealogical researchers.

"I pulled this information that might be helpful." Charles stood. "Time for me to go back to work."

I touched his arm. "Charles, thank you. I really appreciate your help." His ears turned red.

I read about different places in the county and lost track of where they were located. I headed toward a detailed and colorful wall map of Talbot County, dating back to the 19th century, to help orient myself. But I never made it. As I turned by a book shelf, I glanced in a cubicle and saw the young woman Cookie sitting at the table, crying.

It's none of your business. Don't get involved. You have enough going on.

But I couldn't ignore Cookie any more than I could ignore a crying child. I lightly tapped on the door jamb to let her know I was there. When she looked up, she madly wiped her wet cheeks.

"Hi, I was walking past and… Are you okay?" I asked.

Cookie nodded her head in a very unconvincing way.

"Oh, I got the impression that something was wrong." I added.

Cookie started to shake her head, then gave up and nodded.

I stepped into the cubicle. "Is there anything I can do?"

Cookie stared at some unremarkable spot on the floor and shook her head.

I glanced at the book in front of Cookie and saw it was about real estate exam preparation. I dredged up words of encouragement just in case. "Did you get the results of your test?"

"I did. I passed, just like you said I would. I bought a new dress." She hiccupped. "And wore it to the office to show off my new license. The broker put it in a frame and hung it on the wall…even added my name to the list of working agents right then." Then her body slumped forward a little as if the air was leaking out. "Then it all went wrong."

"Why? What happened?"

"Belle walked into the office." There were tears in Cookie's voice. "When she found out what I had done, she started screaming at me. 'What about my business? Where am I going to find another assistant?' My new license was all about her." Cookie took a moment to wipe her nose. "I told her I would keep working for her. I needed the money while I began developing my own business. I promised I would keep doing a great job for her. I pleaded with her to believe me."

What a terrible situation. "What did the broker say?"

Cookie gave me a fleeting stab of a smile. "The broker was cool with that arrangement. She tried to calm Belle, told her that she should accept my offer to keep her business going." Cookie shook her head a little, remembering. "Belle agreed, but she wasn't happy. All because I did something for me." Tears began to fill her eyes again.

After I told Charles we were taking a short break and would be back soon, I hurried Cookie down the street to a little coffee shop. But we couldn't walk very fast, because I didn't want Cookie to fall or twist an ankle while she walked in those ridiculously high heels. She was a little thing, about 5'2" with bouncy black curls. But now, she stood almost up to my shoulder.

"Don't try to walk so fast. I don't want you to hurt yourself. It must be hard navigating in those shoes.".

"Oh, they're okay," she assured me. "Once you get used to them,"

I laughed. "I'd probably break my neck."

Cookie smiled. "I'm so tired of being short, looking up at everybody. I hate it when people talk over my head as if I wasn't there. This way, they have to pay attention to *me*, include *me* in their conversations."

I held the door for Cookie when we got to the coffee shop and noticed they had red soles, the signature of the famous shoe designer, Christian Louboutin. Distinctive and very expensive. "Those are really nice shoes."

"Thanks, they belong to a friend... my boss lets me wear them." Then she said quickly, "I love this place. It always smells wonderful."

I made sure that Cookie sat with her back to the rest of the shop in case there were any more tears. Once we settled in, I gently picked up the thread of our conversation. "Do you want to tell me more about what happened at the office?"

Gently, she nodded. "After things quieted down, Belle gave me a wonderful opportunity. She had a listing for a house that had been on the market for several months. She'd promised the owners to hold another open house that weekend. Of course, Belle didn't want to sit on the house. Any good leads would have come up in the first weeks of the listing. She offered it to me and I jumped at the chance. I knew I would be lucky to get any traffic at all but holding an open house would give me the chance to practice, get used to being alone and in charge." She took a moment to inhale the aroma of her hazelnut-flavored coffee, took a sip and moaned her delight.

She went on with her story. "I was so surprised when this couple walked in the front door, I didn't have time to get nervous. I showed them around the house, pointing out its advantages just as I'd practiced. They raised some good questions and I had the answers. They thanked me for the tour and left. I was so proud of myself I did a happy dance. They looked surprised when they returned a few minutes later and found me gyrating around the kitchen. I think my jaw hit the floor when they said, 'We would like to make an offer.'"

"That must've been very exciting for you." I thought it was great news and couldn't figure out why she'd been crying. "Then what happened?"

"I wrote the contract. It was a dream. They were pre-approved by a local bank. They were patient as it seemed to take forever for me to fill in all the information which was silly. I'd worked with Belle's contracts for a long time."

"But this was *your* first one."

"You're right. I was so excited when they both signed the contract offer and handed the paperwork to me." She looked into her coffee cup with a glum look on her face.

Something was wrong.

Cookie sighed. "I did what everybody says not to do. I dreamed about what I would do with the money."

"And that was?"

"I wanted to buy a special wedding dress I'd found. I looked like a princess in it. It was perfect, just what I wanted."

"But it was outside your budget," I added.

She nodded.

I gave my head a little shake. "But you'd written your first sales contract. Wasn't that good? I don't understand why you are upset. Did the owner turn down the offer?"

She leaned forward. "No, nothing like that. It was a full-price offer." Then she dropped her eyes again. "After the buyers left, I called Belle. She was excited by the news then was very matter-of-fact about our next steps. I was to get the buyers back to the house. She was on her way. Fortunately, they were outside talking about the landscaping. When Belle arrived, she took the contract out of my hand and went over it, page by page. She kept saying, Good... until she got to the last page."

"Was something wrong? Had you made a mistake? Surely, it could--"

"It was the page where the selling agent's name was listed."

"Where you had written your name, right?" I said.

"Yes, and that's where I'd made my mistake," Cookie said in a voice so soft I could barely hear her.

"I'm sorry, Cookie. I don't understand."

"Belle said I should've written in her name," she said in a small voice.

"But you sold the house."

"But she said that she had shown the house to the couple once before," Cookie countered.

I closed my eyes remembering a rule I had run into when I bought my condo: the first agent to introduce the buyer to a property, gets the sales commission. "Did the people tell you that they had seen the property before?"

"No, they didn't say anything. I told Belle they acted like it was their first time in the house. Belle said it was her word against mine. I suggested we ask them, but Belle said we could lose the sale."

"You should have gone to your broker. Let her sort things out," I suggested, trying to hide my irritation at Belle's behavior.

"I couldn't do that," Cookie almost whined. "Belle is the one who makes a lot of money for the agency, and she was in the running for a big award. No one knows what happened but Belle and me, and now you. And you cannot tell a soul."

I wasn't willing to give up that easily. "Maybe you should talk to her again."

Cookie looked at me as if I'd grown two heads. "How well do you know Belle?"

"Not well," I admitted, but she seems like a reasonable person." I knew as soon as the words were out of my mouth that it wasn't true. Dee was right. These twins were very different from one another. "So, what happened?" I didn't really want to hear the result that seemed so unfair.

"She offered to give me a check for $500." Tears quivered on the tips of Cookie's black lashes. "And she said I could keep my job as her assistant."

I gasped. "No." People at the next table looked at me, worried that something was wrong. I gave them a weak smile and leaned closer to Cookie. "I can't believe she would—"

"Belle is all about winning. My fiancé David and I decided the smart thing to do was to take the $500 and keep my job." Cookie leaned a little closer to me and whispered, "I made myself a promise. To protect myself in the future, I would get a broker's license. That's what I was studying in the library today." She sipped her cold coffee. "It's ironic that one of the requirements for a broker's license is to pass a state test about ethics."

I had to stifle a laugh.

"Yeah, I know. It's funny, because Belle has a broker's license. The other requirement is that I have to be an active agent for at least three years."

"Ouch. That can feel like a long time."

"I know, but in the meantime, I can build my life with David and build my career. I'm studying the ethics rules now so hopefully no one else can take advantage of me again. I'll be ready when it's time to take the exam."

I perked up to be supportive. "And you can use the check to buy the wedding gown you want."

Cookie glanced down. "Maybe, we'll see."

CHAPTER TWELVE

"We came into the world like brother and brother. And now let's go hand in hand, not one before another."

— William Shakespeare

Back at the library, I hunched over the papers, files, and references Charles had found for me, hoping for more clues.

Then someone whispered, "You're working hard."

I looked up. Strawberry blonde hair was pulled back from a familiar face with twinkling chocolate brown eyes. Belle? But when she turned her head, I saw the ponytail. Then I noticed the woman was wearing a casual top and jeans. It wasn't Belle. It was her sister, Dee.

"Hi!" I stretched my back a little. "Just doing more research on Waterwood. What are you doing here?"

"I'm here more often than you'd think. If I'm fixin' to work on an old house, I look for the original plans and any history on record. But today, I struck out. I did snag a new bestseller though. This Jacqueline of all trades likes to read in her off time. When we take a day off, my boyfriend, Nicky, and I go out on his boat. He'll fish or pull crabs while I read. Enforced downtime. I love it."

"That would work for me, too."

Dee cocked her head. "Look, I'm done here. I skipped lunch today and I'm starved. Want to walk up to the Pub for a quick bite?"

I glanced at the time. I hadn't eaten much of anything all morning. I could go and still be back in time to meet TJ. "Yes, that would be great." I loved being at the Cottage, but it felt good spending time with people and making new friends.

I packed my notes into the tote and met Dee at the checkout desk. Stepping out of the library's artificial light into the warm sunshine of autumn was startling and invigorating. The tang of salt from the surrounding waters of the Bay made the air refreshing. This area was made for walking.

There were three major towns in the county: St. Michaels, Easton, and Oxford. They all had brick sidewalks, tall trees, and large boxwoods, but each had a slightly different feel.

In Easton, I felt I should stand a little straighter, be more formal, more serious. By the Courthouse, men in coats and ties walked with purpose, on their way to a court appearance or a client meeting. Women in business dresses or suits navigated the brick sidewalks in their heels. Yes, shoes pointed out the difference in Easton. There were many professional people in the town, and they were wearing dress shoes – heels of varying heights for women, wing tips or Oxfords for men. This was a place of business.

I think I preferred the more relaxed feel of St. Michaels where people wore boat shoes and visitors stood out if they dressed for dinner in high heels as they would in the city. In Oxford, daily living was quiet, comfortable, often with pearls.

When we reached Washington Street, a man, walking toward us, stopped and did a doubletake looking at Dee. Then he frowned and spread his legs spread apart to block the sidewalk. If I hadn't felt a little threatened, the man would have been laughable. His white shirt was too tight at the neck and its line of buttons down his chest strained over his flabby torso. I guessed he hoped to intimidate Dee by his sheer size.

"YOU!" he thundered. "You have some nerve showing your face in town, you conniving, cheating woman." He spat out the last word as if it put a bad taste in his mouth.

I took a step forward. I wanted him to know he was facing two women, not just one.

Dee put her hand on my arm. "I got this." She stepped up to face him. "You hush up now. You've got a lot of nerve walking up to a woman you don't know and threatening her."

"Oh, I know who you are." He gestured as if he was putting her name up in lights. "Belle Howard, real estate agent extraordinaire. That's—"

"Wrong! You've got the wrong woman. My name is Dee, her twin sister." Dee took another step toward the man. "And I don't appreciate you talking about my sister that way." She put her fists on her hips. "But I know you and what you did, or should I say, what you didn't do. You declined to have an inspection done on that property you bought. I know for a fact that Belle always pressures, yes, pressures her clients to do an inspection. She's a good agent. She takes care of her clients." She took another small step forward. "But no, you knew best. You looked over the property and said it was fine. HA! You couldn't find your way around a tool box. Even I knew that house had problems." She cocked her shoulder in a flirty way and changed her voice to sound like a sweet, little girl. "I'm just a girl and you're a big, strong guy!"

She dropped her hands and added steel to her words. "You're cheap and pathetic. You should have known better." She spread her feet apart. "So, don't talk about my sister and keep your distance from me or I'll teach you a lesson she won't. Now, walk on about your business." She held her position while the man's eyes darted from her to me then around us to see if anyone else had heard this dressing-down. Realizing we were alone, he puffed up his chest, turned and walked down the sidewalk, his heels pounding the bricks.

"You're impressive," I said, peeking over her shoulder to make sure the big lug was safely gone. "If I'm ever in a bind, I want you on my side."

"Being able to stand up for myself is important since I work in a..." She made air quotes. "man's world. The bullies are the worst. They're all bluster."

"Yeah, but..."

"I know how to take care of myself, too. But I appreciate you stepping up for me. That's cool." She flashed a mega-watt smile, the same as Belle's, though Dee's smile was sincere. "Let's get some lunch before I faint from hunger."

We stepped into the warm and inviting interior of the Pub though it took a minute for our eyes to adjust to the dim lighting. The long tile and polished wood bar extended into the narrow restaurant. Behind it, the shelves along the wall featured a vast array of bottles. High stools were lined up for patrons enjoying each other's company and good food. We walked down to the far end toward the table area.

"We can sit at the bar," Dee suggested. "Or maybe we could find the table over there—"

Her words broke off and I followed her gaze. Belle was sitting at the table with an attractive young man. His wavy, chestnut brown hair had been mashed down by a ball cap, now hanging off the back of his chair. At least he had taken the hat off in the restaurant. Most guys didn't because they knew how it messed up their hair. I didn't know who he was but by the strained look on Dee's face, she recognized him. Belle and the man had their heads together, laughing. Then Belle put her hand on the man's arm, pulled him towards her, and kissed him on the cheek.

Dee took a slow step backwards, her chin trembling, her face pale under her tan.

"Dee, what's wrong?" I asked quietly. I looked back at her sister's table. "Who is that with Belle?"

In a voice as taut as a piano string, Dee said, "That man is Nicky, *my* boyfriend."

The air around us thrummed with anxiety and anger. I didn't know what to do. I didn't know what to say.

"E-E-Emma." Dee stammered. "I just remembered I gotta run to meet a client. Sorry." As she spoke, her eyes stayed on the two people sitting at the table who were oblivious to us standing there watching them. "Bye." Dee raced out the front door of the Pub, bumping into two customers.

As I looked back at Belle and Nicky, my mind flooded with memories of my husband. Ex-husband. Once the love of my life, the man who'd cut me to the core.

I couldn't stay in that restaurant. All the way back to the library, I thought of my high school sweetheart. Our love survived the strains of college. We were going to have a gaggle of kids, but that wasn't going to happen when I found out that after he became a doctor, he was tempted by any female form in scrubs. *Men could really derail a woman's life.*

I felt a stab of jealousy as I thought of Emma and Daniel. *Not everyone is lucky enough to find a true love who remains true.*

CHAPTER THIRTEEN

"Let us be content, my sisters, with our neat muslins and our simple merinos, and admire Mrs. Smith and Mrs. Jones in their moiris and cashmeres."

– Godey's Lady's Book 1863 v. 66

When I met TJ at the library, he was full of news about what other farmers were doing. I sat quietly and let him talk about using drones to monitor crop growth and to keep an eye on solar panels some of his friends were putting in their fields. He said it gave farmers a richer picture of their fields, but he lost me when he talked about sensors and digital imaging capabilities. When we got back to the Cottage, I got antsy. I wanted to dash down to the cabin to see if Emma had answered my letter. I had to wait politely for TJ to leave.

Finally, I was free to go to the cabin. I hoped Emma wasn't miffed by my questions. In my haste at the door, I was all fumble-fingers, but finally got it unlocked. I rushed to the antique plantation desk and found Emma's response. And there was that sweet scent again. As much as I wanted to sit down and read her letter, I forced myself back to the Cottage to capture its contents before they could fade. With them safely recorded in photos and emailed to my account, I sat down to read her words.

Dear Emma,

I must admit I am a little surprised at your interest in my life at Waterwood. You're not even a member of the family. Be that as it may, I shall be happy to answer your questions. I must say, my life, though I treasured it, was a small one.

I remember one particularly harsh winter that prevented my good friends, Minnie and Lottie, from visiting. The wind attacked from every direction. Walking was difficult even between buildings. I ordered all fires be kept high. It would not do for anyone—person or slave—to freeze or get sick. My husband did not complain because he was away in Philadelphia so much that year.

Do not judge Minnie by her comment about her wool clothing being of the highest quality. It was her way. For some reason, she wanted people to know that she was upholding her family's position.

Some people thought that Lottie had married beneath her. But love has no care for a person's position. She could not have foreseen a war would come that cast brother against brother, whether by nature or in law. As I said, she was a dear friend. I was happy to offer her support as she suffered the arrows and sharp words of her sister Minnie and others in the neighborhood.

I lowered the letter and stared out the window. Was this the situation Emma was considering when she made the notation? Was she thinking of her admiration for Lottie, standing by her husband? Was she aching for Daniel?

Minnie always championed their family's slave holdings. It probably was prudent considering that the slaves were the basis of their wealth and business success. Minnie was also proud of her husband's decision to leave the Federal army and join those fighting for the honor and lifestyle of the Confederacy.

It was a very complicated time. The War Between the States brought out the worst in many people. People tried to make us declare our support for one side or the other. Our loyalties, morals, and economic interests were often in conflict.

But that time of upset is behind us now.

A smile came to my face when I read your question about the lace. Yes, the pieces you found are my handiwork. Making lace was a tradition in my mother's family, passed from one generation to the next.

When I was still a little girl, my mother began my needlework education. She was a kind woman who had great patience. I was not always willing to practice the basic stitches. I wanted to jump ahead to the more complicated patterns.

The pattern must be one I cut out of Godey's Lady's Book. Was it labeled Point de Gaze? I fell in love with its delicate look the first time I saw it. It works well with the rose pattern.

I spent many hours attending to the needs of my family and the plantation. Whenever I could, I would steal a moment for a walk along the creek or to sit quietly with my sewing basket making lace. Those were my favorite things to do.

About the skeleton key, I misplaced it during the last days of my life. I am glad you found it. You may be surprised to learn that your two questions are linked. I feel it is safe to share my secret with you. He cannot hurt either one of us.

After my mother died trying to give birth to a boy child, my dear father brought the lace mistress from Philadelphia from time to time to help me perfect my stitches. It helped cushion the deep loss I felt. With her help, I achieved a level of accomplishment.

As I grew older and learned the desires of my heart, I dreamed of the day I would marry Daniel. With the help of Sally, my house slave, I retrieved my mother's wedding gown and secretly began making alterations. I also made yards and yards of lace in the Point de Gaze pattern with the rose flower. It was my fondest desire to wear that gown when I was joined in marriage to the love of my life.

The Almighty does not always grant our wishes. When it became clear that Daniel would never return to Waterwood and that I was to marry the son of a nearby plantation owner, I took my wedding gown up to the attic and locked it away in a secret room. That room became my sanctuary through very difficult years. Please be content to know that in that secret room, I was surrounded by things that brought me comfort and peace. I spent hours there thinking about what might've been.

That place was all I had left that was mine. When my husband denied me my other special place, his actions ignited a deep and abiding anger in me and smolders to this day. I know it is Christian to forgive, but I cannot forgive or forget his actions or accusations. I cannot talk about him or the little girl I wanted to name Emma. It is too painful to think about my secret room and my last diary. To learn more, you will have to find my last diary and its brass key.

Last diary? Brass key? The one tied to the iron skeleton key? Another little girl?

Waterwood House has always kept my secrets, but if you wish to use the big iron key, you have my permission. Go to the attic and search for the shelves that form a bookcase built against a brick chimney. Do not try to move it for it is built in to the structure of the house. Instead, remove any items from the top shelf then remove the shelf itself. Use the wood crate that may still be close by that I always used to reach the hidden lock. If it has survived, you will find the lock that the key was designed to open.

The other key, the small one, will lead you to my last thoughts. It will unlock my secret place where I hid my final diary. It is in my bedroom where I would stand to watch the morning sun rise.

With great affection,
Emma

I never thought that lacemaking and an old iron skeleton key would have a strong connection. The attic room held Emma's secrets and I had her permission to enter it. I wanted to sprint to Waterwood House and climb its many stairs to the attic, but I had to consider TJ's feelings. It was his home. I had to respect his privacy. Should I show him this letter now? Should I wait until he gave me access to the attic and then show him what I found there?

I had to admit that a little part of me was afraid that TJ would say *Enough! w*hen I asked for access to the attic. I wanted to learn more about Emma and her life at Waterwood. I felt we had a connection that went beyond the fact that we shared a name. But TJ was angry because I was trying to reestablish communication with a ghost.

His life was caught up with today's events and plans for the future. He had to think about what seeds to plant, what fertilizer to use, when to irrigate, how to balance the effects of weather. He was well settled in the here and now. I was looking to the past. The last thing I wanted him to do was to close off access to Waterwood House and Emma. I had to be patient and plan my approach carefully.

CHAPTER FOURTEEN

"DIARY: a daily written record of the writer's personal experiences and observations."

— *New Webster's Dictionary*

The first thing the next morning, I sent TJ a text.

8:04 AM

< TJ

Hi! Could I meet you at Waterwood House in a little bit? Need to talk.

8:03 AM

TJ Sure. Everything OK? I'm working on accounts. Come anytime.

8:04 AM

8:04 AM Yes, all good. See ya soon.

I put the iron skeleton key in one pocket of my jacket, a folded copy of Emma's latest letter in the other and set off for Waterwood House. I walked slowly so I could rehearse what I was going to say to TJ. I didn't want to upset him, but I wanted him to know how important it was for us to follow the clues Emma had left us. I didn't think he would throw me out of the house, but after the outburst on the path, I wasn't sure. So, I practiced as I walked by the drying cornstalks in the fields.

TJ greeted me in his normal, lighthearted way that had been muffled by the stress of bringing in the harvest. He poured me a cup of coffee. "What's up?"

"Let's sit down," I said.

He plopped down in his chair. "Uh, oh."

"No, it's nothing bad. I just want you to hear me out." I took a sip of coffee and changed my mind. I decided to let Emma make the case. "You know I wrote a letter to Daniel's Emma." Quickly, I held up the palm of my hand for him to stop. "I know you don't approve. I should have told you before I put it on the desk, but it's done."

Softly, he asked, "What happened?"

"She wrote back."

TJ's eyebrows shot up.

I was gratified to see his response. "Yes, and she was a real lady about it." Mentally, I held my breath before I said the next words. "And we've been exchanging letters." I braced for an explosion... that didn't come. Pleasantly surprised, I continued. "I asked her about the iron skeleton key I found in Aunt Louisa's box. I wanted to know what it opened." I took it out of my pocket and laid it on the table. "The answer may surprise you."

I could tell I had snagged TJ's attention when he asked, "What did she say?" He lifted his coffee mug with one hand to take a drink while letting the fingers of his other hand play with the key.

I was tempted to pull out the letter but described her response instead. "She said there's a secret room in the attic and invited us to take a look."

His mug stopped in midair and he stared at me.

I shrugged. "That's what she said. Are we going to accept her invitation?" I crossed my fingers under the table so he couldn't see.

It seemed like forever before he said, "I don't see how we can turn down her offer."

I let out a sigh of relief and scooped up the key. "Can we go upstairs and take a look now?"

He chuckled. "I don't think I have a choice. I really have to commend you for sitting quietly in that chair for so long." He took a last swig of coffee, stood up, and got a flashlight from a cabinet. "Let's go."

He led me to the foyer and up the stairs. I couldn't help but let my eyes sweep upwards, drawn by the design of the stairway. Up, past the ancestral portraits and landscapes that lined the walls. Up, along the hand-carved banister touched by generations that offered a solid handhold as it curved at the landings. Up, to the window that framed a panoramic view of Waterwood.

We went past the second level where the family slept and up again to the third floor used for servants' rooms, storage, and a non-descript door. TJ opened it. I reached into my pocket to check that I had Emma's iron skeleton key, the key that would unlock her secret place. I took a deep breath to prepare myself to face musty smells, maybe even the odor of a deteriorating dead animal and a maze of spiderwebs. With a flash of strong determination, I walked in.

I was surprised that the attic wasn't as unpleasant as I expected. The air was fairly fresh which surprised me and worried me because it meant that somewhere the area was open to the elements. That was something for TJ to manage.

"Well, here we are," TJ announced. "One big centuries–old attic. Now what?" His phone rang. He checked the screen, sighed, and clicked accept. "Hey, Jeff. Hold on a minute." He hit the mute button. "I've got to take this call. It's business. Are you okay here?"

"I'll be fine," I assured him. "You know where to find me."

He nodded, handed me the flashlight, and walked back to the stairway with his cellphone, leaving me alone with Emma's past.

I was glad I'd worn an old pair of jeans, socks and a long-sleeved T-shirt that were enough to keep me warm as I began my quest for a bookcase that wasn't a bookcase. I glanced around to get my bearings. There were many trunks and boxes stacked on top of one another. Pieces of furniture that were no longer wanted or needed in the main parts of the house were stored here, too good to toss out, but no longer valued to be part of the décor. I could get lost up here just looking at the things placed closest to the door, but I needed to find the bookcase built against one of several brick chimneys.

I glanced around the massive area and finally spotted bricks at the far end. I made my way around things placed randomly. I tripped over the runner of a rocking chair and almost fell. At the last minute, I grabbed onto a stack of boxes that almost tumbled down on top of me. Once I steadied myself and the boxes, I continued through the labyrinth of the past. Some things had to be pushed out of my way, but it was easy work. Nothing too heavy. Then the toe of my shoe nudged something heavy.

It was a frame that should have been hanging on a wall. The front was turned away from me, so I picked it up and turned it around. It took me a moment to realize that it was an antique version of the plat Belle had shown me. This map of the property, used to identify boundaries, was drawn by hand on thin parchment paper. The word *Waterwood* was written prominently in heavy black ink. Below the name of the plantation, the year was written clearly: 1871. The thick black boundary line showed that Waterwood Plantation was much bigger than it was today. I could understand why TJ would covet the additional acres now lost to him.

The map showed Waterwood House and many of its outbuildings. I found the creek and the Lone Oak, which was marked by an artist's representation of the actual tree. It was shown much smaller than it appeared today so many years later, but it was still portrayed as an impressive landmark. Across the creek from the Lone Oak was a section carved from the heart of the plantation. A thick black boundary separated it from Waterwood. There was no structure noted but it clearly marked the property that I now owned.

Seeing it presented this way rekindled my curiosity about why this land was cut out of the heart of Waterwood. Why had someone framed it? I had come up to the attic to find answers and so far, I'd only added to my list of questions. I moved the frame to a prominent place so I wouldn't forget about it.

I scanned the attic again, looking for the bookcase that would lead to Emma's secret room. Finally, I caught sight of something that looked promising. But it wasn't really a bookcase. More a set of wooden shelves braced against the bricks of an old chimney. I quickly made my way to it. All kinds of things were stashed on the five shelves, among them were books with disintegrating leather covers, some small boxes, and a man's top hat. They were all adorned with dusty cobwebs, a clear sign that nothing had been touched for a very long time. Gently, I moved each item to a safe place.

The shelf I wanted was the second from the top, high above my head. I couldn't imagine how someone of average height in

Emma's time could reach it. Following her instructions, I found her small wooden crate and dragged it over to the shelves. Gingerly, I tested its reliability and was surprised to find it was solid. I planted my left foot and pulled myself up.

I grabbed the shelf to remove it, but it was stuck solid. Had I gotten the instructions wrong? Was Emma leading me down a garden path, unwilling to share her secrets?

No, I wouldn't accept the possibility that she might be playing with me.

It had been a long time since someone had moved it. It was probably just stuck. I compared it to the other shelves. This one was a little thicker than the others which suggested it was special, different for some reason. I positioned my feet carefully so I would be stable while I wrestled with it. At first, it didn't move. I reset my feet and gave it a stronger tug. I felt the shelf begin to give way. Then with no warning, it came away in my hands and toppled to the floor. It threw me off-balance and I teetered backwards for a breath-taking moment. I grabbed onto the other shelves and held on tight until I regained my balance and caught my breath. When I had recovered, I found I was facing an old-style lock. Pulling the skeleton key out of my pocket, I inserted it in the slot and tried to turn it.

It was frozen in place.

I was too close to give up. I reset the key and strained against it. This time, it moved. There was a loud click followed by a scraping sound. I almost lost my balance again when the bookcase bounced toward me with a jerk. Emma's secret room might have been testing me, but I had won. Almost panting with excitement, I jumped down and moved the crate to the side. One end of the bookcase had moved outward. I grabbed its edge and pulled.

I was surprised how easily it moved. It revealed a dark opening, like a hidden passageway leading to a secret room, a sanctuary for the lady of the manor.

This part of the attic was not wired for electricity, so the flashlight and a small, dusty window were my only sources of light. I stepped to the entryway and moved the cone of light into a darkened area.

And I screamed! A ghost!

I stumbled backwards, out of the secret room and crashed into a tall dresser. My heart was beating so fast I thought it was going to jump right out of my chest. I knew that was a cliché, but it was exactly how I felt. I had just seen a ghost. Not the kind that corresponded by letter. The kind that wore a sheet and showed up in cartoons by the name of Casper.

After a few deep breaths, I stood up straight and smoothed down my shirt. I scoured the area until I saw the flashlight that had hit the floor and rolled under a chair. Fortunately, the crash hadn't affected it. I retrieved it from the dusty floorboards.

I moved forward into the doorway and swung the beam of light around the secret room again until it fell on a sheet of muslin thrown over something about five feet tall. I wasn't going to deal with anything else in the room until I had identified what had scared me. A lot of dust had settled on the muslin cover. I raised it carefully to peek at what was hidden underneath.

My eyes were amazed by a vision of creamy white, a gown fit for a bride. This must have been the gown she was making for her wedding to Daniel. A huge skirt of exquisite silk was overlaid with the most delicate lace I'd ever seen. In the middle were two intertwined initials:

$$E \& B.$$

I remembered the story TJ had told me about Elizabeth and Benjamin, Emma's parents. How they had fallen in love at a *glittering* ball and they never wanted to be apart again. If there had been a love story like theirs in my family, I too would have wanted to keep the gown worn by my mother when she married her true love. I had learned the hard way that marriage was not easy and that every bride needed strength and energy and yes, good luck.

Even with all the hope this gown represented, it was obvious that it had not been used again. Emma must not have worn it when she walked down the aisle to meet Joshua at the altar. Having experienced Daniel's love, she must have known it was not a love match. Knowing that, she must have resigned herself to making the best of each day and caring for Waterwood and all it represented. To see this gown and all the tiny stitches that created the lace made by her loving hands was indeed a gift. In these moments, I felt closer to Emma than ever before. Slowly, I lowered the protective cover back in place.

On the far side of the room, was a full-length cheval mirror. Did she use it to admire herself in the wedding gown? That was yet another question that might go unanswered.

Near the mirror was a small carved wooden table. On the top, lined up in a neat row held in place by two iron bookends, were small leatherbound books. There were no titles on their spines. I carefully picked up one from the middle of the collection. Gently, I opened the cover and turned to the first page where I read the words, *My Diary.*

I'd found them, Emma's diaries! This was better than letters. Writing in a diary was like writing a letter to yourself.

Looking at the line of journals, she must have kept many volumes. My hands shook with excitement. I looked back at the open diary in my hands. Below those first words were the numbers *187_* but I couldn't read the last number. I squinted, but it was too blurry. I turned the page and even here, the writing seemed to blur a little. Could it be? I turned the page and the next and the next. The words had blurred. The handwriting was no longer legible.

No! No!

I fanned through more pages. The paper was mottled. The ink had run so badly that I couldn't even tell if any words had been recorded there.

No! No!

I picked up another journal and found damaged pages. The same was true with several more journals. I looked up at the sloped roof over my head and saw the problem. There were water stains on the wood. Signs of a leak. The bane of handwritten words. In her day, Emma must have visited this hidden room often but in the intervening time of more than a century, the roof had allowed rain to seep inside. I was sure that if TJ had seen evidence of the leak from outside, he would have repaired it immediately. This was the result of a little water working its way along the rafters until it found a place to drip. In this case, the rainwater had destroyed a valued record. I was overwhelmed by the enormity of the loss.

I sank down on the rough wooden floor and began to cry. So close, I felt so close to this woman and now to be separated by a little rainwater, was almost too much to bear.

"Emma? Where are you?" TJ's voice drifted through the attic, getting louder. He was close. "Are you… in here?"

"Yes," I called out. "I'm here. Keep coming."

"EMMA? Are you all right?" TJ's body filled the doorway to Emma's sanctuary. It must have been the one thing that Emma never wanted to see: a man standing in the entrance to her secret room. I felt certain that if she knew TJ, she would be delighted.

I quickly wiped the tears from my face and tried to make my voice steady and upbeat. "As you can see, I found Emma's hiding place. I think the things your aunt wanted to find are all in here." I flashed my light around the room, avoiding the ghost-like dress form, and let it rest on the books sitting on the tabletop. "I found Emma's diaries."

"Really? That's fantastic!" He said as he stepped carefully into the hidden room once locked away by the bookcase. As he glanced around, he said only one word: "Wow."

"But I have some bad news for you." My voice cracked. "There's a leak in the roof."

He frowned as he looked up and searched the ceiling. "Where is it?"

"I don't know, but rain has dripped over her journals. They're ruined, TJ. They're all ruined. Her words are gone. We'll never know why she hid these things away. There's so much we'll never know or understand."

TJ knelt down and put his arms around me, and I cried into his shoulder.

CHAPTER FIFTEEN

"The emerging woman ... will be strong-minded, strong-hearted, strong-souled, and strong-bodied...strength and beauty must go together."

— Louisa May Alcott, *An Old-Fashioned Girl*

TJ agreed to let me take Emma's journals back to the Cottage to try and dry them out. We found a box and laid each one carefully in it before he drove me home. I set up another area of the dining room table for the diaries. I did an internet search about drying wet books then went to work.

First, I did a quick scan of the pages. Fortunately, there was very little mold. The diaries that had lost their entries went into baggies and straight into the freezer. Later, I'd explain to Maria why part of her domain was filled with books. Next, I had to concentrate on the words I could salvage. According to the information I gleaned from the internet, I had my work cut out for me.

First, I put each diary between paper towels and pressed down hard. When no more moisture squeezed out, a paper towel went between each page, page after page, then I pressed down again. Each diary that still had a chance to be read was set on end with its cover as wide open as possible to allow air to circulate. I set up the fan from the hall closet to send a gentle stream of air to help the drying process. Later, I'd add pressure so the diary pages might have a chance of flattening out. Each step was part of a long process, but there was some hope that some entries could be saved.

Once the drying process was set up, I took a break to fight the temptation of finding entries I could read. The white gloves Charles had given me were soaked so they spent some time in the dryer. When I came back later, I was greeted by a light sweet scent, almost. I still couldn't identify it. Maybe Maria had used an air freshener. Even though the air outside was chilly, I opened a window to get some fresh air moving in the room. Emma had left twenty journals. Too many of them were in the freezer with little hope of being read. I had great hopes that the volumes at the two extreme ends, earliest and last, would have some readable entries since the leak seemed to have dripped over the diaries in the center of the collection. After putting on the dry cotton gloves, I picked up the diary from one end, a small book about eight inches tall, its soft black leather cover water-stained. Inside, cream-colored pages had rounded corners. I saw no signs of mold, but even this one had not escaped damage. I opened it and on the first page, Emma had written with a flourish:

Diary
of
Miss Emma Elizabeth Ross

On the next page, the writing area was outlined with a thin black line. Some of the pages were coming loose from the binding. Emma's handwritten words were smooth and beautifully aligned straight across each page, an achievement that required patience, practice, and good pen nibs.

Dear Diary,

It is 1861, the year I will become seventeen years old. I will be old enough to accept invitations to social events. I long to attend dances and fancy dinners. Papa promises that I shall have ball gowns and evening dresses of silk and velvet. He gave me a subscription to Godey's Lady's Book. I love reading every word and looking at all the fashion plates and woodcuts.

Godey's talks about the latest colors that are in style. I think my favorites are violet and rose. Peach-bloom velvet sounds like heaven. Godey's wrote about a green silk ball dress with a white satin apron front decorated with white and red roses. It sounds divine!

Papa hopes that if we go to the cities on the Western Shore, I shall meet eligible gentlemen of whom he would approve and perhaps form an attachment. I dream they will be handsome and charming.

A few entries later, I read:

Dear Diary,

I am afraid I am not meant to attend parties and balls. It is not meant for me to have pretty gowns. I am not meant to travel to Baltimore or the great city of

Philadelphia any time in the near future. The world is in a state of turmoil and fear. There is talk of secession. What if Maryland seceded from the Union while we were away in another state? How would we cross enemy lines to get back to Waterwood?

It is hard for me to think of not being part of the United States. Would I no longer be an American?

But to give up our slaves? How would Waterwood survive?

Would Sally leave? She has taken care of me since I was a baby. I love her. To think about losing her breaks my heart.

I wanted to read more, but the next pages were still damp, and I was afraid of tearing them. I had to be patient. I returned the book to its upright position so it could continue to dry.

Looking for a diversion, I went to check my email.

Hello Emma,

I hope all is well and you are making progress with your book idea. Our next writer's meeting is coming up. You are coming, aren't you?

I will swing by and pick you up, say 6:00? (Notice I'm not taking No for an answer.)

See you soon!
Maureen

I'd forgotten all about the writing group. I'd started reading some of Maureen's books and jotting down some ideas about characters and plot elements, but the thought of writing a book was still daunting.

Should I wait until ...

A voice boomed in my mind: *If you're going to do this, do it NOW!*

I didn't know I had a voice that could scream at me, but there she was. And now I was truly painted into a corner. I did not want to admit failure to myself and certainly not to Maureen, someone I respected. I hit reply:

Then I guess I'm saying yes to the meeting. And I'll think about your kind offer Thank you. See you soon. –Emma

---

Okay, the commitment was made. It was time to move forward. I'd have time while I waited for the drying process. I decided to follow Emma's example and keep a journal of my book ideas. It would give me a place to scribble down plot ideas, character traits, snippets of dialogue or description to consider using later instead of trying to keep it all in my head. I dug around in the den closet and found a blank spiral notebook. But before I returned to the dining room, I took a white sheet from the stack of origami paper and sat down to fold an origami figure.

Origami helped me relax, even in stressful situations. When I started teaching, I discovered that a room of rambunctious children would calm down to watch me fold a figure. Today, I decided a unicorn would be appropriate. It was a little more complicated than other forms, but I'd had a lot of practice. The children, especially the little girls, loved unicorns. With each fold, I missed them more and more.

And my brain was flooded with questions. Why had the universe yanked me from my quiet, organized world and plopped me down here on the Eastern Shore? Why had it challenged me to fix my broken body instead of facing the fact that I'd never walk again? Here, I was amid an avalanche of memories from my childhood with Uncle Jack, filled with love, excitement, and hope. Now, I had no clear way forward. The unicorn was known as a source of power. Maybe that's what I needed to stay on this path of history and discovery that would lead to who knew where.

When I finished, I put the little unicorn in front of the line of Emma's diaries. Maybe it would help preserve her words on the damp pages. A feeling of sadness was starting to creep over me. Sadness that Uncle Jack was gone. That I hadn't been with children for a very long time. That Emma's words might be lost forever.

I remembered one of my dear uncle's bits of wisdom. If I was spending too much time in my head and it was getting me down, I should take a walk and let the earth nurture me. I grabbed a sweater and headed out the kitchen door.

Across the creek stood the Lone Oak. Back in the day of Captain John Smith, who might have been the first white Englishman to sail the waters of the Chesapeake, much of this land was covered with oak and pine trees that soared into the bright sky. I could imagine Daniel and Emma as young children, playing around its massive trunk. Had Daniel ever climbed the Lone Oak? Now that most of its leaves had blown away, it was easy to see the structure of the tree. Its broad limbs reached out to me with an invitation to come, climb and explore. It would have been an irresistible call to a young boy. I wondered if Emma refused to be left behind. Would her curiosity and spirit driven her to follow him up the tree? I could almost see them sitting on a limb high above the ground, taking in the view, talking, and dreaming together.

This tree had witnessed times of desperate attempts to protect a loved one. It was rumored that Emma's father, with Daniel's help, had buried a chest there. A chest said to contain money, silver, and other valuables. More than one life had been lost or ruined by the quest to find it. From what I knew, Emma never found it. Emma's descendants, Stephani and Josh hadn't found it either, as hard as they tried.

Stephani and Josh. I heaved a deep sigh. What a waste. Instead of chasing their dreams, they were sitting in jail, awaiting sentencing. Had someone else gone looking for the treasure chest over the decades, found it, and carted it away? Or was it still waiting quietly under the soil of Waterwood?

It was amazing how one wrong decision, one wrong step, one comment between siblings could change a person's life. I thought about the sisters who'd written letters to Emma about the tensions between them. Did they ever reconcile? One could only hope they did.

Sisters. I knew that relations could be tense, even strained between sisters. I had an older one of my own. I wasn't sure if the great difference in our ages made it harder for us to have a close relationship. It would explain why almost everything my sister did irritated me. I wasn't sure if it was because we had different priorities and different ways of doing things or if we annoyed one another just by breathing.

Maybe age didn't matter. There was friction between the twins. Dee looked stricken when she saw her boyfriend Nicky with Belle at the Pub. It might have been an innocent situation, but I wasn't sure. I remembered the surge of jealousy I'd felt when Belle flirted with TJ that first day I'd met her. There was no reason for me to feel possessive. TJ was a friend, not a love interest. I was surprised by my reaction. But in Dee's case, Nicky was her fiancé. I could only imagine how she felt.

A chilly blast of air reminded me that the warmth of early fall days was giving way to winter. As I turned to head back to the Cottage, my legs felt heavy and my shoulders slumped. I hadn't realized how tired I was. I had been busy doing things, sure, but I was tired. A little too tired. I thought of the feelings barely disguised in Emma's letters to me and the emotions she'd hidden away in her secret room and between the pages of her diaries. Plus, the sentiments expressed in the letters from the sisters…all of these things had drained my energy. I decided that it might be prudent to slow down my pace a little. I didn't want to undo all the good rehab work I'd done for my body.

But the thought of Emma's trunk sitting in TJ's attic, waiting for me, rekindled my enthusiasm. I wondered what treasures and stories it might reveal when I raised the lid.

CHAPTER SIXTEEN

"Well, if I can't be happy, I can be useful, perhaps."

— Louisa May Alcott

What a treasure trove of information was lined up on the dining room table, drying out. I put on the cotton gloves and settled down with one of Emma's diaries. The next readable entry gave a clear look at how she made life-changing decisions.

Dear Diary,

The decision is made. I am to be married. Not because I love a man. I lost that chance when Daniel did not return from an expedition to deliver supplies to the Confederates down South. Papa has allowed me to make the choice to determine my future.

First, I can live with him until Papa is called home to be with Momma. Who knows what I may face when that time comes, alone on the plantation, without family to protect me? This option is fraught with too many unknowns and dangers.

Or I could leave Waterwood and live with relatives in Baltimore or Philadelphia. I cannot live away from Waterwood. It is the life force that flows in my body like the creek and river flow through our land.

Or Papa can arrange a marriage to the son of the family that owns the plantation adjacent to Waterwood. His name is Joshua Collins. I understand he is handsome. Papa would set certain safeguards so they could not steal Waterwood away from me. This is what I choose. It will not be a love match, but by doing this, I will protect that which I love most in the world after Papa and Daniel: Waterwood.

A knock at the front door drew me back to the present day. There, I found TJ and Dee on the steps.

"Oh! Why didn't you call?" I said with a smile that felt forced. I hoped I hid my surprise and discomfort at seeing Dee. I hadn't talked to her since that day at the Pub when we saw Belle and Nicky together. I felt so awkward. I hadn't even mentioned what had happened to TJ. Not knowing what else to do, I followed their lead.

"I guess I should have at least sent a text," TJ said. "Sorry. It's just that Dee was up at my house working on the electric and I thought it might be a good idea to check out the Cottage. We don't want any surprises. I think it's all okay, but Dee is here and…" he shrugged. "Okay?"

"Of course." I stepped back. "Come in. I haven't a clue where the breaker box is or really anything else mechanical."

"Not a problem, I can find my way around." She lifted a large tool box in her left hand as if it was nothing. "I've brought some things I might need. If it's okay for me to poke around to find…" Her voice went flat as she recited the list. "The electrical box or boxes, access to the attic, best way up to the roof… You know, that kind of thing."

"And you'll see if I need more insulation?"

Dee nodded and set off to check out the Cottage.

"I think this is a smart thing to do." TJ touched the brim of his baseball cap emblazoned with some seed company's logo. "I'll leave you to it."

"Oh, TJ!" I called after him. "There's a writer's meeting tomorrow night. Maureen, one of the writers, is going to give me a ride to Gretchen's. Do you think you could pick me up?"

He looked down, shook his head, and laughed. "Emma, you're a piece of work." He raised his head and gave me a broad grin, his eyes dancing with amusement.

"Why?"

"I'm just thinking back to the last time. Are we going to have any drama—"

"Hey, look at me." I held my arms straight out. "I'm healed. I'm healthy. We will have no problems."

He didn't look convinced. "But it's a meeting of writers. You said—"

"I said a lot of things," I countered quickly. "I'm committed to working, or at least trying to work on this book idea I have. Maureen said she'll help me and if there's anyone who knows what she's doing creatively, it's her."

Then, he said with the thick accent of a Southern gentleman, "Ma'am, I commend you for your fortitude. It would be an honor to ferry you home." He touched his hat. "Ma'am, until this tomorrow evening."

I found Dee in the kitchen fiddling with the electrical box. Maria gave me a look but, I suspected, prudence overruled her tongue. If the Cottage burned down, she would be out of a job.

I focused on Dee. "You look like you really know what you're doing." I winced, not believing I'd just said that. "I'm sorry. What I meant was, it's great to see a competent woman working in the building trades." I winced again. "I mean—"

Dee gave me a big smile. "Don't worry about it. I hear it all the time."

"How did you ever—? Was it hard breaking in?"

She shrugged with one shoulder. "Yeah, I guess it was. Still is. At least once a week, some yahoo makes a comment, but I can handle it. I noticed you have some big project going on in your dining room with all the books and papers."

"It's really several projects," I said, not wanting to be reminded. "Some of them are going fine. One isn't *going* at all. Not yet. Getting started is tough."

"I get it," she said, pulling a screwdriver out of the tool belt at her waist. "When I first go to work on a house, there is so much to do that I have trouble picking a place to start."

That makes sense, I thought.

"Emma?" Dee's eyebrows were scrunched together. "You okay? You checked out for a minute."

"Oh, sorry. Guess my mind is focused on the project that's giving me trouble."

"Then you should get back to it." Dee cocked her head toward the dining room. "It's the doing that gets things done."

But I stayed to watch as she took the panel off the electrical box and poked around. It was a relief to learn the Cottage wasn't still running on fuses.

"It looks like your Uncle Jack upgraded everything," Dee said. "That's good, but there are a couple of little things I could do here to make it better."

"If you have the time, please do it." I found myself staring at Dee while her attention was focused on the electrical wires and connectors. "Even though you and your sister look alike, you two truly are different. How did you choose this profession?"

Maria glanced at the doorway reminding me of the project waiting for me in the dining room, rolled her eyes, and went upstairs to putter.

"It's kind of a long story." Dee raised an eyebrow. "Are you sure you want to hear it?"

"I'm curious and would like to know. Coffee?" I offered.

"Sure, thanks."

While I made the coffee, Dee half disappeared under the sink to check for leaks. "We were born and raised in Dorchester County," she said. "It's just south of here. As kids, we went and did everything together, but it was always Belle's way."

"That must have been difficult," I suggested.

Dee shrugged. "No, it was easier to go along with what she wanted. It made her happy, which was always good. And so many times, she manipulated a situation for someone else's benefit."

"How did that work?"

"Well, while we were in high school, she had a parttime job at a shop in town. A dress shop, I guess you'd call it. Belle was always good at getting people to buy things. She definitely has the sales gene. We got our prom dresses from the shop at a discount, of course. We had a good friend who fell in love with a dress in the window but there was no way she could afford it at full price. Belle went to the owner, suggesting that she sell the dress at a discount. The woman, who was an old crow, said discounts were for family, not friends.

"I was there and was so impressed by my sister. Belle didn't lose her temper. She calmly thanked her for the job and said she couldn't continue working for such a mean-hearted woman. Then we walked out of the shop. The old bat followed us halfway down the street, screeching that she would sell the dress to our friend. But Belle kept walking. The bottom line was the story traveled through the town and Belle got a raise."

That memory brought a bright smile to Dee's face, but the smile fell away without warning. She looked down at her boots and shuffled one foot. In a soft voice, she continued. "Belle is a good person, deep down." Dee shrugged. "Sometimes, she goes too far." Her left hand curled into a fist. "She doesn't realize what she's doing sometimes."

"And how she might be hurting someone?" I added.

Dee raised her eyes to mine, and I could tell that we were both thinking of that moment in the Pub when we saw Belle with Nicky. Her other hand tightened into a fist. "You have no idea."

I waited for an explanation, but Dee didn't go into detail. We stood there like statues without saying a word for the longest time. Then, without warning, she opened her hands and spread her fingers wide. "We'll talk. We'll work it out. We always do." She gave her head a little shake that sent her ponytail bouncing, as if ridding herself of any negative ideas. Then Dee brightened. "Did you know she's helping with Cookie's wedding?"

"Really?" I was embarrassed that I was so surprised—about Belle helping with the girl's wedding, that Dee had neutralized her anger so easily, and that I was still upset for her.

Dee didn't notice my confusion. "Yeah, she thinks of Cookie as another little sister."

I was feeling a little emotional whiplash, but I followed Dee's lead. "So, Belle is the older twin?"

"Yes, by fourteen minutes," Dee said with a smile. "And growing up, she never let me forget it."

"Your parents named you Belle and Dee? Aren't twins usually given names that go together, like Faith and Hope or Chloe and Zoe?"

"Those aren't our real names. Mom liked to garden and named us after her favorite flowers. Belle got Rosabella—beautiful rose."

"That's pretty, but a bit of a mouthful."

Dee nodded. "Probably one of the perks of being born first. She didn't mind it much until more and more girls started showing up with that name. She shortened it to Belle. Thought it was pretty and feminine, kinda like her only she never lost all her thorns.

"I got off easy. Mom named me Daisy. When I was old enough to be teased in school, the kids, especially by this one girl, used to say my name through her nose, all nasally and singsong. One day on the playground, I punched that whiny voice right in the mouth.

"No!" I was shocked. "What happened?"

"Knocked out a couple of her baby teeth. When the teacher asked her what happened, she took one look at me and said she'd fallen. Seeing that blood running down her chin made the other kids think twice about calling us names." Dee's face darkened. "We took care of things at school. At home, things weren't so great." Dee waved the comment out of the air. "But that's another story. The important thing is home is always where Belle is. She is always there for me, to protect me. She's doing that now with Cookie, her assistant." *I don't think she's taking such great care of you right now,* I thought.

But it wasn't my place to say anything. "I guess it's a good way to grow up. I've had students, little ones in my kindergarten classes, who could have used a guardian angel or sister."

"Oh, she can be that," Dee said looking away. "The downside is that it gives her the idea she is in charge. Kind of like it's her right."

"Was that okay with you?"

She gave a little nod. "Yeah, usually." A little steel came into her voice when she said, "When we were growing up, I drew the line at boyfriends." Her shoulders sagged a little. "At least, I tried."

"It didn't always work?"

"No, but that was another time, another place. We're good now, as always."

She breathed a deep sigh. Was it a sigh of relief? I wondered as she moved to the bathroom to check the pipes.

"After we finished high school," Dee continued. "Belle took a few college classes but got tired of people telling her what she could and couldn't do. So, she rebelled. She resented the fact they gave her deadlines that were hard to meet and for what? A mark on a piece of paper or in her virtual record. No, that wasn't for her. It didn't help that she thought Dorchester County, where we grew up, was *beneath her.* You've met her. She's a clothes horse. She has more shoes in her closet then I will ever wear in my lifetime. She likes fancy things. We didn't grow up in a fancy place. It's a beautiful county and the people are truly salt of the earth. She just wanted more."

Dee paused and looked down for a moment. "She met with the college counselor to talk about what to do with her life and the woman mentioned real estate. Belle figured that was a perfect fit. She is good with numbers, can talk rings around people, and her persuasive powers are unmatched. I think between the two of us, she got all the nerve. I have to admit sometimes she needs to rein in her personality, but real estate requires an independent, entrepreneurial spirit and if that doesn't describe Belle, I don't know what does. The possibility of making good money didn't hurt either."

I followed Dee upstairs as she continued the checkup of the Cottage and her story. "I remember how her eyes sparkled as she studied and attended classes without one complaint. In no time, she had taken the state test and gotten herself an official Maryland real estate license. Then she had to decide where she was going to live and work. She never considered going to the Western Shore. Too many people, too much traffic, and too much competition. She looked around the Shore and set her sights on this area, Talbot County. It's close to family and friends, and there are more people here with more money and big properties."

"Is that why she's interested in Waterwood and my Cottage?"

"Probably. Right now, she is working a deal on a big farm across the river." Dee looked out from the linen closet in the hall bathroom. "I think there's a tiny leak here. I can fix it, but not today. It should be okay if you don't use it a lot."

"It can wait until you can come back. I use the master bath." I followed her as she headed in that direction. I wanted to hear more of their story. "So, Belle moved out and left you?"

"She really didn't want to go out on her own at that point. She'd never really been alone. She'd always had me."

"So, she persuaded you to move?"

Dee nodded. "Sure did. Even though we're very different and she was a pain in the neck sometimes, we're still sisters, twins." Dee chuckled.

"What did you do?" I was fascinated how this all unfolded.

"While she was getting straight with her real estate studies and all, I went to Belle's counselor hoping she could point me in the right direction, too. I'm no scholar and I don't like spending a lot of time with people. I like to fix things, build things. Always have. The counselor suggested that I check out the certificate programs at the community college. For fun, I took a welding course."

"Welding?"

"Yes, it looked like fun and the hourly pay possibilities looked good. I discovered I really liked it. I breezed through the course and got a good job right away." She leaned over and whispered, "And I think the boss man liked seeing a woman in tight jeans working that hot flame."

We laughed.

"I got different construction certificates, like electrical, heating & air conditioning. I also took the course to be a home inspector and I'm prepping to take the exam. I'm all about having choices. With my experience, I could be a general contractor, but not right now. I like getting my hands dirty." She gathered up her tools. "Okay, everything looks good in here. I can do a quick visual inspection of the roof, but I don't have time to go up there today."

"Anything you can do would be great." I followed her downstairs and outside. "I had no idea a community college offered programs like that."

"It's great, because not everybody is going to be an English teacher, medical doctor, or get a Ph.D. in something. They even have a training course to get a Commercial Driver's License. You can make good money—six figures even—driving a long-haul truck. If you want to stay home, the hourly pay for driving a school bus is pretty good. I didn't go for that license. I cringed just thinking about being around kids all day."

"You really have to love working with kids. Wiping their noses, putting up with their antics and drama is part of being with little ones. Teaching is what I've always wanted to do."

"That's good. We need people like you," she said with a smile.

We tromped through the fallen leaves the wind had driven past the nearby pine trees and piled up around the Cottage's foundation.

"What happened?" I was fascinated with the idea of a person seeing herself moving through the same world.

Dee stepped back to get a better angle to look at the roof. "I got some experience and ended up going out on my own. There are a lot of women living alone who need work done on their houses and prefer working with a woman! Belle has me do some work on her houses, too. But I preferred working in the county where we grew up. I knew people and knew the roads. Talbot County felt foreign."

"But this is where you're working now. What changed?"

A little smile touched Dee's lips. "My truck broke down late one afternoon down in Dorchester County. It was always breaking down. All of my go-to buddies were out fishing or crabbing or who-knows-what. A towing service would take hours to come to the middle of nowhere."

"What did you do?"

"Desperate, I called my sister and braced for an abrupt turn-down, like I'm busy, I'm with a client, whatever." Dee's face took on a glow. "But that's not what I got. She dropped everything, went by the garage to get the tools I needed and found me by the side of the road. I got the truck running in no time and followed her back to town." Dee got a faraway look in her eyes. "I got to thinking while I was following her shiny new SUV with a sunroof. I was driving a rusting out truck on its last legs. I wanted a shiny new vehicle, too. If I had to work in Talbot to get it, that's what I'd do. If Belle could make the change, so could I." She shrugged. "After all, we're twins."

"Are you glad you made the move?"

"Yeah," she answered slowly. "Yes, I am. It's different than the way I grew up. Pace is faster. People are a little more sophisticated maybe, but nothing I can't handle. And the money is much better. I bought a new truck almost right away. Belle helped me with that. She said I had to look successful to be successful. Hate to admit it, but she was right."

"Do you live together?" I wanted to know more.

"We did in the beginning," she said with a wistful look as if remembering that time. "I didn't date a lot like Belle, going to fancy parties and nice dinners at yacht clubs. I didn't have time. I was all about the work, still am. When I had enough money, I bought a small place of my own. It was a real fixer-upper. A good investment and gave me my independence. Finished it up, moved back in with Belle for a short time and sold my house to a nice older couple who were downsizing. Went to settlement yesterday."

"You do all this work alone?" I asked, amazed.

"I bring on people as I need them, but it's usually me, my truck, and my tools. Figure I have only so many years to do the heavy work, then I'll have to start hiring on and training other people. I'm thinking about getting a dog. It would be good company, drivin' around to the job sites."

"TJ takes his dog Ghost everywhere." I looked down at my cooling coffee. "I've even toyed with the idea of getting a puppy, but I think I have to wait until I figure out what I'm going to do."

"I know that feeling." Her face clouded. "My boyfriend Nicky and I..." Her voice shook. "We were talking about buying a place together." Her voice went soft. "But now...I can't live with Belle either."

I remembered what Dee and I had seen at the Pub. Belle and Nicky at a table in the corner, nuzzling and flirting. I was so sorry I'd reminded her of that scene.

"I have to finish up." She tapped her watch. "Sorry."

"My fault. I've been distracting you."

"No problem. I'll check in with you before I leave," as Dee pulled out a small pad and pencil to make notes.

It reminded me of Emma's diaries. "I'll be in the dining room." Eager to continue that project.

CHAPTER SEVENTEEN

"...what I would give worlds to become in truth, your loyal, loving wife!"

— From *Godey's Lady's Book* 1863

Whenever I was near the dining room, I wanted to devour whatever was still readable in Emma's diaries. I punched up the heat on the first floor to help the drying process along.

Then I turned to my emails and cleared them out. The only important message was from my attorney Mr. Heinrich who was looking forward to settling my accident claim soon. *And getting paid*, I added silently. There were a few messages from friends, but most were falling away, tangled up with their own lives. They say absence makes the heart grow fonder, but I'd found that if somebody wasn't an active part of someone's life, it was easy to be forgotten.

I turned back to Emma's diaries, a more constant friend, and found some readable entries.

Dear Diary,

My time of deliverance is drawing near. Though I have given birth to two sons and a daughter who survived, I have great hopes for this baby. She has not been a moment's bother. Yes, I wrote She for if I am allowed a preference, I would love to have another daughter. I have so much to share with a little girl. My Anna Grace has been a joy and comfort to me. I love my boys, but I feel such trepidation for them. Their father always wants the boys with him when he is here. He wants to teach them about Waterwood, but I fear they will absorb his unpleasant habits and outlook on the world. No one would quarrel if I kept a little girl by my side.

So, I hope for a girl, for me and Anna Grace. Above all, I hope for a healthy baby and I pray it is a safe delivery for us both.

What a unique window I had into the very different lives of these five women. In today's world, Belle was a wildly successful star in the real estate world. There was her twin, Dee, shy and careful, who people confused with her vivacious look-alike. But Dee wouldn't be left in the dust. She'd made a career for herself by learning a collection of skills, unexpected for a woman, and she did them well.

And there were the three women who lived more than a century earlier, who experienced the Civil War in different ways. Minnie was frightened by the possible changes to her life and insistent on maintaining appearances. Her sister Lottie suffered the subtle barbs and blatant charges of her disloyalty to her family and public disapproval of her husband's actions. And, of course, there was Emma who had faced the sad reality of loss of Daniel but stayed focused on a bright future with a new baby and the future of Waterwood and her family. The war brought them all isolation and shortages.

Each woman reacted in her own distinctive way, some which were baffling to me. I decided it was easier to understand the little ones in the kindergarten classroom than adults today or long ago.

I could still hear Dee puttering around so I turned to the next entry.

Dear Diary,

My heart is broken. Through a veil of pain, Sally told me that my baby did not survive the birth. She was fearful that I would give up my hold on this life to be with my dear baby girl. Sally begged me to stay for the sake of my sons, Waterwood, and for her. My husband stood silently and watched me cry an ocean of tears. He called for a grave to be dug in the family plot and the next day, he buried our daughter. That was weeks ago. Under Sally's care, I am slowly regaining my bodily strength, but I am still wrapped in sadness.

I was relieved that Emma recovered, though I could feel her disappointment. I loved working with little ones. That's why I became a teacher. When I married, I'd hoped to have a lively family of children. After the divorce, I had to reevaluate my life. Now, after recovering from the accident, I had to do it again.

Dee walked into the room just as I finished reading. "Okay, I've checked things out and you're all set. This Cottage is in much better shape than Waterwood House. You're lucky. TJ is facing a lot of work."

"I wish there were something I could do to help him. He's been so kind and supportive to me during this rough time in my life."

"Better to give him words of support and leave the actual work to the professionals." Dee winked. "It would be a shame if anything horrible happened to that house."

I stood up, ready to walk her to the door. "I agree. It's a gorgeous house and must have a lot of stories to tell. You know that old saying, *If only the walls could talk*?"

Dee smiled and nodded. "I've been in a lot of houses, and I've often wondered what they could tell me. Sometimes, marks or holes in the walls suggest a dark side. Things I don't want to think about." A smile crept over her lips. "But sometimes there are crayon marks a foot above the floor, a budding artist starting her drawing career on her mom's walls. Those always make me smile." She glanced at the table laden with papers, books, and my computer. "It looks like you've got a lot going on here."

I grabbed at her invitation to talk about my projects. "I stumbled into some historical material dating back to the Civil War. This area is so rich in history. I had no idea that the Eastern Shore was sympathetic to the South. I'm finding it all fascinating."

"There are a lot of historical houses around the county. It feels like each one has its own story. I try to work on them whenever I get the chance, doing what's needed to maintain them." She took a deep breath. "We can't afford to lose them."

I suddenly realized that Dee might be able to help me. "Have you ever heard of Safe Harbor House?"

"I guess that would be the name of the main house on Safe Harbor Farm."

"So, you know it?"

"Know it? Is this too weird? I'm on my way there right now. The property is up for sale and my sister has the listing. I'm supposed to meet her there in a half hour to look at some of the outbuildings. She likes to be able to suggest ideas to a potential buyer but checks with me first to see if they're feasible."

I had to tamp down my excitement. "Do you think there is any way I could go with you? I'd stay out of your way. It's part of my project, or one of them, that is all over the dining table. You see, during the Civil War, two sisters lived across the Miles River from each other and exchanged letters with one of TJ's ancestors at Waterwood House. One of them lived at Safe Harbor House. It would be great to see her home."

Dee shrugged. "Nobody's living there. I guess you could follow me out there and look around as long as you don't go inside the main house." I didn't respond. "Or you could call Belle and make an appointment."

I had to make a confession. "I don't drive," I said quietly. It was embarrassing to admit that I, a woman over thirty, who thought of herself as independent, didn't drive.

It didn't take Dee long to put it together. "That's why you told TJ that you needed a ride from that writer's meeting." I nodded. "That's right, you were in one bad accident, then you were in the middle of that horrible thing at the Lone Oak."

I braced for her pity, but that's not what I got.

Instead, she said, "You are one lucky woman. Tough, too. I don't blame you for not getting behind the wheel." She looked me straight in the eye. "Don't worry, you will drive again when you're ready."

I let out a little sigh of relief. "Thanks."

She looked at her watch and thought for a moment. "If you don't mind being on your own while I work, you could come with me to the farm now." She held up her index finger to show she wasn't done. "I don't think I'll be long, but—"

"I can wander around, get the feel of the place. Imagine the people who lived there." I pointed to the letters tucked safely in plastic baggies on the table. "I could imagine the women who wrote those letters. I'd be happy just looking at the river."

"Okay then. Grab a warm coat and scarf. The breeze can be cool if it's coming off the water. It's my last appointment of the day and I'll bring you back."

I jumped at the chance. "Thanks. I'll be ready in a minute."

After hanging a warm scarf around my neck, I followed Dee outside. Feeling confident about my injured leg, I swung myself up into her truck, ready to take a ride back in time.

We rode up Route 33, took the turn to Unionville, and headed toward the Miles River Bridge.

"Why don't they call it the St. Michaels River, do you know?" I asked.

"Belle collects all kinds of trivia to keep the clients entertained while she's driving all over the county. I think she said the people from England called it by that name, but Quakers moved into the area. They didn't recognize saints, so they called it the Michaels River. Over time, people got sloppy in their speech, and it became the Miles." She gave me a shrug. "Simple, if you know the history."

As we crossed the bridge, I saw a stone building, or what was left of it, by the side of the road. "Can you stop here for a minute?" I leaned closer to the window, looking at the ruin. Nature was slowly reclaiming the site. The walls, made of large stone blocks, had tall arched windows. They were almost obscured by climbing green ivy and the bright scarlet leaves of a rambling vine. The roof was gone.

Dee pulled off to the side of the road. "Everybody marvels at it," Dee said, taking a moment to look at the structure.

"It looks like a little Gothic church." I glanced around. There was no town. Just fields and a few houses. "But why here?"

She flashed me a smile. "You have a nose for this historical stuff. It is…or was, St. John's Chapel."

"Why did they build it so far from St. Michaels and Easton?" I wanted to know.

"On Sundays, people living on this side of the river had to travel to the Christ Church in St. Michaels, an all-day trek. Families came in carriages to this point, crossed the river by ferry, rode to St. Michaels, attended church services then made their way home again.

"It sounds exhausting," I said.

"It was. That's why they built this chapel about twenty years before the Civil War." She reached up and tightened her ponytail. "The locals were supposed to maintain it, but they didn't. Around 1900, part of the roof caved in during a morning service. The parishioners abandoned the chapel rather than repair it, because they had a wood bridge by then and better ways of getting around. The chapel served its purpose for about fifty years."

"And now it just sits?" I eyed the graceful structure, nestled in the trees by the river, next to a little cove. "It's a shame."

"Yes, but that's one restoration project I wouldn't want to tackle." She turned left on the road that ran down the other side of the river. "There's another story about this area, kind of a Romeo and Juliet story."

Would that remind Dee about seeing Belle with Nicky?

Dee continued without losing a beat. "Families brought their children, relatives, workers, everybody came to worship. A teenage boy and girl met at the chapel and fell in love. He was the son of transient farm workers that showed up for the harvest. She was the daughter of a large landowner. One night, she went to the chapel to meet the boy and run away. Her daddy found out, grabbed his gun, and went after her." Dee sighed. "He shot the boy dead. They called it an accident, but…" Dee shook her head. "You saw the little cove behind the chapel?" I nodded. "The story goes that she drowned herself there rather than live with a broken heart. People couldn't forget what happened and I think that's why they let the chapel deteriorate."

"No," I breathed, not wanting to believe such a sad story.

"There's more. Every spring since, two swans have shown up here. They mate for life, you know. People say they are the spirits of the young lovers returning to the one place they were happy, the chapel." She shrugged. "I'm not a real romantic, but it's kinda nice to think it might be true." A faraway look came over her face as we drove past empty cornfields now. She spoke, but her words were almost lost in a whisper. "It would be nice to find a true love who loved me."

"You and me both," I agreed.

She heaved a sigh. "I guess there's no such a-thing as a man you can count on. A man who wouldn't be tempted by someone else. A man who would stay true."

Before I could respond, she announced, "We're here." She slowed the truck and turned onto a gravel driveway.

There was nothing imposing or dramatic about the entrance. It had two square brick pillars about four feet high with lanterns on top to mark the roadway. It was an estate entrance like so many others in the area. Usually, the houses at the end of those driveways were large and luxurious, but the entrances said we have nothing to prove. The thought made me smile as we came around the bend approaching Safe Harbor House. I had a flash of disappointment as usual and had to remind myself that these houses were built with their imposing frontages facing the river. That was the way visitors once arrived. It was only with the advent of the car and truck that homes were usually approached from the road. By that time the houses were fifty, eighty years old and there was no way to pick them up and turn them around.

We were on our way to the main house when she steered to the left toward an oddly shaped building. It looked more like an igloo made of brick and wood.

Dee put the truck in park, sounded the horn, and pulled the key. "Belle is around here somewhere. She'll come find me. She said you can wander around as much as you please, look at the outbuildings, but she can't give you access to the main house today."

"That's fine," I said as I slipped out of her truck. "I only want to get a sense of the place. It might give me some insight into the people who once lived here."

"We're going to look at this outbuilding. It's got possibilities. It was built as an ice house. From here, it looks like a building that has sunk down into the ground but when you go inside and down a few steps, the space is great. Belle thinks it'll make a great man cave for a new owner. Its high peaked roof and open floor space without roof supports have her mind racing. She looks at all kinds of design magazines and TV shows then asks *me to do that*. Then, of course, I have to figure out how." She smiled and shook her head. "Of course, this building has one big problem."

"What's that?" I squinted, trying to visualize the man cave Belle wanted.

"There's a big ole hole in the middle of the floor that goes deep underground. That's where they stored the ice. She wants me to figure out a way to close it up safely, repair the brick walls, and refinish the wood ceiling. It's all doable and I think it would look pretty special." Dee shrugged. "All it takes is money."

Dee got out of the truck. "I'd better get inside. I see her big SUV. You okay wandering around?"

I nodded, "But can I ask you something?

"Sure."

"Why does she have an angel in her car? It just seems..." I stuttered. "I'm sorry, I didn't mean..."

"No problem. It doesn't seem like it fits with her strong, successful agent persona, but ever since she was a little kid, she's loved angels. All kinds. And you should see her collection at home. Whew! She has dozens and dozens.

"Now, I've got to get inside. With spotty cell coverage out here, remember to keep a sharp ear out in case we don't meet up. When I'm done and ready to go, I'll hit the horn rather than wandering all over the place looking for you."

CHAPTER EIGHTEEN

"It takes two flints to make a fire."

— Louisa May Alcott

I was thrilled to have permission to wander around Safe Harbor Farm to let my imagination run wild. "Sounds like a plan."

Dee put a fat carpenter's pencil behind one ear and rummaged in her truck for a notebook and measuring tape while I headed toward the house. Once I got around to the front, I was struck by the expansive view of the river. No, it was more of a vista. At this angle, I could see all the way across and down the river toward the Bay. The water reflected the robin's egg blue of the sky. The shoreline was bordered by tall green pines, fiery red maple and oak trees, and the golden stripes of birch. I knew how much I enjoyed living at the Cottage and watching the daily changes of nature on the creek and of the Lone Oak. It was almost overwhelming to think of living with this breathtaking view every day. Then I remembered that the people who lived here at the time of the Civil War did not have much time to sit and appreciate the view. There were constant demands on their time to be sure that the plantation produced enough food and products for survival. In comparison, our lifestyle today was downright lazy.

As I walked across the front of Safe Harbor House, the breeze shifted so it was coming directly off the water. Fingers of cold air reached out and touched my skin, a sign of the winter season to come. I wrapped the scarf tighter around my neck and pulled the knitted hat down over my ears. I walked down toward the water for a reason. When I figured I'd gone far enough, I turned and got the full impact of this elegant home.

The main part of the house was similar to Waterwood House, including a set of white columns. There were pairs of black shutters at every window on both floors. The main difference between the two centuries-old houses was Safe Harbor had more additions on each end, beginning with two-story sections then single-story additions as the house tapered down on each side, making it seem bigger.

I wanted to go inside, but that would have to wait for another day. My research had identified the outbuildings commonly found on a plantation such as Safe Harbor and Waterwood. I hoped I could recognize some of them as I walked around the other side of the house.

A round building had a single door slightly ajar and what looked like a vent in its curved wall. As I stepped closer, it still gave off the strong acrid smell of wood smoke. In order to preserve food for the family, fish and meat were smoked in a small building with a large fireplace inside.

Close to it was the outdoor kitchen or cookhouse. It was kept separate so the main house didn't overheat or become inundated with various cooking smells.

Next, rather far from the main house, was a building—no, that was too generous a description. It was a small, crude house. There was a small porch across the front. Something was written on the wall by the door. Someone had burned coarse letters into one of the planks of wood that made up the walls. They read, *Overseer.* This is where a man lived who was a necessary evil on the plantation. He was not welcome in the main house. The man's job was to make the plantation *produce.* That meant getting as much work out of the slaves as he could, even if he had to take a whip to them. Slaves, the source of prosperity and fear. It was this man's job to make them produce and prevent a slave uprising against the master and his family. A shudder ran through me. I couldn't imagine how someone could treat people as property, as chattel, just because their skin was dark.

I walked away quickly to a large open area adjacent to that house. The land wasn't planted. It was just an open area. It must have been where the slave quarters were located, never substantial, now long lost to the ravages of time.

My imagination took off. I could hear heavy boots striding across the wooden porch and down the steps. The overseer yelling at the top of his voice. A young man standing still, eyes wide with fright. Accusations flying. A whip cracking the ground, sending up puffs of dirt.

A voice shouted again, but it wasn't in my imagination. "Y'all better stop that. Don't you do that again"

This wasn't a voice from the shadows of history. It was a woman's voice, close-by. Yelling right now.

I turned away from the illusions of the past and looked at the other nearby outbuildings, trying to pinpoint the source.

"I said y'all better stop that." The words had a sharp edge like a knife.

I whirled around. Those words came from the squat building with the pointed roof. The ice house. The place Belle wanted to convert into a man cave.

Slowly, I was drawn toward it. I didn't want to interrupt the sisters if they were working, but something was wrong. The air felt ripe with danger. I stepped next to the light red brick structure. Here, in its shadow, was a small feeling of safety that kept me apart from what was happening inside. My feet slowed. All was quiet now. Had I imagined the words heavy with threat?

Then a woman keened, "No, noooo."

Her pain nudged me forward. My footsteps moved faster, though my brain was screaming for me to run away.

"No, Nooooo."

The woman cried out again. It was one of the sisters, but which one?

Silence hung heavy in the chilly fall air. It lay on my shoulders like a millstone threatening to take me to my knees. I waited. Nothing. No more sounds. No activity.

Maybe the girls had disagreed about something and were overly dramatic. I should keep my nose out of their business. But the sound of the voice crying out *Nooooo* still echoed in my mind and prickled my skin.

I took a few tentative steps toward the door, just in case. Then the crunch of footsteps reached my ears. They were coming, closer. I stopped. They stopped.

Another voice, a man spoke with the gentle air of disbelief. I couldn't understand his words, but his voice rose higher and higher until it split the air. A wail.

The sound froze my blood.

Then there were footsteps, heavy footsteps. Running. A flash of blue. Then gone. There was no other sign of him.

I moved again toward the door. What had he seen? What was he leaving behind? I reached the open doorway and peered into the shadowy space inside.

It was just as Dee had described. Steps down into a large, open, but darkened area. A flashlight lay discarded on the ground, shining upward. I pulled out my phone and turned on my flashlight app. It lit up brick walls leading up to a peaked roof. Plenty of room for the tallest man to stand comfortably. Plenty of room for screens suspended in front of rows of recliners. But all that was in my imagination. This place was part of Safe Harbor House, but there was no delicate lace or flame mahogany furniture here. Inside, the smell of old dirt long laid bare and undisturbed hung in the air. Musty. And there was the sour smell of sweat from work done so long ago. My nose tightened to keep out as much of the odor as possible.

Where were the sisters?

I grabbed up their discarded flashlight and shone it around the open space of rough brick walls, a wood roof and a floor of dirt, straw, and gravel. To the side, a piece of rotted muslin fluttered from a handle of an old wooden wheelbarrow. I made myself scan the murky area. And then my eyes fell on what I feared most.

A body sprawled on the ground. Face down. Ball cap with a ponytail pulled through the back.

Dee! Blood was everywhere. I leaned over her and saw she was breathing.

But I'd heard two voices. Where was Belle?

A circle of darkness in the middle of the floor drew me toward it. A ladder with rotted rungs lay next to the opening. Standing as close as I dared, I angled the light down, down into the ice pit. To the horror below.

A body lay draped over the wood supports halfway down the hole. A woman with strawberry blonde hair hanging loose like a halo around her perfectly made-up face. Her head was at a crooked angle.

Belle.

I dropped to my knees and held out my hand. There was no way I could reach her. I whispered her name. She didn't respond. I looked away. It couldn't be. No. I forced myself to look again.

Wait! There was a sound, a creak. Had she moved? No, nothing had changed. One high-heeled shoe with a bright red sole dangled from her right foot. Her arms and legs in a provocative position, but there was nothing sensual here. Only death.

Beautiful Belle was... My body slumped forward from the shock. Another creak. Was the support about to give way, sending her down into the unforgiving darkness? I had to jerk back before I too tumbled down. Bits of dirt sprinkled down the side of the hole.

Move! Move! Before the old hole gives way.

I scrambled back, out of danger. That's when I heard a moan. Behind me. Dee!

I crawled to her and knelt beside her body. Dee's jeans and shirt were stained with mud. And blood. It was everywhere. The smell was sharp. She had a gash on her head that was bleeding. Gushing. Crimson and thick. Dripping down Dee's face knotted up in pain. Soaking into her shirt. Creeping across the dirt floor.

I pulled off my scarf, bunched it up and applied it to the gash to help stop the bleeding. She moved. I laid a hand on her shoulder to hold her down on the floor, not sure what kind of damage she could do if she tried to get up.

"Dee, it's okay," I said, trying to soothe her. "Don't move."

She raised a hand toward her head. I pushed it away gently. "No, just lay still."

Her strength leaked away, and she melted back into the floor.

"That's good." I glanced at my phone's screen, plenty of battery, but no bars. "Just lie still for a minute. I'll be right back. Don't move."

I raced across the floor, up the few steps and outside, whipping my phone around in every direction hoping for a signal.

Nothing.

I ran on, holding the phone up toward the sky, coaxing a signal out of the ether.

Then, two bars. I stabbed 911.

CHAPTER NINETEEN

"...we're twins, and so we love each other more than other people..."
— Louisa May Alcott, *Little Men*

With lights flashing and a siren wailing, Dee was rushed off to the hospital. I stayed behind, sitting on the back bumper of the ambulance, a blanket pulled tight around me. The flashing lights of the emergency vehicles including the police were out of place in this serene spot. Only a few wispy white clouds marred the blue-sky dome that reached down to the horizon. A breeze brought the salty scent of the river to me though I don't think it could ever drive away the distinctive metallic smell of fresh blood.

I closed my eyes and again saw the scene I'd found in the ice house. Blood. Blood everywhere. Was it on my shoes? I looked down. It was. Without thinking, I reached down hoping to wipe it away. My hand stopped inches away from my shoe and started to shake. I couldn't touch it. I couldn't wipe away the blood from my shoe or the memory from my mind. Was this all Dee's blood? Had I stepped in some of Belle's?

A voice yanked me back to the present. "Ms. Chase?" he asked.

I met the man's deep brown eyes. I knew them. I knew that face.

"Emma?" Homicide Detective Craig Mason leaned in closer. Lines of concern creased his forehead. His mouth was poised to speak, but he was waiting for me to respond.

"Detective?" I finally managed to say.

He seemed to sigh with relief. "Good. Are you okay?"

I managed to nod. I reached out. My hand was shaking. I looked down. My other hand was shaking wildly and I couldn't calm them. Maybe the shock of everything was getting to me. I couldn't think what I was supposed to do to counteract the PTSD. I couldn't think of much of anything.

Craig spoke gently. "Emma, I have to ask you some questions, but we can wait a few minutes."

An EMT handed me a cup of water. I wished we were in England where they would ply me with heavily-sugared hot tea. That thought was reassuring. I still had my sense of humor. I started to speak.

"Sh-h-h," the detective told me gently. "Don't say anything now. Just drink your water. I've contacted TJ. He's on his way,"

"Don't want to bother—" I began to say, then the magnitude of the situation started to penetrate my brain again. Water sloshed out of the cup as my hand shook.

Craig cradled my hand in his. "I'll be the judge of that." He guided the cup to my lips. "Drink."

I did as instructed and felt a little better. He put the cup down. "Now, sit back and catch your breath. I'll be right back."

He slipped away before I could ask him any of the many questions whirling around in my head. *Was Dee okay? Belle?* I'd hit overload and withdrew from everything around me. Everything but the drop of blood on my right index finger.

"Emma!" TJ's voice was filled with concern but hearing him call out brought such comfort. TJ would make everything all right.

"I'm okay." I looked down at my shoes and grimaced. "A little bloody, but it's not my blood." My body shot up straight. "But the girls, the sisters?"

The detective walked up. "We're attending to them. Don't worry. You and I—"

I had to interrupt. I had to know. "Tell me! Are they okay?"

Craig glanced at TJ who was adjusting his cap, then he delivered the truth. "I'm afraid Belle was badly hurt in the fall. But thanks to your quick action, Dee has a chance. That's what the paramedic said. We'll have to wait and see. Good work, Emma."

"But Belle is dead?" I wanted to know, but didn't want to hear the answer.

"Yes. I'm sorry." The detective wouldn't let me dwell on that news and moved the conversation right along. "Can you tell me what happened?"

In fits and starts, I filled him in on our little excursion to Safe Harbor Farm. I'd lost that warm feeling of strolling around the old house and grounds, trying to visualize what life was like more than a hundred years ago. Then I remembered the angry voices that had pulled me back to the present.

"The voices must have been really loud," I said.

TJ looked at Craig and said, "If they were yelling in the ice house, the acoustics might have amplified their voices."

"That's where they were meeting to discuss turning the old building into some kind of a man cave," I added.

"Did anyone else know they were going to be there?" Craig was quizzing me.

I shook my head. "I have no idea."

TJ was getting antsy. He bounced from one foot to the other while the detective questioned me. "Did you see anything unusual? Someone else maybe?"

I shook my head again.

Strain was showing on TJ's face. "Can I take her home now?"

"Not yet." The detective held out his hand. "Do you feel like walking a little bit, Emma? Not far."

TJ hissed at Craig. "Is this necessary? Now?"

"It would really help. It will only take a minute. Emma, can you show me where you were when you first heard the twins yelling?"

I finished the last drop of water in the cup, slipped the blanket off my shoulders and rolled to my feet. TJ put out a hand to steady me.

Maybe talking about what happened would help.

"I think I was walking over there." I led them to the far side of the ice house. "I couldn't see anyone, but I could hear their voices. One was screaming. The other was snippy."

"Could you tell which was which?" Craig was ready with his notebook.

I almost burst out laughing at his ludicrous request. "You must think I'm genius. The girls are twins. I don't think their momma could tell them apart like that."

"But you said you could tell a difference in what they were saying."

I shook my head. "Not *what* they were saying. *How* they were saying it. One was red-hot mad. The other was goading her, toying with her twin. But I have no idea which was which. Then there was a scream." I turned to TJ and squeezed his hand. "Now I know what a blood-curdling scream sounds like." A shiver ran down my back. "And then, nothing. Nothing that I could hear. Sorry, detective."

TJ set his jaw. "Okay, that's enough for now. Talk to her later or better, tomorrow after she gets some rest." He put his hand under my elbow, ready to guide me to his truck.

"You're right," the detective agreed. "I've got enough to start. Plus, we'll see what the crime scene people find. Emma, thank you. You're very brave."

Funny, I didn't feel brave. TJ's hand on my arm was steadying and reassuring as we walked to his truck. I kept my eyes on the ground, so I didn't trip over a rut created by the ambulances. Every step drained a little more energy away. I looked up to see how much farther we had to walk.

And I stopped, frozen like a statue.

"Emma, are you all right? What is it?" TJ searched my face, but I wasn't seeing him. I saw the land, the main Safe Harbor House, the back of the ice house and other outbuildings. I saw it all, before the emergency vehicles—the ambulances and police cars—were called to the farm. I heard the voices, the girls yelling at each other. But there was something else.

I gripped TJ's shirt in my fist. "Get the detective. Get the detective!" The urgency in my voice got him moving while I stayed rooted to that spot. Staring, but only seeing what was there before. Not what.

Who.

The men ran toward me.

The EMT stepped in front of them. "Are you okay, ma'am? Maybe you should—"

"No, I'm fine." I kept staring. "Where is Craig? I remembered something."

Craig waved away the EMT and came closer. "I'm here. What did you remember, Emma? Can you tell me?"

SUSAN REISS

I moved my eyes and focused on the detective. "There was someone else here." My words were coming out on little puffs of air, faster and faster. "Someone. Not the twins. Someone else. I saw someone. A man."

I barely heard TJ ask, "Who?"

Craig put out his hand to prevent any interruption. "Emma," he said softly. "Tell me what you saw."

"After the scream, everything went quiet. Then there was another scream. No, it was more of a moan or a whimper. I could barely hear it, but I remember it." I paused and rubbed my arm, feeling the icy waves of anxiety settling in. I didn't want to revisit the memory. I knew I was safe, but it didn't matter. I didn't want to dip into that pain again. But the detective needed to know.

"It was so quiet. Even the birds were afraid to sing. I was standing outside, close to the door. I didn't know what to do. It wasn't any of my business. It was between the sisters. Sisters fight all the time. It wasn't my place... Then there were footsteps, footsteps on the gravel."

Craig encouraged me to go on. "What happened next?"

"Someone else was there and things were quiet..."

"What did you do?" Craig demanded.

"I went toward the door."

Craig wanted clarification. "Which way?" I pointed to the side nearest the main house. "Then what?"

"I heard more footsteps. Outside now."

"Did you see anybody?" Craig pulled out his notebook.

"No," I said, trying to remember. "Just heard somebody. I thought one of the girls was leaving. But the footsteps..." I looked at TJ. "They sounded heavy like a man.

"Did you see anyone?" Craig asked again.

"No, not then." I shook my head. "I hung back. Didn't want to get in the middle... But those screams...they scared me. I heard a man's voice. Then I had to move… needed to know the twins were all right. I came around the side…" I turned my head to my left as if I was walking around the ice house again. "Yes, I saw …" I perked up at the memory. "Yes! I saw a man. A big guy, not fat, just big. He came out the door and headed in the other direction. He was running, running away. I made it to the door… I went in …" My eyes prickled with tears as I remembered the awful scene inside.

"You can stop there, Emma. That was great," Craig assured me. "You're doing great. Just one more question. Did you recognize the man?"

I stared into the distance, the tears finally started streaming down my cheeks. I shook my head. "I only know it was a man. Blue jeans. Some kind of shirt. Boots. Nothing special. Oh, he was wearing some kind of ballcap."

"Did you see…"

I was already shaking my head.

Frustration weighed down Craig's words. "The one time I need the guy to wear his hat backwards. Can you tell me the color of his hair?"

Again, I shook my head. "Only caught a glimpse…as he ran. Never saw his face." I looked at Craig, the tears flowing freely now. "I'm sorry. I'm so sorry. If I had moved faster…"

But Craig was shaking his head. "No, if, IF this man hurt the twins and he had seen you, he wouldn't have hesitated to hurt you. You were right not to try and stop what was happening. I'm glad you're okay."

TJ's arm went around me as the sobs shook my body.

"TJ, take her home and watch out for her," he added quietly.

When we got back to the Cottage, TJ wanted to stay the night in the living room chair as he had once before. That time, nobody died. I was just an idiot, falling down and hurting myself, after the first meeting with the writers. This time, after we had a quiet dinner of pizza and salad, I shooed him out of the Cottage. He was too busy with his farming responsibilities to lose sleep because of me. Protesting the whole time, he finally left, and I locked up everything tight. If I could only lock out the images flashing in my mind.

CHAPTER TWENTY

"Women work a great many miracles."

— Louisa May Alcott, *Little Women*

My mind kept going back to what happened, what I'd seen at the ice house. I figured that was normal, but the trauma and endless questions were taking a toll. I couldn't seem to settle. I needed a calming distraction. I wandered into the dining room and picked up another diary, hoping for a safe, unemotional distraction.

I settled back to see how Emma had chosen to go on with her life after losing her baby. I scanned for readable entries. So many were damaged. In places, only a few words had escaped the rainwater. I was able to glimpse some details of Waterwood, like overseeing the smokehouse operations, a horse Emma had grown to love, and the doctoring skills she was required to use. I read with great surprise that it was the mistress who oversaw the all-important hog slaughter. If it was modest or failed in some way, the people of the plantation – slaves and those who lived in the main house – would feel the effects of hunger.

Then I came to an entry that was intact.

Dear Diary,

Today was one of the saddest and most shocking days of my life. I walked out to the front porch and found Anna Grace playing with dolls. She is almost sixteen years old, much too old to be playing with dolls. But she surprised me. She said she was practicing for the day she would have her own baby. She said she wanted a little girl she could dress in pretty things.

She held up a baby's day dress. When I saw it, I forgot how to breathe. I recognized it instantly, because I had sewn the rosettes, stitched the seams for the little inset sleeves, and crafted the lace edging myself. It was made for the baby, my baby girl, who was not destined to survive the perils of birth. She would not walk with me along the paths of my beloved Waterwood, learn to thrive in this magical place at the knee of her mother. When the time came to bury my baby, she could not be dressed in her christening gown for she had not been blessed. Though too sick to move from my bed, I asked my husband to let her wear the little day dress I'd made. The same dress that Anna Grace was holding.

I choked down hot tears and bewilderment for I did not want to frighten the child. Child? She is almost a woman who will wed sometime soon. She is too old for dolls, but not too young to sense the tension between her parents.

As calmly as I could, I asked where she had found the little dress. She responded that she had found it in her father's office, tucked at the bottom of a small chest.

Neither I nor any of the children are allowed in his office. The thought of him finding out that Anna Grace had been there and taken something made me fretful. I instructed her to return the dress to the same place and never speak of it.

She resisted until I promised that we would work together to make a baby day dress like it that would fit her doll and perhaps her own baby someday.

When she ran inside with the sweet little dress, I collapsed against the solid wall of Waterwood House. I could not let the children see me shed tears, but my heart cried out in dismay. Was my tiny daughter not laid to eternal rest in the dress fashioned by her mother? Or was she lying cold in the grave without the warmth of her mother's love?

I struggled to control myself as the memories of that time flooded my mind. I remembered the day when I was finally able to rise from my bed after her birth. I made my way to the family graveyard with Sally's help. I wanted to kneel at the grave of my littlest one. But her grave was not there. I was distraught, but dear Sally calmed me. She found the mound of dirt that covered her. Why was my baby buried so far away from where I am to lay?

Why? So many questions fill my mind even now.

From the day I told him I was with child again, I felt he looked at me with contempt. Did he think the child was *not his? Having known me for all these years, did he truly think that I could betray my marriage vows? I could not.*

But here in the quiet of my diary, I must add the words, unless Daniel walked in the door.

I returned the diary to the dining room table so it would continue to dry. My brain was in a whirl. I put on Uncle Jack's warm coat and it gave me comfort as I wandered outside in the clean air.

CHAPTER TWENTY-ONE

"My sister and I, you will recollect, were twins, and you know how subtle are the links which bind two souls which are so closely allied"

— Arthur Conan Doyle, Sherlock Holmes, *Ovun Basladt*

T he next afternoon, the doctors said Dee could have visitors if we didn't stay too long. TJ and I stood outside the private hospital room Detective Craig Mason had arranged for Dee. He felt the need to protect her until he found the man who might have attacked her and killed her sister Belle. He needed to talk with her and thought that if we were in the room, it might be easier for her. I wasn't sure what we could do to help, but I was willing to try, especially if all it meant was that I had to show up.

The three of us entered the room and I fussed with the flowers and the Get-Well balloon we'd brought. I was surprised that there was just one vase of flowers from Belle's real estate firm to take the dreariness out of the dreary, but functional hospital room. Because of the unusual circumstances, maybe happy, bright things were not appropriate. Sending a sympathy card to a hospital seemed out of place, too. I was glad we'd brought something. The detective positioned TJ at the end of the bed and put me in a chair where I could hold her hand. I guess Craig thought a woman could offer more comfort, if needed, than a male friend she'd known for a long time. But this was the detective's show, not mine.

It broke my heart to see Dee lying on the white sheets that seemed to drain all color out of her face. The big bandage on the left side of her head didn't help either. That must have been where the man had hit her. Craig said the forensics team had identified the weapon as an old brick they found lying on the ground. If the man had wanted to kill her, he hadn't made a real effort. Still, he'd almost succeeded. The brick had broken the skin, that's why there was so much blood. It was a miracle that it didn't fracture Dee's skull. She had a concussion, but nothing life-threatening. TJ and I were making appropriate comments when the detective cleared his throat.

"Dee, thank you for seeing us all today. And let me begin by saying we're very sorry for your loss." Craig tipped his head toward us. "I'm glad your friends could come to lend support while I ask you a few questions. So, why don't we start by you telling me what happened."

I could see her body tense. I was about to say something, that this was a bad idea, when she began to speak. Her voice was a little raspy, probably from not talking much.

"I don't know what to tell you. I didn't see that much. My sister..." Her voice caught and I almost reached for the tissue box, but Dee rallied. "We met, she wanted to turn the old ice house into a man cave. She wanted my okay so she could suggest it to potential buyers."

Craig encouraged her. "What did you think?"

"It's got a vaulted ceiling. No supports to get in the way. Plenty of room for a pool table, seating, screens and…" Dee relaxed as she talked about the work she loved. It was clever of the detective to get her talking about familiar things. Her voice grew stronger and stronger. Then her expression became uncertain. Was it the memory of what happened next or something else? "But we started talking about other things, I think. I don't…"

Craig must have seen the change, too and jumped in again to keep her talking. "That place in the middle of the floor. You had to do something with that. Would you cover it up?"

She started to nod her head, but a flash of pain stopped her. It took a moment for the wince on her face to relax. The detective was patient.

"Yes," she said finally. "That's right. We'd need to build a support and cover it over. An easy fix… no one would know it was there."

Craig smiled his reassurance. "You're doing really well, Dee." He took a deep breath and looked down at his notebook. "Tell me what happened next."

"I'm not sure. I—I needed to take measurements. Belle always wants—" Dee choked on those last words. After she got control of the tears that threatened to fall, she spoke again. "She always wanted details for buyers. That's why she was so good at her job. Her buyers believed she had their best interests at heart."

"Did she?" Craig asked softly.

The simple question caught Dee off guard. "W-what?"

"Do you think that Belle had her clients' interests at heart?"

Dee shrugged a shoulder a little against the pillows. "Her clients? Yes."

The detective kept his eyes on his notebook. "What about you? Did she take care of you?"

"Y-Y-Yes, since we were kids." Dee was starting to sound a little defensive.

"But she made your life miserable sometimes?" Craig suggested.

"No. What do you mean?" Dee squinted at him, confused.

He cocked his head to the side. "She wanted you to give her details and costs on repairs and renovations. Did she pay you for that information?"

"Sure, and she always recommended me for the work. She paid me for any work I did for her."

He looked up and shot a question at her. "Were you two fighting… about money that afternoon in the ice house?"

"What? No!" Dee's hand gripped the blanket.

Craig shot back. "But you were fighting, weren't you?"

"I, we… why would you say that?" Her voice was strained.

Craig cocked his head. "Somebody heard you two having some angry words, Dee."

Now, it was my turn to tense. Was Craig going to square us off against one another? I hoped not. I didn't sign up for a confrontation.

Dee spoke up. "We were having a little disagreement, that's all. It's what sisters do."

"I heard that your little disagreement was pretty loud and pretty angry." His words dripped with sarcasm.

"Do you have any brothers or sisters?" Dee demanded. She was finding her attitude again. Craig shook his head. "Then you don't know and haven't a chance of understanding," she snarled at him. "We're twins. We may have different personalities, but we're both passionate."

Dee's eyes strayed to the window and stared at nothing. In a voice that was so taut, it matched the tone of the highest tones of a piano, she said, "Oh no… the last thing I said to my sister… I didn't mean to yell at her… if she had only… she had to stop…I can't believe I'll never talk to her again." And Dee dissolved into agonizing sobs.

My nostrils flared as I shot a furious look at Craig. Instead of lashing out at him, I reached for the tissue box and tried to comfort Dee. The men talked in murmurs in a corner away from the bed. I couldn't hear what they were saying, and I didn't want to know. Hadn't the girl been through enough? Did he have to push her like that? It was obvious that she wasn't used to the idea yet that her sister was dead. People needed time to let a loss like that settle in, especially without family to cushion the blow. I was still dealing with the loss of my Uncle Jack, and it had been almost a year. Dee had only had a day. Especially with the head injury, it was unfair for the detective to push like that.

When Dee's tears began to slow, Craig moved to the other side of the bed. "I apologize for asking you to talk about this very sad situation. Again, I am sorry for your loss."

The words of compassion helped calm Dee and began to renew my faith in the man.

"I get it," Dee said. "You're doing your job. I wish I could help you more."

"Thank you. I appreciate that." He pursed his lips. "Do you think I could ask you one more question?"

I was about to insist that he stop when Dee looked at him with a quivering grin. "If I can ask you a question?"

Craig nodded. "That's fair."

"Okay, you go first." She took a tissue and wiped her eyes dry.

"Dee, was there anyone else in the ice house with you?"

Dee screwed up her face in confusion. "What?"

"You know that Belle ended up in the ice hole. Did she slip and fall? Did someone push her? Did you?"

Dee tried to straighten her shoulders. "I didn't hurt my sister," she declared. "Sure, we'd yell at each other. But hurt her?

Kill her? NEVER!" She held his eyes in a steely stare. "And she wouldn't hurt me. Find out who hurt her and hit me over the head. And now, you and I are done."

Craig mumbled his standard statement of thanking a witness for her cooperation which gave me some time to swallow my fury.

We started to say our good-byes and shuffle to the door when Dee said, "You can't leave, Mr. Detective. You haven't answered my question."

Craig was done as far as I was concerned, so I jumped in. "And what do you want to know, Dee?"

She shifted her gaze to me and spoke in a small voice. "Why hasn't Nicky been to visit me? They won't tell me anything here."

I looked at the two men. I didn't have the answer.

TJ jumped to the rescue. "Dee, he wanted me to tell you that he sends his love and wants you to get better fast. He'll come as soon as he can. You concentrate on getting better so you can go home. We'll talk soon."

We all turned toward the door again to leave when her next words stopped us. "Home? Where is that? I just sold my little house and moved back in with ..." She stumbled, not able to say her sister's name. "I can't live there now. Where is home for me now? Where can I go?"

Now, it was my turn. "Don't you worry about that. You concentrate on getting better."

"But Emma, I can't ... she isn't coming home." She took a breath and continued. "I could stay with Nicky, but something must be wrong. He hasn't come to see me. I don't understand."

I hoped she couldn't see my concern. "Don't you worry. We'll work it out. Now, get some rest."

CHAPTER TWENTY-TWO

"You are like a chestnut burr, prickly outside, but silky-soft within, and a sweet kernel, if one can only get at it. Love will make you show your heart someday, and then the rough burr will fall off."

— Louisa May Alcott, *Little Women*

As TJ steered through traffic, we were both quiet, lost in our own thoughts. It was a relief to turn on Route 33, back to open fields and tall trees showing off bright colors before their leaves fell. Here, I could take a deep breath and feel sheltered.

Yes, it sounded crazy. The Cottage is in the middle of nowhere, far from people. True, but here, Mother Nature always nurtured me. Of course, the summer months offered breathtaking vistas of open sky and azure waters. But the soaring evergreens were always there, even in the bare winter landscape, with their emerald boughs dancing gently in the wind. The Shore had a strong effect on my mental well-being. How could I ever go back to the noisy, smelly city where the only way to see the sky was to stand still and look straight up? Where did I belong?

Where was home? That's what Dee had asked, and she was right. I too needed answers, but Dee's need was urgent.

With Belle gone, it was logical to think of Dee's fiancé. "TJ, where is Nicky?"

He pressed his lips together and finally admitted that Nicky was being held as a person of interest.

"What?" I was shocked. "The police think that Nicky…"

With a little shrug, TJ said, "I don't know. They must have their reasons."

Still unable to wrap my mind around that idea, I concentrated on the immediate problem. "Where do you think Dee should go when she is discharged from the hospital? Does she have any friends who will step up and offer her a place to stay?"

TJ took one of his hands off the steering wheel and rubbed the back of his neck. "I don't know. If that room was any indication, I'd say the answer is no."

"I noticed the lack of flowers and cards, too." I shrugged one shoulder. "But this is an unusual situation. Do you send a bright, happy Get-Well card when her sister was just murdered?"

TJ was quick to say, "They haven't determined that it was murder yet. Best not to say anything like that for now."

I wiggled around to face him as much as my seat belt would allow. "But what else could it be?"

"Well, according to Craig," TJ said carefully. "It could have been an accident and—"

"An accident?" I didn't mean to interrupt him, but I was stunned. "How could it have been an accident?"

"You saw the inside of the ice house. In the 1800s, they lowered blocks of ice down the hole so they would keep into the summer months. The hole is right in the middle of the dirt floor. No barriers or guardrails. The crime scene people might be able to tell what happened. Even if the floor was dry, it's easy for dirt to break away at the edges. That's how cave-ins happen. There was nothing to prevent Belle from losing her balance and falling into the ice pit."

"If Belle was dead before she slid into the hole, it would be murder. But if she wasn't..." I paused.

He jumped in. "It might still be murder... or it could be an accident. It's a puzzle and just a flat-out mess."

"You're right about that."

"We should stop speculating. If we jump to the wrong conclusion, Emma, people could be hurt,"

"Especially Dee," I added quickly. "There's one thing I know for sure."

TJ took his eyes off the road and looked at me with a frown.

"Belle didn't choose to jump into that hole. It would have ruined her cashmere slacks and matching sweater set. She would have hated losing a shoe." TJ looked mystified. "Shoes, TJ. It's a woman thing." And the little joke eased the strain caused by the talk of murder hanging in the air.

Here we were, two people in a truck, driving home from a police interview where we talked about a death. I felt some comfort as I drank in the natural beauty of the landscape. But something kept pushing at my mind. What about the shoes, the outrageously expensive shoes? Were they important? I'd think about them later as TJ slowed down to enter St. Michaels, always a place of activity and distraction.

People on the brick sidewalks ambled between shops and restaurants, enjoying a day that didn't require a coat or scarf, yet. We passed two women laughing as their husbands followed along behind with lighter wallets and bags of unique finds. A young couple blocked the walkway with a huge stroller while they smiled and cooed at their baby. A short man with gray hair and glasses walked with purpose, threading his way through the people toward the pharmacy. Probably a resident. Except for him, they were happy. They were all happy, without a worry. I hoped he would be okay. But the others…I wanted to stop the truck, jump on top of the cab, and scream at them.

Stop it! Stop laughing. Stop acting like everything in the world is fine. There is a young woman dead. There is a sister who doesn't know where home is anymore. How can you act so normal, without a care? You acted like this when I lost Uncle Jack and my heart broke. You're doing it again. STOP IT!

But it wouldn't do any good to yell at them. They wouldn't hear me. Everyone is tied up in their own lives with barely a thought for anyone else. It happened in my own family when Uncle Jack died. My sister said it was sad, but he was an old man. My mother wondered what price the Cottage would bring. When she heard my tears on the phone, she said I was too attached, and his death was part of life. If I couldn't make *them* understand, what impression could I make on these strangers?

I reached out and squeezed TJ's arm.

"What's that for?" he asked.

"Oh, I'm just glad that we're going through this together." I put my hand back in my lap, hoping the gesture had said it all. That without friends and family, life might be too hard to live. Friends and family. That reminded me of the main unresolved question.

"TJ, where is Dee going to go?"

He thought a moment. "I don't know. She said she doesn't want to go back to Belle's apartment."

I felt a little shiver. "I don't blame her. I wouldn't want to be there either, at least not until things are resolved." I couldn't voice the one thing I was sure we were both thinking. *If only she could stay with Nicky.* But that was out of the question until we were sure it wasn't Nicky who hurt the twins.

TJ grunted softly. "I guess she could stay at Waterwood. Heaven knows I have plenty of bedrooms."

"And how many of them are ready for a guest? I know your heart is in the right place, but she needs someone around to help her, at least for the first few days. I think she should come and stay with me."

"That's not a good idea, Emma," TJ exclaimed.

"Why not, TJ? She can use my old bedroom at the Cottage. Maria keeps the house squeaky clean and she can cook for us, too. Maria loves taking care of people. The Cottage isn't as big as Waterwood House, but it's big enough for her to have her privacy and find company if she wants or needs it. After all, she is recovering from a serious head injury."

He cleared his throat. "That's what I mean. She has a head injury."

"If you think she'd be safer not using the stairs, we can make up a bed on the sofa—"

"No," he said with such force that I shrank into my seat. "No," he repeated in a gentler tone. "The point is, she was hit on the head with a brick, at least Craig thinks it was a brick. It didn't just fly up and hit her. And she didn't hit herself on the head. Someone took a swing at her. Somebody wanted to hurt her."

My breath caught. "I didn't think of that. That could only have been Belle or…"

"The same person who hurt Belle." He hesitated. "And might try again." He closed his mouth and squeezed his lips together. There was something he didn't want to say aloud.

So, I said it for him. "It could have been murder. Almost a double murder." Suddenly, that idea became a very real possibility. "But why would someone want to kill the sisters?"

Neither of us had the answer. We rode along in silence. I rubbed my hands, trying to rub away the chill triggered by the thought that somebody murdered Belle and tried to kill Dee. Was that why they were both yelling, using words to fight off their attacker? Was it someone they knew, someone they believed wouldn't hurt them? Did Dee scream when she saw her sister manhandled into the ice pit?

Why, oh why didn't I get closer to hear something? I know, I know, I didn't want to intrude. But if I'd heard something, anything, it might have condemned or freed Nicky or given Craig another lead.

TJ interrupted my thoughts. "That's why I don't think it's a good idea for Dee to stay with you. If it wasn't an accident, that *somebody* might come back... and hurt you both." TJ took his eyes off the road for a moment to look me straight in the eye. "I think she'd be safer at Waterwood House."

"And be there all alone during the day? No, together we'll be fine at the Cottage. Anyway, that somebody would have to know where to find the Cottage, to find us. Besides, I have a landline so we can call the police if we need them."

TJ shifted his gaze back to the road. He swung his eyes, now narrowed to slits, back to me, then back to the road. "You know, you can be pretty frustrating sometimes. Ornery is a better word. Yes, ornery."

I banged the back of my head on the headrest of my seat. "Oh, no..."

"What? You don't like to be called ornery? Well—"

"No," The word came out almost like a moan. "No... the meeting of the writers is tonight." I started digging into my tote.

"It's a dinner meeting, right? So, you've got time," he assured me.

"I have to find my phone. Maybe I can catch Maureen before she goes by the Cottage to pick me up."

"I guess I could take you and then go back and pick you up," he offered.

"No, I can't go to the meeting, not after everything that's happened." I hoped he heard the resolve in my tone. I didn't want to go, and I didn't want to have a fight about it. Dealing with Dee was more important and had taken a lot out of me. I couldn't handle a room full of writers, too.

I hadn't noticed that he had picked up speed and was making the turn to the Cottage. What I saw made me sigh. Maureen was getting out of her car, a bright red Porsche Cayenne!

CHAPTER TWENTY-THREE

"You cannot fail unless you quit..."

– Abraham Lincoln

When TJ came to a stop, I jumped out of the truck. "Maureen! Here I am."

Even casually dressed in black slacks and a black and white silk tunic, she had an elegant flair about her.

"I'm so sorry," I said, rushing forward. "I totally forgot about the meeting. You see, we had to go to the hospital..."

She frowned as she ran her eyes up and down my body. She knew about the challenges I'd faced in recovering the use of my leg. "You didn't hurt yourself again, did you?"

"No, no, I'm fine. TJ's fine, too." Her face relaxed. "We went to see Dee."

Maureen frowned again. "That poor girl. To lose her sister like that and to get hurt herself. Is she all right?"

"Yes," TJ answered. "They're going to discharge her soon."

"And she's going to come and stay with me." I sent a look of defiance at TJ that meant, *And that's that.* "With so much going on, I'm sure you can understand that I can't go to the meeting tonight."

I was surprised to hear TJ say, "I don't understand." He looked at his watch. You still have time to get cleaned up and go."

Maureen agreed. "TJ's right. We don't have to leave right away. I came early to bring you one more book. Don't worry, it's short."

Looking from one to the other, I said, "But I wouldn't want to put you out."

"It's no bother," Maureen said with a smile.

TJ raised his eyebrows. "She's willing to take you. You'd better get moving."

I knew I could flat out refuse to go, but here were two people eager to help me work toward my dream. That didn't mean I had to like it, but I couldn't turn my back on their support. I went inside to get ready for the meeting, but on the steps where no one could hear me, I let out a long, low groan. Dreams could take so much work.

It didn't take me long *to get all cleaned up*, as TJ put it. I scurried down the steps as fast as I dared and burst out the front door to discover Maureen leaning against her car enjoying the surroundings. TJ's truck was gone.

"Oh, good, you're ready," Maureen said as she tucked a soft wave of her thick silver hair behind her ear. There were some lines on her face, but she'd earned every one of them as the creative director of a successful advertising agency in New York. She probably could teach me everything I needed to know about writing. "I told TJ he didn't have to wait and that he didn't have to pick you up. I'll bring you home. I got the impression he was a little relieved."

How did I feel about that? Glad that he'd have the evening to himself ...and a little hurt that he'd given up so easily on the opportunity of driving me home. He probably didn't want to chance a repeat performance. I'd been an absolute dolt after the last meeting, acting out my frustrations like a spoiled child to the point that I'd hurt myself. Just the thought made my cheeks grow hot, again.

She must have noticed and looked at me with her eyebrows together, worried. "Did I do something wrong?"

I took a breath and tried to bury my embarrassment. "No, not at all. And thank you for offering to drive me home."

"It's no bother. Now, we need to get going." She handed me a slim book. "Take a look at this one. It's a favorite of mine. We can talk about it in the car."

In no time, Maureen had her Porsche on the main road, happily shifting through the gears. I had no idea that this sedate woman would opt for speed. I didn't get a terrifying sensation in this car that would make me reach for the grab bar with both hands. Maybe it was because it was a Porsche, a car built for speed. But to make sure I didn't spiral down the fear hole, I directed my attention away from the road to the book in my hand. The title was *Bird by Bird*. Was Maureen suggesting that I take up birdwatching, so I'd relax into the zone to write? I thumbed through the pages expecting to see lots of color photos, but there were none. I wanted to ask her about the book but didn't want to distract her from driving at a speed I was sure exceeded the posted limit. I hazarded a glance her way and saw her smiling.

"I'm proud of you," she said.

A comment I hadn't expected. "For what?"

Her smile broadened. "For not gripping the chicken bar... also known as a grab bar. But you are gripping that little book. Worry not! All those years I lived in New York City, I never had a car. Why should I? The expense for parking alone was exorbitant and the stress of driving in-town..." Her shoulders and head shuddered a little. "I had enough stress on the job. Didn't need more just to get home."

"So, how did you end up with a bright red Porsche?" I asked, relaxing into the leather seat.

"When I decided to move down here to the Shore, I knew I'd have to have a car." She lowered her voice to let me in on a secret. "In fact, I think it played a part in my decision. New car. Open roads." She nodded. "Oh yes, a perfect combination! It always thrilled me to go fast. Maybe that's why I like watching NASCAR."

NASCAR! My hands squeezed into a death grip on the book. If I'd known, I would never have gotten into this spiffy red car with a stick shift. But I wasn't going to grab onto anything for dear life. No way!

Not noticing my anxiety, Maureen continued. "The first thing I did was go to the Porsche Driving School in Atlanta. They have an incredible operation there. I had my own driving coach who put me through my paces on this fabulous, closed track they have. The coach explained the capabilities of the car and why it responds the way it does. While there, I opted to drive a 911 Cabriolet, though I was tempted by the 911 GT3. Its top speed on the track is 197 miles per hour."

I gasped.

She chuckled. "Don't worry, even I thought that was a little too fast. I went through the training twice to make sure this New Yorker knew what she was doing. I picked the Cayenne so I could transport groceries, go to meet with writers, and have a little fun. My one nod to the feeling of speed was getting a manual transmission. Feel better now?"

I did and relaxed in my seat. To turn her attention away from my initial nervous response, I said, "But what I don't understand is…" I raised the bird book. "What does bird watching have to do with writing?"

She chuckled again. "That little book by Anne Lamott can make all the difference in how you approach your writing. I can't tell you how important that is. Writing a story, any story, can feel overwhelming. You have to develop characters, map out the plot and subplot lines, create the setting where it all takes place… and, yes, determine what genre you're going to work in. Science Fiction is so different from Women's Fiction and Mystery. Yes, it can be overwhelming, but that little book, *Bird by Bird* will put writing… and life into perspective."

She made the turn onto a gravel driveway marked only by a split rail fence. The huge wraparound porch with white rocking chairs helped disguise the fact that this large Victorian house at the end of the drive was new construction. It didn't have the feeling of age and permanence of Waterwood House, but it was in keeping with the historical feeling of the Shore.

Maureen paused for a moment before we got out of her racy car. "I'm glad you came, Emma. These women aren't bestselling authors, probably never will be, but they're enthusiastic and willing to study the craft. With the books I brought you, my mentorship, and the support of these women, you'll have a good base to build on." She released her seatbelt. "We'd better get inside before they come out here to get us."

We were met with exuberant welcomes by the ladies who had already fortified themselves with a glass of wine. Gretchen, who opened her home and cooked for the group every month, stepped forward to give me air kisses of welcome. Her ramrod-straight posture reminded me to stand square and not favor my right leg in any way. "I'm so glad you've come," she said.

As usual, Denise was right behind Gretchen. I wasn't sure if this pale, hesitant woman was offering support to her friend or was following her like an obedient puppy. She welcomed me in such a soft voice, I had to imagine that was what she said.

Zelda, loud in both voice and clothes, rumbled in front of shy Denise to add her greeting. Didn't this woman know that a bright yellow horizontal striped sweater did nothing for her sallow complexion or her overweight figure? Remembering her comments from the last meeting, I was thankful that she had a better handle on elements of writing than fashion.

Catherine, who had first introduced me to the group, looked amazing in her signature white pantsuit that matched her hair and white Jaguar parked outside. When she gave me a little hug, she whispered, "I'm glad you're here… after what happened the last time." When she stepped back, she gave me a wink. I guess my foolish act with the cane was going to be our little secret, but I suspected everyone knew by now.

It was an eclectic group, but I was learning that they might have something worthwhile to share. I smiled at Maureen to let her know I understood what she had said in the car, and I was grateful. Then I was hustled into the kitchen for a glass of good wine and some wonderful food.

The evening of conversation and writing exercises were worthwhile, now that I'd relaxed and was able to absorb what they were saying. When we left, I felt inspired to the point of thinking, *Yes, maybe I can do this.*

CHAPTER TWENTY-FOUR

"...but, dear me, let us be elegant or die."

— Louisa May Alcott, *Little Women*

E arly the next morning, I was ensconced on my living room sofa under an afghan my mother had made for Uncle Jack years ago. I'd read some more of Maureen's book *Bird by Bird*. Since I was thinking of basing my book on Emma's story, I was about to check out another diary entry to see if there was something I could use when my cell phone rang.

"Craig called." TJ sounded stressed. "About the situation."

An alarm went off in my head. Was he about to deliver more bad news? "What's happened? What's wrong?"

"Nothing, except Belle is dead," he said with a lilt of nasty irony. "I'm sorry. I still can't wrap my head around what's happened. Craig called to ask if you would be willing to go to Easton for a meeting."

"Why did he call you?" I was beginning to feel like I was on a merry-go-round.

"To save time. He knows you don't drive and was asking me if I would relay the message and arrange a convenient time without a lot of back-and-forth. You do need a ride, don't you?"

"Yes, thank you." I relaxed a little. "Sounds smart. When does he want us?

"This morning, if that's convenient for you."

"If it works for you, it works for me." I heaved a sigh. The last thing I wanted to do was crawl out from my comfortable little nest, but I'd promised to help. "If we have to go, we have to go."

"I know how you feel. I don't want to go either, but we have to," he said.

"You're right. Will you let Craig know?"

"Sure will." He paused. "Emma, there was nothing you could have done to change what happened."

I was about to fight him on that point, but he continued.

"Two women were attacked. If you had gotten to the door sooner, it might have been three."

I was startled by those words. I didn't want to believe I was in danger. But there was no denying that someone had hurt the twins. "I know, thanks. And TJ, I may need to go to the library afterwards for a little while?" I could sense a smile in his voice when he agreed.

It was easy to get ready. Nothing fancy was required. It would be a little while before TJ was due and I needed something to occupy my thoughts so I wouldn't dwell on the idea of *three* women could have been hurt.

In the dining room, I picked up a diary and started to look through it. Page after page was water-streaked making the handwriting unreadable if there was any left at all. Seeing a word here, a line there, kept me going. When I was almost to the end, I got lucky. I found a fragment.

... a framed map of Waterwood with all its lands. It was wonderful to have a bird's eye of the property I love so much. Then Joshua pointed to the pink area. Yes, it was my favorite place in the whole world of Waterwood, across the creek from the Lone Oak. I love to walk along the shore and take a book to read there. For some reason, it is different from all the other lovely places around the plantation. It's where Daniel and I played as children and grew closer as we got older.

The man I'd married stabbed his finger on the spot and declared I was never to go there again. He said the new owner...NEW OWNER of part of Waterwood's soul! This new owner has the right to stop me, even shoot me on the spot if I trespass. He took the framed map from my sight and left me to mourn the shock and unfairness in private. But hammering drew me to the foyer. He had a slave drive a nail into the wall and hang the Waterwood map in a place so I will see it, be reminded of his cruelty, every time I mount the stairs. I shall never write or say his name again. He will only be a nameless man in my life—X forev~

She was talking about the framed plat I'd found in the Waterwood House attic.

TJ's horn interrupted my musings. I grabbed the letters I'd found and headed out to meet him. Going to the library later would help balance things. We arrived at the red brick police building in Easton and were ushered into a small room with a large window in one wall looking into the next room. Just like on TV. Craig explained he had arranged a lineup to try and identify the man I had only glimpsed at the ice house.

"You have a suspect? You know who did it?" My head whipped around toward the window, wondering who was on the other side of the glass.

"Let's take this one step at a time, Emma. The men have been placed in the room next door with their backs to us because that's the way you saw the man running away." He took a breath and let it out. "It's a stretch but worth a try. If you recognize anyone, give me the number associated with that person."

"Okay," I said in a small voice. I closed my eyes, trying to conjure up the memory of that moment at the ice house. Yes, it was fleeting, but I did see a man. He was tall with broad shoulders. The man had worn his jeans pulled up to his waist, not slung low. He'd had on a cap which gave me no clue to the color of his hair so it must have been cut short.

I opened my eyes to see the line of men standing on the other side of the one-way window. And there he was. I wanted to burst out, *That's him*. But tamped down my initial reaction so I didn't accuse someone unfairly.

As if he was reading my thoughts, Craig suggested, "Take your time, Emma. Look at each one and let me know what you think."

I did. When I had gone down the line, I jumped back to *him*.

"Number Four," I said.

"Are you sure?"

My jaw tightened in determination, and I gave him a quick nod. Craig raised his chin in acknowledgment and flicked the intercom button.

"Okay, thank you. Number Four, please see the officer in the waiting room."

SUSAN REISS

As Number Four turned to leave, I saw his face. My knees went weak.

TJ caught my arm to steady me. "Emma?"

Craig stood on my other side. "Do you know him?"

I nodded as I straightened up. "Yes, yes, I do." I looked at TJ. "You do, too. It's Nicky, Dee's fiancé."

When TJ and I got outside in fresh air, it was a little easier to cope with the shock. But still...

Had Nicky hurt the twins? How was that possible? He is in love with Dee. They have plans. They are going to get married. But I'd seen him with my own eyes, cuddling up with Belle in the pub.

As we walked toward the parking lot, TJ broke the silence. "Emma, do you think—"

"I don't want to talk about it right now, okay?" I said in a weak voice.

"That's fine," he agreed. "It must have been a shock seeing him."

When someone said, I don't want to talk about something, why did people keep on talking about it. Time for me to change the subject. I tried to make my voice sound light. "Oh, look, I didn't realize the library was so close. I can walk there. Is that okay with you?"

"Sure, but first, I have a surprise for you." He handed me a baggie with an envelope inside.

"You found another letter?" It was just what I needed to distract me.

"And I put it in a baggie for safekeeping like I've seen you do. Now, you go to the library. I have an errand to run." He pulled out his keys. "Take your time. You deserve a break from this whole mess. I should be back in an hour."

I thanked him and rushed ahead, hoping Charles was on duty. I was relieved when I spied him at his desk through the windows of the Maryland Room. Instead of asking for more information and whipping out the new letter TJ had found, I greeted Charles in a polite, civilized way. He was old-fashioned like that.

Every time I thought I'd finished researching things at the library in Easton, something else popped up and back I'd go. I began this visit with yet another question for Charles, because he knew where to find everything.

"I found a land map…"

"A plat?" Charles suggested.

"Yes, a plat for the Waterwood Plantation, dated 1871. It shows my property, not the Cottage itself, but the boundaries of my little piece of land. Where would I find the deed?"

"Didn't you get a copy after settlement?" he asked.

"It's probably in a stack of legal papers. I'd like to see the original deed. Is it here?" I ran my eyes around the Maryland Room toward the file cabinets against the wall, hoping it would be a few steps away.

"Oh, you'll have to go to the Clerk's Office."

"Oh," I groaned a little. "Where is that?"

"It's part of the Talbot County Circuit Court." Charles grinned. "The office is right across the street in the courthouse."

"In the meantime, I brought you some more letters." His eyes sparkled as he looked at the baggies and bounced from one foot to the other in excitement. "I'll copy the originals while you're getting the deed."

I was grateful that so many places were within walking distance. I dashed across the street and found the office. The staff couldn't have been nicer. The clerk assigned to help me was a little surprised by my request but went to work with enthusiasm. We sat down at the computer meant for public use and she talked me through the search. The deed popped up on the screen, containing the usual descriptive information, but

SUSAN REISS

there was an attachment dated later. It was beautifully handwritten, but ugly in content:

> *It is hereby agreed that the purchaser will not allow any member of the Collins Family, especially Mrs. Emma Collins, access to this property under any conditions. If the purchaser violates this caveat, the property will revert in its entirety to the seller, Mr. Joshua Collins, with no remuneration.*

What an outrageous thing to do to Emma. How unfair, to bar her from any part of the land that originally belonged to her family. I was thankful that the roof leak hadn't ruined Emma's diary entry.

With a copy of the deed and caveat safely tucked away, I went back to the library with my latest puzzle piece. I found Charles working with copies of the letters at a library table.

"I thought we could read the letters together if you have time."

I checked the library's grandfather clock and sat down. The missive he handed me began in a rush of emotion:

My Dear Emma,

I can barely contain my anger and frustration after reading the local results of the election.

I leaned toward Charles and spoke in a soft voice. "Minnie was very upset about the local results of an election, evidently a national election. Do you have any idea which one it was?"

He went to a file cabinet and brought back a folder. "I think she's talking about the presidential election of 1860. As you know, Abraham Lincoln won overwhelmingly, but the election

174

was hotly contested. It caused deep divisions here on the Shore. According to these notes, there were two other candidates on the ballot along with Abraham Lincoln and Stephen Douglas. They were the ones that mattered to the people on the Shore. They were John Breckinridge who supported the Deep South, and John Bell, a Tennessee politician, who wanted to preserve the Union without abolishing slavery. Breckenridge carried the Eastern Shore which wasn't a surprise considering all the slaveholding plantation owners with strong Southern leanings. What shocked people was Lincoln received two votes. Maybe that context will help."

Understanding the conditions and sentiments at the time this letter was written was so important. I eagerly began reading Minnie's letter again.

My Dear Emma,

I can barely contain my anger and frustration after reading the election results. There is little we can do about the national election, but how people voted locally is of great concern to us all.

We ought to run them out of the county. I don't care who they are. There is no place for them here.

It's bad enough having a dear sister trapped in a marriage to that man who once served in the Federal Army. True, when the troubles began, he resigned his commission, but instead of supporting his brothers in the Southern states, he continues to work for the Union interests in Philadelphia. I must say, Emma, that I can barely abide that man when the family gathers.

My own dear husband served in the Federal Army as well. When the Southern states seceded, he resigned his commission. Though it has brought some hardship to us I do believe he did the right thing. He could not watch this conflict from a safe position. He offered his training and experience to the Confederacy and has received a commission of high rank. I must take up the mantle of maintaining our life here. I do it gladly. He must not be distracted or worry about the workings of our plantation.

 There are so many things I must consider as mistress of Miles Bend Farm. It concerns me how many Unionists there are in the neighborhood. I do not know what to expect from them. Also, I fear a slave uprising. Why can't we all live united here on the Shore?

 These worries lay a burden on my heart, but I keep my eyes to the future when I believe the South will triumph. For now, I hold my head high and with great pride.

    With admiration, your dear friend,
      Minnie

"I had no idea people on the Shore were so divided," I whispered.

"Wait until you read the next letter. Miss Minnie gets personal with your Emma."

My Dear Emma,

I read your latest letter with some concern. You wrote that many women were able to show their support for the Union through local churches, hospitals, and other organizations. Of course, we cannot do that since our sympathies lie with the South. Your dear father does not want you to take a public position regarding the coming war. He is right to ask you to focus your attention on Waterwood and gentle interaction with friends.

However, you must not forget where your future success and well-being lies. Of course, we must always remember to maintain our ladylike manners. I hope you will not mind me saying so, but I believe that your husband should speak up more in defense of our way of life and our Southern brothers and sisters. What would Waterwood be without its slaves? Where would any of us be without them? We are fighting for survival.

With so many of our neighbors confused about what is important, I believe we should be clear. With concern to your social position in our community. I wish with great expectation that you will stand with us as we stand with our sisters and brothers in the South. I would not want your social advancement to be thwarted. You only have to look at how my sister Lottie is treated.

This whole situation is exhausting. The days have been so gloomy with the brutal thunderstorms rolling over the Shore one after the other. I must remind you to take care of yourself.

Remember the dangers of drafts. They can bring on a variety of maladies. You must keep your constitution strong. You cannot ignore the importance of daily exercise. When you walk every day, always take your shawl to repel the chill. Remember, there are many people who depend on you. You must be both doctor and caregiver for all the people of Waterwood. If you are sick, whatever would they do? Though you are young, take extra care, my dear.

Wishing you only the best,
Your "Aunt" Minnie

Wow, this Minnie didn't hold back. I was getting the impression that there was little room for constructive conversation between sisters or neighbors, let alone with politicians. Not much had changed in the past century when highly emotional issues were involved.

I was eager to discuss the letters with Charles when the grandfather clock by his desk chimed the hour. I automatically counted the bongs. And jumped out of my chair.

"Oh no, I have to go. I have to go right now!" I started gathering my things into my tote. "Thanks for your help."

He stood, always the perfect gentleman. "What's the problem?" Charles asked in his quiet, librarian voice.

I followed his example. "My friend is waiting for me outside."

"Oh, in that case, you should go. I've read Minnie's letter and it's a doozy. The only thing you need to know right now is the people in St. Michaels had strong Union feelings even though they were surrounded by large estates and plantations that relied on slave labor. They weren't shy about letting their feelings be known, as you'll see in that letter. Thank you for sharing them with me, Emma."

"Thank you for all your help. I'll see you soon," I said in a rush.

As I headed out of the special reference room, I knew what he was thinking. *No running in the library.*

CHAPTER TWENTY-FIVE

"TO THE EDITOR: *Godey's Lady's Book,* which has always been foremost in every good word and work relating to women, seems to me a proper channel through which to express the sentiments, exhortations, hopes, and fears called out by this unhappy war, so far as women alone are concerned. From a Lady of New England."

— *Godey's Lady's Book* 1863

Desperate, I charged through the library and through the automatic sliding doors. I'd have to apologize profusely to TJ for losing track of time. I didn't want him to think I was taking him for granted. I truly appreciated his patience and willingness to drive me around. I didn't know what I'd do without his help.

Oh yes, I do. I'd have to start driving again. The thought turned my blood to ice. I wasn't sure I would, could, ever drive again.

I went out to the sidewalk and looked around. No TJ. No sign of his truck. All the parking spaces were taken. *Should I call him? And say, what? Where are you?* That would go over big. That's what he should be saying to me. I needed to apologize face to face, not over the phone, so he could see how sincere I was.

I walked down the street and scanned the parking spaces on either side. No truck. With creeping panic, I checked the parking lot. There! His truck was in a space on the far side. And a man was standing by the driver's window. Who was it? His back was to me so there was only one thing to do. I sprinted over to the truck and found Craig, the detective. Upset about seeing Nicky this morning, I'd forgotten that I needed to speak to him.

After exchanging pleasantries, I asked him if he had a moment. And asked TJ if he could wait a few more minutes. Everyone agreed and Craig led me over to a little memorial area on the corner for fallen emergency responders.

"What's up, Miss Emma?" He slipped his hands into the pockets of his slacks and rolled forward and back on his feet that looked unusually large, even for a man. I had to stifle a giggle when I realized they looked like flippers stuffed into black leather shoes.

"Emma?"

Hearing my name brought me back to the present and the serious nature of our conversation, serious at least from my perspective. I chewed on my lower lip for a moment then began. I told him about the confrontation with Belle's irate client on the sidewalk in Easton, the man who had mistaken Dee for her sister.

"That's good to know. Did you get a name?" he asked.

"No idea. I was overwhelmed by his anger and rudeness."

He nodded. "I'll ask Belle's broker if she knows anyone who fits that description."

I was about to head back to TJ's truck when Craig said, "Anything else you can tell me?"

I hesitated. The last thing I wanted to do was to get someone in trouble. Someone who was innocent. But how was I to know who was innocent? That was the detective's job.

I finally formed the words. "Do you know Cookie?"

"You mean Belle's assistant, Catherine? We usually don't deal in nicknames. Yes, I do."

Reaching into his inside jacket pocket, he asked, "You don't mind if I open my notebook, do you?" Before I could respond, it was open and he'd found a fresh page. With his pen poised, he said, "Tell me about her." The man's dark chocolate brown eyes drilled into me on a quest for some new detail that would blow the case wide open.

I closed my eyes so I could avoid his intensity. "I've been spending time in the research room at the library."

"Like today? Yes, TJ told me."

I took a little breath to steady myself. "That's where I first met Cookie. Oh, I mean Catherine. She was crying."

"Why? Boyfriend trouble?"

Why did men always assume that if a woman was crying, it was over a man? I'd thought better of the detective, not to jump to conclusions, but I let it go.

"No, boss trouble." I couldn't hold back. "And Cookie is engaged, happily."

"Oh, wait." Craig put the pieces together. "She worked for Belle? Was there trouble?" He frowned making two little dents between his eyebrows.

I nodded. I told him about the open house commission. "You should ask her about that, maybe talk to their broker, too."

I paused and glanced at TJ who had Ghost out of the truck and was throwing a ball for him on a little patch of grass nearby.

I opened my mouth but still couldn't meet the detective's eyes. I felt like I was telling a tale out of school. "It's your job to determine what is important and what isn't, right?"

Craig went straight to the point. "Tell me what you know."

"I've seen Cookie wearing Belle's shoes."

Craig let out a huff of air. "Women and their shoes." He pursed his lips.

I couldn't let him dismiss the detail without considering its possible importance. "They weren't just any shoes."

"I know, I know, my mother is always talking about —"

I interrupted. "These shoes sell for more than $800."

He let out a low whistle. "That's one pricey pair of shoes."

"They were only basic black heels with an open toe."

"So, what makes them so special?" He squinted, trying to understand.

"The undersole, the bottom of the shoe, was bright red."

Craig's eyebrows shot up. "So?"

"It's the signature of the famous shoe designer, Christian Louboutin. I know because I looked it up," I said, feeling a little proud of myself.

"$800, that's a lot of money on an assistant's income," he mused aloud.

"No, no, they were Belle's shoes," I corrected him. "And I think Belle had them on when she went to the ice house."

Craig looked at me with disbelief. "She wore high heels to walk around a farm? Shoes that cost that much? That's crazy."

"Unless she was meeting someone, somebody important, somebody she wanted to impress." I added quickly, "Somebody other than her sister Dee."

My comments made an impression on the detective. He had a faraway look on his face now as he considered what I'd said. I hoped I hadn't gotten Cookie in trouble, but Craig needed to know about the shoes that could point to a man, a man who meant to hurt Belle.

In the truck on the way home, TJ asked what I had told Craig. I gave him the briefest summary only because I didn't want to think about the ugly incident anymore. TJ felt the same way, because he perked up when I told him about the letter to Emma he'd found. He asked me to read it to him.

"This is another letter from Minnie to Emma." I scanned the beginning. "I have to warn you that when this woman gets upset, she doesn't hold back. Here goes."

Dear Emma,

I had to write as soon as I heard what happened in St. Michaels. I find the actions of the people there most disagreeable. I believe they are misguided in their support of the Union, but they have gone too far. The rally and the 100-foot flag pole with a gilded eagle on top are most insulting. They were most disrespectful when they paraded around that local group of tottering old men, veterans of the War of 1814. It was an ordeal for them to raise a huge American flag all the way to the top.

The Easton Star newspaper reported what happened next. Did you read about it? I know some husbands and fathers prefer that their women do not read the news, but this is too important.

It was reported that a giant eagle appeared and perched atop the pole. As the flag made its way to the top, the flag snagged on something. Ten stars were torn away. I am sure it symbolized the secession of the ten Southern states. To think that the eagle took off to the South to tell Jefferson Davis what had happened, warms my heart.

Oh, if it was only good and proper, I would shout my support from my rooftop. Since such actions are not acceptable, I can only encourage women to inspire the men in their lives to speak out.

Yours in unity,
Minnie

"Whew! You're right. That woman didn't hold back," TJ said in surprise.

"The direct approach must have run in their family. We have one more letter from Lottie.

Dear Emma,

My sister crows about her husband going South to work for the Secessionists. But he has left his wife and family alone, abandoned his responsibilities. To me, he must first take care of his own hearth and the people he loves. I do not know how she can allow him to devote himself to some ethereal idea that reaps almost nothing but the dead bodies of sons and brothers and husbands. Why must he put himself in danger of a bullet or cannonball? I pray nothing happens to Minnie's husband. It is beyond my rational mind that he should put his family in the bullseye of possible ruin.

With great trepidation and prayers,
Lottie

"Wow! I used to think Southern ladies were polite and genteel. Guess I was wrong."

"But our Emma doesn't strike me as that type of woman. I'd like to know more about her, TJ. I think I'll find a lot in the trunk. May I visit your attic again tomorrow?" I bit my lip in anticipation of his answer, hoping he'd say yes. Needing him to say yes. It would be the perfect escape from the unhappiness I was living today.

"I have places I have to go tomorrow…" he said.

I could feel my face fall with a thud.

"But if you don't mind being in the house by yourself—"

I almost jumped for joy. "It's fine. That's perfect." And we made a plan.

CHAPTER TWENTY-SIX

"Girlhood's bloom and the garments of mourning, the heart of youth and earth's sorest grief, these are combinations which cannot pass unnoticed."

– Godey's Lady's Book 1863

I showed up at Waterwood House the next morning a few minutes early. I barely talked to TJ before I raced up the stairs calling out, *It's okay. I know where I'm going. See you later.*

At the attic door, I skittered to a stop. I couldn't storm inside. I would stir up a cloud of dust that might drive me sneezing from the attic. Things inside were not organized. I could break something by accident. I could break my body and that wasn't an option. I took several deep breaths before opening the door and moved into the past with slow, measured movements.

Gingerly, I moved through the unwanted accumulations of stuff from past generations. There were so many things strewn around, TJ would need to set aside a large chunk of time to sort through everything.

One framed land map of Waterwood leaned against the dresser. Now that I wasn't obsessed about finding Emma's secret room, I took some time to look at this handmade drawing of Waterwood Plantation rendered in pale green. Water was represented in pale blue. The colors must have faded over time. The year 1871 inked in the corner, a time when Waterwood itself was much larger. It was obvious why free labor—slave labor— was needed to farm so much land profitably without the modern techniques and equipment that we had today. That didn't excuse the fact that Emma's family owned slaves. It only helped explain it. Waterwood House and outbuildings built almost in the center of the plantation were clearly marked. I found the creek and the Lone Oak, drawn tall with lots of leaves. The detailed work was impressive.

Then my eyes fell on the part that interested me: the ground where the Cottage now stood. The cutout was almost a perfect square, shaded pink, in stark contrast to the green for the rest of the plantation. I'd found the original of what Belle had, but it was too late to be of any use to her. The memory of her death started crowding in again and I needed a break from it. I put the frame by the door to the hallway so I wouldn't forget it again and went back into the attic.

I slid into the entry to Emma's secret room that we'd left partially open. Seeing the muslin sheet draped over the mannequin made my breath catch in my throat, but only for a moment. I knew it was there, but still, it was so lifelike, or should I say ghostlike. I'd have to make a conscious effort to remember that it was nothing but a protective covering to preserve Emma's gown.

Things were as I'd left them. The table still had the dust-bordered outlines where Emma's diaries had stood all lined up for more than a hundred years. They were drying at the Cottage.

Now, I was eager to see what Emma had hidden away in her trunk. It was an impressive piece. I estimated it was almost a yard wide, about twenty inches deep and almost thirty inches high. Big enough to hold many treasures.

My internet search had turned up some historical information about such a trunk. The planks used to construct it were probably pine and oak that now had a warm patina. Today, the trunk would be valued for itself, not just as a sturdy piece of luggage. The heavy-duty cast-iron clamps and hinges would have survived many arduous miles of travel, but I wasn't sure that *this* trunk had seen a lot of use.

I remembered reading that the round top was significant. It ensured that this trunk would be placed on top of flat top trunks when they were loaded on rail cars or ships. That was a clever way to minimize any damage to the trunk or its contents. There was one more advantage: other trunks couldn't be stacked on top. Upon arrival at one's destination, trunks on the top were unloaded first, eliminating a long wait in baggage claim at the train station or dock.

Even after I carefully inspected the exterior, I couldn't find any scratches or dents that would signal normal wear and tear during a trip. It confirmed my suspicion that Emma might never have traveled far from Waterwood. The plantation supplied almost everything she needed. For anything else, she would have shopped or placed an order in Easton. She probably traveled to Baltimore or Philadelphia to visit family from time to time. In that case, the packed trunk would travel on the cart or carriage, under the careful control of her servants.

I wanted to satisfy my curiosity, so I went out to the main part of the attic. Scanning the large area, I spotted several trunks pushed together. Two were piled on top of one another. They didn't have the rich patina of Emma's secret trunk, but they bore the scars—heavy nicks, scratches, and dents—of extensive travel. I wiped a place above the lock on the top trunk and saw initials burned into the wood: **JTC**. Joshua Collins, I guessed. Emma's husband must have roamed far and wide, leaving Emma to run Waterwood and maintain the family.

As I went back into Emma's secret room, I grabbed what looked like a sturdy wooden chair so I could sit by the trunk and not kneel on the dusty floor. In position, I released the lock and I raised the lid on Emma's keepsakes.

The interior of the trunk was a work of art. Divided into four paper-lined sections, each was marked by a printed color lithograph. Guarding the lower section on the left was a picture of a stern woman squeezed in a fine burgundy gown by her corset. A straw hat with an impressively large flower of burgundy and cream fabric sat squarely on the top of her head. It almost looked like she was balancing it. The no-nonsense outfit was probably appropriate for travel.

Above the austere traveler was another painted lithograph marking a compartment in the lid. It featured a younger woman with curled ringlets, dressed like a Roman matron in draped rose and gold fabrics. She had a sweet face with red cupid-shaped lips.

On the right side was a lithograph of a young girl with long wavy blonde hair. Her turquoise blue dress with white lace and matching wide-brimmed hat underscored her glow of innocence.

While all these decorations were lovely, I wanted to see what they concealed underneath. To lift the cover featuring the Roman woman, I had to release a leather latch. There, I found a garment that took my breath away. It was a delicate dress in pale yellow for a baby. Fine embroidery of tiny flowers and leaves done in white thread danced across the front. I put on the cotton gloves Charles had given me. Then, ever so gently, I took hold of the shoulders of the dress and raised it up from its place of safety. As it was freed from the compartment, the dress unfolded. And kept unfolding. I had to stand up and hold it high to free the whole dress from the trunk. Not a dress. More of a gown, a christening gown, with intricate needlework and an abundance of lace. The little top and long sleeves were lavishly embroidered. The skirt, handsewn with elaborate stitching, must have been four feet long. I could only imagine a tiny baby almost lost in the yards and yards of fine yellow fabric. It was in great condition, as if Emma had just finished the gown and placed it here in the trunk. Had it ever been used?

I was about to return the gown to the trunk when I saw the rest of the ensemble nestled in the compartment: a cap with matching embroidery, lace, and ribbons and little booties, again heavily ornamented. The baby who wore this ensemble would be one lucky little one. I assumed Emma had crafted these pieces. It must have taken the full nine months of her pregnancy to complete all the pieces. I replaced the tiny things and carefully folded the christening gown back to its place.

Then a thought hit me. Emma had given birth to four children. Two sons and one daughter survived infancy. Based on the small stone in the graveyard by Emma's plot, another boy had not survived. Was this his christening gown stored unused in her trunk because he died before he could be blessed by the church? And why was there only one gown here? Perhaps Emma had later given the boys' christening sets to their wives for use with their own children. Yes, that was a possibility. But where was her daughter's? Sadly, she had succumbed before she married and had children. Wouldn't her mother have kept her christening gown?

I examined each piece in the ensemble. The ribbons had never been tied. The fabric hadn't been fingered in any way. No, this outfit had never been used. Were these things made for the baby Emma had referred to in her letter?

But I hadn't seen another small stone by her grave. Emma would have had the child's body in the family graveyard, not cast aside like trash, of that I was certain. This was not the time to puzzle out that mystery.

My next area of exploration was the section guarded by the very proper older woman balancing her hat with the huge flower. On top was a child's sampler, the kind stitched by every little girl of comfortable means at that time. I lifted it out and laid it on my lap. Near the bottom, Emma had worked her name. Though the stitches were not yet refined like the work on the baby's christening gown, she declared that this was her work by sewing her name and age in large letters:

Emma Elizabeth

Age Ten Years Old

She must have been proud of her sampler that was used to teach her letters and numbers while building her needlework skills. This was the beginning of a lifetime of crafting beautiful things. I thought of my own mother who loved to work needlepoint canvases. I really should dig them out of storage and have pillows made or something.

Under the sampler, I found another lace fichu or scarf. It was finely done and in excellent condition, not like the one Aunt Louisa had put in the box. Emma must have used that one every day. The one in the trunk was a wonderful example of her work as an accomplished lacemaker.

I pulled open a tiny drawer cradled in the larger compartment to find two pieces of black jewelry decorated with jet black beads. One was a locket that contained a curl of grayish-white hair. I had seen an article once about mourning jewelry popular in the 19th century that celebrated the life or held a memento of the person who had passed away. Who had Emma lost? The hair color was not right for a baby. I doubted it was a curl from her mother's head, not yet turned gray since she was quite young when she died in childbirth. Emma was very close to her father. Was this the locket she wore during the days of deep mourning for him?

There was one more piece in the drawer that solved this little mystery: A tiny gold ring with a piece of jet, a black gem, in the center surrounded by tiny white pearls, often used to symbolize tears. Inside the band were engraved the words *Papa - Heart of Waterwood*.

I thought back to Daniel's letters filled with love and respect for Emma's father and there was TJ's story of how Emma's parents had met at a ball in Philadelphia. Benjamin had forsaken his Grand Tour of Europe so he could bring his beloved Elizabeth home to Waterwood and settled down. He must have been an extraordinary man. His death must have deeply affected his daughter. I tucked the pieces back in the drawer and latched it. TJ would want to keep them safe.

It was time to look under the tray of the trunk, but first…I couldn't deny my curiosity any longer. I had to look under the cloth sheet covering the mannequin to see the whole of Emma's creation.

Moving gingerly, I began to pick up the bottom of the muslin sheet. A cloud of dust rose, and I started to cough like I would never stop.

"Oh good," TJ said. "I'm here just in time to see you die from a coughing fit."

His comment made me laugh, so now I was choking, too.

TJ pulled me out of Emma's secret room where I could catch my breath.

"Wow. What set that off?" TJ wanted to know.

"The sheet over the mannequin has over a century's worth of dust. I wanted to see the gown underneath."

He looked down the hall for a moment. "I have an idea. All that dust can't be good for the trunk or anything else in that room."

"And the special something underneath the sheet that it has been safeguarding all this time, the protection will be undone as soon as we take off the sheet."

"I think we should move the mannequin and its sheet out of that small area to a large room with good ventilation and uncover it there." Pleased with his idea, he nodded his head. "Yes. But what do you think?"

"You are not going to ask me if I can heft a little lady's dress form and carry it downstairs, are you?" He pushed up a shirt sleeve to show a well-developed muscle. "With this farmer's arm?"

He laughed and so did I. He went to check out the rooms where we could uncover the dusty form. While he was doing that, I went to finish my initial exploration of the trunk.

"Oh," I jumped up and followed him. "I wanted to show you something else." I led the way to the framed land map leaning against the door jamb.

TJ's face lit up. "This is a great find. It's dated 1871. It must include all the land when the plantation was still intact. This is great."

I pointed to the pink square close to Waterwood House. "It shows the Cottage or at least its land. Emma's husband Joshua carved it out of Waterwood, but why would he do that?"

"No idea, but I bet you're going to find out." He smiled at me. "This belongs downstairs. Thanks, Emma, for finding it."

He left carrying the land map and it was time to discover what treasures lay in the large compartment under the tray.

CHAPTER TWENTY-SEVEN

"Preserve your memories, keep them well, what you forget you can never retell."

— Louisa May Alcott

B ack in Emma's secret room, I removed the trunk's large tray and found some beautiful silk fabric of deep violet. When I lifted it out, it unfolded into a long gown with a high waistline and a bit of a plunging neckline. I recognized the design because the Empire style was still popular today, especially for a formal event. But seeing this gown was unique. It had been made close to the time when Napoleon's Empress Josephine had made it popular.

Much to my surprise I found books nestled underneath the gown. Quickly, I dusted off the table that had held Emma's diaries and moved it clear of the leak drip area. As I reached for the book on top, I wondered why she would keep books hidden away? Didn't they belong in the library downstairs that was easily accessible? I kept the questions in mind as I identified each book in turn.

First, there was a beautifully illustrated *Alice in Wonderland*. I gently opened it and looked at the publication date. It was 1865. I should point out the possible value of these books to TJ. If they were first editions, their monetary value might surpass his interest in Emma's reading tastes.

Next were two books by Jules Verne. *20,000 Leagues Under the Sea*, published 1869 and *Five Weeks in a Balloon*, 1863. Both were stories of adventure that would have taken her imagination far beyond the boundaries of Waterwood. *The Innocents Abroad* by Mark Twain, published in 1869, might have balanced the disappointment of being left at home while her husband Joshua traveled far and wide. *Water Babies* by Charles Kingsley, 1863, was a story of escape from a life of toil and drudgery. Was Emma dreaming of a way out? Finding *Great Expectations* by Charles Dickens was a surprise. I would have thought its content was a little racy for a tender young woman born and raised on the Eastern Shore. Perhaps others thought the same and that's why she'd hidden it in the bottom of her trunk. Then I saw the book that almost broke my heart. *Little Women*, 1869, by Louisa May Alcott. True, it had its challenging and tragic moments, but I could imagine Emma would be drawn to this story about family love and support.

I still hadn't reached the bottom of the trunk. What else would I discover?

There was a magazine sitting on top of some white fabric. It was an 1861 copy of Godey's Lady's Book. Several pages were marked with lace ribbons. I took a peek at one and saw an illustration of several lavish bridal gowns. There also Peterson's Magazine dated 1866 Volume 49. Two pages were marked: one illustrated lace stitches and the other showed a pattern for a lace border and embroidered letters of the alphabet. I set them aside for later.

I reached for the white fabric wondering why such fine material would be used as a trunk liner when muslin would do. I was wrong. The fabric wasn't a liner. When I lifted it up, my jaw dropped. It was a wedding gown of fine oyster white silk. The design was plain, almost severe. Simple pearl buttons adorned the bodice, and a length of ribbon was sewn at the waist. Small cuffs at the end of the sleeves featured a narrow lace accent. When I compared this lace with the other pieces in the trunk, it looked sparse.

Of all the things in the trunk, this wedding gown did not seem to belong. Why was it packed at the bottom so that the creases formed by the weight of the books might never be removed? Surely, Emma must have known the gown would be damaged, perhaps permanently? Yet, this is where she chose to store it. Why had she banished it to the bottom of her trunk?

I heard TJ's footsteps sounding through the attic, so I wasn't surprised when he appeared in the doorway to Emma's secret room.

"How are you doing?" he asked, his voice charged with excitement.

"Just finished getting to the bottom of Emma's trunk. I found treasures that you—"

"Good. I've got a room ready for your companion here." He gestured to the mannequin covered by the dusty sheet. "Ready to move it to its own room?"

TJ didn't wait for a response. I think the curiosity bug finally latched on to him. He had overcome his resistance to learning about Emma and early life at Waterwood. His enthusiasm presented a new problem. We needed to move slowly and with great care, but it was a problem we could handle.

Now, I was ready to see what she had hidden under the sheet. It took a while to wrestle the mannequin through the narrow walkways of the attic and out to the main part of the house. On our way to the room TJ had prepared, we had to stop twice to step away from the dusty cover. TJ had his own coughing fit. I hoped there wasn't anything toxic in the attic air that might have collected on the sheet. Oh well, we were both exposed at this point. We could only hope for the best.

When we reached the doorway to the room, TJ carefully placed the stand on the floor.

"I have a plan. I'm going to stand here, in the room, and lift the sheet from this side. I'll hand it to you over the top of the form. Can you reach that?"

I extended my arms. "Yes, it shouldn't be a problem."

"Good. You take my end of the cover, pull it over the top and put it down on the floor on your side. I'll quickly move the dress form into the room and close the door. That should help trap most of the dust inside the sheet and outside the room."

"Clever idea, TJ. Very smart. I'll bundle it into the corner of the hallway so it's away from the door."

"Good. When the dust calms down out there, knock on the door to see what you've found."

"All right, I'm ready." I held up my hands, ready to grab the muslin and knock down the dust we'd disturb.

He counted us to action. "One, two, three…GRAB!"

He raised the sheet and handed it to me. I took the edge and pressed it to the floor. He moved the dress form into the room and closed the door. There was a dust cloud, but it was much smaller than I'd expected. Gingerly, I wrestled the bundle to a nearby corner. I took a deep breath, eager and ready to see Emma's treasure.

I knocked on the door. TJ called out for me to come in. I reached for the doorknob and was about to touch it when I realized it was glimmering. I bent over to see the antique clear glass knob had a little silver mirror inside. Waterwood House had an abundance of little surprises. I turned the doorknob and what I saw took my breath away.

There, in the center of the empty room lit by indirect rays of the sun, stood a magnificent bridal gown. The silk was rich. Its texture was as smooth as ice. The silk skirt billowed under the finely worked lace that lay over it. I wondered if Emma had worked the lace while she waited to come of age to marry. The neck was high. According to Godey's Lady's Book, it was in keeping with the French designs to preserve the modesty and delicacy of the bride. The sleeves were wide but did not weigh down the dress. They almost created a cloud to allow the bride to float through her special day.

TJ spoke, breaking the enchantment. "This was on top but fell off when I moved it. I didn't know what to do with it." He held up a wreath of ivory roses with a veil of whisper-thin tulle attached.

My first thought was a question. How did she preserve the beauty of the fresh flowers? But, as I reached to take the wreath from TJ's farm-hardened hands, I realized that the roses were made of translucent ribbon. I couldn't imagine how many hours of time and concentration it had taken to make such exquisite flowers.

"Put it on," TJ said.

"Oh no, I couldn't."

"Yes, put it on." He folded his arms across his chest.

I turned my back to him. The long train of tulle trailed across the floor. I raised the wreath over my head and settled it into place, wishing for a mirror. I turned to him, the veil draped around my body like a formal bridal portrait.

With a little intake of breath, TJ said one word.

"Beautiful."

CHAPTER TWENTY-EIGHT

"Few they were, but oh, how heavily laden with grief and woe."

— *Godey's Lady's Book* 1863

I wanted to do so much with the things I'd brought down from Waterwood House and the work was starting to pile up. All the running around and making discoveries in the attic was taking a lot out of me. A fresh cup of coffee would help me relax and concentrate on what I had to do. While the machine was brewing, I carefully transferred the diary I'd been reading to the kitchen table. Promising myself I'd be very careful, I settled down to read while I sipped.

Dear Diary,

My tears stain your pages as I write these words. Today, my dear Sally went to the Gates of her Heaven. She has known me from the first moment I drew breath.

As a babe, only minutes old, Momma handed me to her. Years later, when Momma died, she dried my tears and made sure I never felt alone.

Sally always knew the yearning of my heart. She knew my innermost secrets and my meanest thoughts. And she always loved me. I will feel her loss most keenly. In her leaving, she has given me a most precious gift. Hope.

With her last breaths when we were alone, Sally spoke to me of the time I gave birth to my last child. I was so sick, she feared I would die. She told me of the happenings in the hours and days following the birth of my daughter. I had no knowledge of them.

She cried as she apologized for keeping the secret so long. She told me how my husband had sworn her to secrecy. How he had threatened her. That if she breathed a word, she would lose her own daughter. He vowed he would sell the girl down South if Sally breathed a word of what he'd done.

I felt overwhelmed by what Emma had written. I got up to walk around the house when I glimpsed a car in front of the Cottage. Not TJ's truck. A car. And its owner, the detective, was heading back to it. I put down my mug, scurried to the door, and threw it open.

"Detective! Craig! I'm here."

He headed back and we settled in the kitchen, each with hot coffee.

"There's a chill in the air. Winter is coming," he said.

Why was he stalling? He didn't come all the way out to the Cottage to talk about the weather. "I'm surprised to see you here. Is there something I can do for you?"

He sipped his coffee. "I wanted to thank you for telling me about Cookie's problems with Belle and about the shoes. You were right, about the shoes, I mean." He leaned forward as if eager to talk about something other than death. "I looked them up on the internet. *Pricey* doesn't do them justice. I think women are buying more than shoes when they raid their bank accounts for over $800!" He pulled his notebook out of his jacket pocket. "I wrote down a quote from the guy's website. 'Red is said to symbolize love, passion and blood—"

"Seems like that's what Belle got," I commented almost morbidly.

"He went on to say, 'which empowers women and unleashes their inner confidence, allowing them to break the constraints of society, whilst wearing the *forbidden shoe.*'" He flicked the notebook closed. "By the way, those red soles are known as 'sammy-red bottoms.' Don't ask me why."

"Thank you, I'll file that away." It was my turn to lean forward. "Did Cookie tell you why she had the shoes? Did she admit they were Belle's? Was there a man at the ice house, I mean a man other than Nicky?" He seemed like such a nice guy. Deep down, I didn't want him to be the one who hurt Belle.

Craig held up his hands. "One question at a time. Yes, Cookie admitted wearing Belle's shoes. But I don't think Cookie killed her for them."

"No, they ended up going into the ice pit," I said feeling a little disgusted.

"Oh, the shoes you saw at the ice house weren't the same ones Cookie has been wearing," Craig explained.

My eyes opened wide. "You mean Belle had more of those shoes with your sammy-red bottoms?' I liked shoes, but that was ridiculous.

Craig nodded slowly, sharing my amazement. "Belle thought Cookie should wear really high heels for her upcoming wedding and she was willing to share. Belle didn't want the girl to look like a child next to the groom. Evidently, he is tall. Not that we would think 5'10" or so was tall, but Cookie is only what five feet tall so he would tower over her at the altar and in the pictures. Belle came up with the solution of sky-high heels. She told Cookie she could wear her shoes around the office to practice. It seems that Belle kept them there if she had to impress a client."

"But I saw her wearing them at the library." I was confused again.

"I asked her about that and she started crying. She knew that Belle was down on the Lower Shore in Salisbury that day and wouldn't be back for a long time, so she extended her practice area… and liked that people noticed her instead of discounting this really short woman-child."

I could understand that, but…

"And that wasn't the only time she cried," Craig went on.

"Oh dear. I didn't realize that they were that close." I thought about Uncle Jack and the hole he'd left in my life.

"It seems that Belle had taken Cookie under her wing," said Craig gently.

"What? But Cookie had that dispute with her about the house sale commission."

Craig nodded. "I asked the broker about that. She said she didn't know, but she speculated that Belle wanted, needed every sale so she could win some award that was important to her. She also explained that Belle thought of Cookie as a little sister and treated her well as long as she stayed within the boundaries of Belle's control. Cookie's surprise about getting her license infuriated Belle. Sure, she wanted Cookie to become an agent. It was the natural progression, but not yet. She wanted Cookie to excel but only when *she* was ready."

"So, that's probably a dead end." I was relieved. "What else then?"

"We're doing the best we can." Craig sounded a little defensive. "We're following all leads."

"Like what?" I wanted to know. "Who are you investigating?"

"We call them the victim's known enemies… or in this case, *their* known enemies."

"*Enemies*? You think they both have enemies?" I asked. "Why?"

"All you had to do was look at them to get the answer to that question. I couldn't tell them apart, could you?

"Well…"

"Remember the guy you and Dee met on the street? It could have been him or another of Belle's disgruntled clients stalking her. If so, he could have lashed out at Belle then saw Dee and figured he'd pushed the wrong woman. He swung the brick to make sure he'd gotten his target. Or he went after Belle thinking it was Dee then saw Dee and the brick flew again."

"No, I don't buy that second scenario." I shook my head emphatically. "Anyone who knew Dee would not mistake Belle for her. No, doesn't fly."

Craig cocked his head. "But you have to admit that someone going after Belle does make sense."

"I'll give you that," I admitted reluctantly. "But why hurt Dee?"

"Dee saw him kill Belle."

"Ah." was all I could say. There was no disputing that logic.

"I'll give you another scenario, but I can guarantee you're not going to like it." Craig loosened his tie a little.

"Okay, I'm ready."

"You're sure? Because you're really not going to like it," Craig assured me.

"Go on already."

"Okay, hear me out." He arranged the salt and pepper shakers and his coffee mug on the center of the table. "It was a love triangle gone wrong."

"What?" I slowly shook my head. The detective was truly reaching. "You mean—"

He held up his index finger for me to wait. "Hear me out. Maybe it was a love triangle involving both sisters and Nicky." Describing it, he moved the pieces into a triangular shape.

"No, no—" I didn't want to go down this road.

"Let me explain. Nicky starts off with Dee." He moved the shakers together. "But Belle is flashy, flirty, more exciting." Enter the coffee mug. "They start seeing each other on the sly." He scoots the salt shaker over to the mug. "Dee finds out." Craig moved the salt shaker around the other two. "Then she makes a plan to meet her sister in the ice house. There, Dee accuses Belle of stealing her man, maybe the same way she did in high school."

"How did you know that?" I demanded.

He shrugged. "A wild guess, but it makes sense. Anyway, the two sisters fight. Dee pushes Belle into the ice pit." He tipped over the empty coffee mug. "Nicky walks in." The pepper shaker hops into the scene. "He sees what Dee has done. Looks down at Belle. It's obvious she's dead. Enraged, Nicky turns on Dee." Craig makes Nicky's salt shaker jump up and down on the table at Dee's pepper shaker. He yells, 'You killed my love!' then goes after Dee with a brick – the only real weapon at hand. He swings it to kill her." Craig knocked the pepper shaker down. "Then Nicky runs away…except he doesn't know he's botched the job."

"That's crazy. You do a good puppet show but your idea is wrong."

The detective raised his shoulders in a dramatic shrug. "Don't be so quick to dismiss the idea. There are two ways I could prove it."

He was acting a little too cocky for me. I was ready to call his bluff. "All right, what are the two ways?"

"I can prove it when Dee recovers her memory and can tell us what really happened."

"Or…" I wanted to make all this go away.

"The other is a dead giveaway, pardon the expression. If the medical examiner finds that Belle is pregnant and the DNA confirms that it was Nicky's child…"

I grabbed my head with both hands, afraid it was going to explode. That idea was outlandish and I told him so.

"You could be right." But the way he said it, he wasn't convinced. "Don't worry. We're following up on other sources of evidence."

I steeled myself for other off-the-wall ideas. "Like what?"

"Our forensic team is analyzing the ground inside the ice house. The ground may have been soft enough for a shoe print. Match the print to one of those three people and we'll know the truth of what happened."

Finally, he was making sense.

"They are also looking at the dirt around the lip of the ice pit and down the sides. If someone is falling, she might reach out, clawing the ground to catch herself to stop her fall."

Again, I had to admit he had a point. "That makes sense."

"…unless she was already dead before she went into that pit."

Just the thought made me shudder.

"So, the medical examiner is checking for strangulation marks on the neck, bruising. Her entire body will be checked. She could have been hit on the back of the head before the fall. There are lots of possibilities and they'll check for them all."

I was struck dumb by all the ways the tragedy could have happened in the ice house, leaving one twin dead and the other alive but with no memory of what happened to cause her to lose half herself.

Craig got up to leave, but there was something bothering me. I motioned for him to sit down again.

"You've made some points, I'll give you that, but there's one question you haven't answered, except for the idea of Nicky's retaliation. Tell me, who hit Dee on the head with the brick?"

The detective was a good sport. He moved back into the chair and prepared to play my game of what-if.

"Okay, I'll take that challenge. If there was a third person in the ice house, that person could have hurt both twins."

"That's obvious." I gave my head a quick shake. "No, no, I'm sorry. I didn't mean to sound glib. What I meant to say was that's one possibility. If I may…"

The detective bowed his head for me to continue.

"Belle could have hit Dee with the brick for one of the reasons you pointed out. If she had a thing for Nicky, she could get rid of her competition and knock off Dee."

"And we'd consider that a credible alternative idea if we found Belle's DNA on the brick. She attacks Dee who pushes her away. Belle loses her balance and falls into the ice pit."

"That's an intriguing idea," I said, getting lost in the thought.

Craig looked down at the table and gave a little laugh. Not a ha-ha laugh. More of a chuckle at a personal joke. "Of course, there is another option."

I looked at him, though already exhausted by all the possibilities he'd presented. "Okay, let's hear it," I said as I leaned back in my chair.

"Dee hit herself with the brick."

I closed my eyes. "That's an outrageous idea."

"Hear me out," he said quickly, leaning forward. "Dee pushes Belle or the girl slips and falls into the ice pit. Whatever. Then Dee sees what has happened to her sister. She is distraught. Grabs a brick and hits herself in the head as punishment." He rocked back in his chair, full of pride.

No, no, I didn't want to think that Dee would do such a thing. I had to find a way to disprove this outrageous theory. What? What? Then I had it. "Dee was hit on which side of her head?"

Craig closed his eyes in thought. Then slowly he raised his hand to his head. His eyes popped open and he said, "She was hit on the left side of her head."

I swung my arms high in the air as if signaling a touchdown. "That proves Dee couldn't have done it."

His eyebrows came together. "How do you figure?"

"Dee is right-handed. I've seen her working with tools here at the Cottage. If you're going to hit yourself in the head and you mean to hurt yourself, you need the strength of your dominant hand." I mimed picking up a brick with my right hand and curling it around my head so I could hit the left side. "I'm not sure you could even do it unless she was hit on her forehead or over her left eye?"

"No," sounding disappointed, Craig said, "No, she was hit over her left ear."

I mimed that maneuver. "I guess it could work if she really turned her head. Would she still have the power to inflict the damage that she suffered?"

The detective slipped lower in his chair, put his elbows on the table, then took a deep breath. "I see your point. I think we can agree it's a puzzle and very sad." He stood. "I suggest we wait and see what the medical examiner and the lab reports tell us."

I too got up. "I agree." And yawned.

Craig caught it and asked, "Did our conversation wear you out? You should take a nap."

"No, that's not it. A nap won't help 'cause I can't get to sleep, at least not for very long. This situation has me wound up. Haven't had a good night's sleep since it happened." I tried to hide another yawn. "I'm sure I'll sleep like a baby when you figure out what happened. I appreciate you going through all those scenarios. And I also agree that this is a terrible mess that I wish had never happened."

"You and me both."

CHAPTER TWENTY-NINE

"Good, old-fashioned ways keep hearts sweet, heads sane, hands busy."

— Louisa May Alcott

I was getting to know my way around the Maryland Room. I no longer had to bother Charles, the reference librarian, for every little thing. It was an empowering feeling. He'd even suggested that I might volunteer a few hours each month to help other people... with some additional training, he'd added. I think he assumed I was driving again. That wasn't going to happen any time soon. I'd gotten all my paperwork to become a substitute kindergarten teacher to the Talbot County Public School system. They still had to do the background check and all. Then, once approved, I would have to wait for a phone call which could come at 6 or 7 in the morning on the day they wanted me. It might be dicey getting a ride to the school on such short notice, but I'd deal with that later.

Everything else has worked out, I told myself. *That will work out, too.*

I was merrily making my way to the vertical file cabinet when I glanced into the little cubicle area that Cookie liked to use. I was surprised to see her there, with tears streaming down her face again and used tissues all around. She must have been deeply affected by Belle's death and it was taking a toll.

I tapped on the door jamb so I wouldn't startle her. When she looked up, I went to her.

"Obviously, you're not okay. Want to go for a coffee?" I asked.

"No, I don't have time, but thanks. I have to be at work soon."

So, she hadn't lost her job. That was good and not the reason for the tears. "Then let's go out to the courtyard for a minute."

Soon, we were under gray autumn skies, huddling against the chill in the wind. Neither one of us wanted to sit down on a bench.

"I'm sorry you caught me." Cookie blew her nose. "I don't mean to be trouble all the time. It's just that I have nowhere else to go where I can be alone to let my feelings out. I can't cry at work."

"Of course not," I said.

"And when David catches me crying at home, he gets really sad and upset. He's such a good guy." And the tears welled up in her eyes again.

I reached out and rubbed her arm. "Oh no, don't start again. Tell me what's wrong. Maybe it will make you feel better to share."

She gulped some air and wiped her eyes. "It's just that we don't have a place for the wedding anymore."

"What do you mean?" I was very confused.

"Nicky knew we wanted an outdoor wedding but can't afford a place like the Chesapeake Bay Maritime Museum or the Inn at Perry Cabin in St. Michaels. We're only going to have a small wedding anyway. So, Nicky said we could have it at Safe Harbor Farm. That's why he closed on the property earlier than he'd planned."

My mouth fell open. "You knew that Nicky was buying the Safe Harbor Farm?"

"Of course." Cookie gave me a quizzical look. "Belle needed my help filling out all the forms, organizing the surveys, filing things with the county. That's some of what I do...did for her. They swore me to secrecy. And I didn't tell a soul. If someone looked at the paperwork, it would be clear who was buying the main house property, but the clerks who handle that kind of information don't talk outside their office. The lawyers don't talk." She looked down at the tissue in her hands that she'd been shredding and added softly, "It always made me smile knowing what happy times were coming to that house with two people who loved each other and would love the house." The tears started to flow again. "After what's happened, we can't have our wedding there. We have to find another place. David and I aren't really church people so..." Her hand flew to her mouth. "Oh no! I forgot. I have to cancel all the arrangements. I don't know what we're going to do."

I shivered. I didn't know if it was from the cool temperature or the reminder of the tragic events in the ice house. "Right now, we're going inside. You're going to wash your face and get to work on time. We'll figure out the wedding later. One thing at a time."

"You were right. I do feel better now." Cookie threw her arms around me. "You're the best. I'm so glad you're my friend." Then her face turned red, and she scampered inside the library.

I stood in the courtyard thinking about that beautiful old house on the river, the main house of Safe Harbor Farm. This was not the first time it had seen trouble between sisters. I had the letters the two sisters had written to Emma. Minnie must have been the older sister, feeling justified in telling her sister Lottie what to do and commenting freely to Emma when her sister didn't fall into line. I needed to find out how the sisters resolved their differences. Did the Civil War and its outcome destroy their relationship and their plantations?

I heaved a deep sigh. Now, I had yet another thing to research. Astonished at how I got myself tangled up in the lives and happenings on the Eastern Shore, such a tiny corner of the world, I followed Cookie inside.

CHAPTER THIRTY

"What do girls do who haven't any mothers to help them through their troubles?"

— Louisa May Alcott

W hen I got back to the Cottage, I looked at the list of things I wanted to research. It was time for something happy and pretty.

I picked up the Godey's Lady's Book dated 1861. It had ceased publication decades before I was born, but I knew of it. I think every woman who has ever walked into an antique shop has seen the framed illustrations of lavish 19th century gowns taken from their original publications. They included lengthy articles about all aspects of fashion along with instructions about home management, food preparation, and all manner of subjects that were deemed appropriate. When I saw my first complete issue, I thought it was demeaning to women, but considering the times of the mid-19th century, I came to the conclusion that it was appropriate, even helpful to them. Emma had marked several pages with lace pieces. Now, I could look at it from her perspective, to see what attracted her interest.

In the fashion section of the book, a headline popped off the page:

Fashions
_____

NOTICE TO LADY SUBSCRIBERS
Having had frequent applications for the purchase of jewelry, millinery, etc. by ladies living at a distance, the *EDITRESS OF THE FASHION DEPARTMENT ...*

The language might have been cumbersome, but the intent was the same as any entrepreneur today, especially those online. The *Editress* was starting a mail order service for those living far away from big city stores. This is where it started. Ladies were discovering the joys of shopping from the comfort of their own homes. They would have loved Amazon.

I read about the Steel Fashion-Plate for December. Godey's stated it believed their illustration of a group of brides was the first ever published in any magazine. I turned the page to see such an important picture:

Five brides wearing ornate gowns with elaborate high-neck tops and billowing skirts draped with yards and yards of veiling, all gathered in a luxurious setting. Red curtains edged in gold tassels and garlands of red and white roses surrounded them. Many of the gowns were covered with lace. It must have taken an army of lacemakers to create even one of them. I looked closely and realized that the gown, second from the left, was the one I'd pulled from the bottom of Emma's trunk.

I turned the page and found lengthy captions about each gown. First, there was a gown that reminded me of the one hanging on the dress form in an empty upstairs room in

Waterwood House. I read through its glowing description. Godey's Lady's Book said the gown would cost between $1,000 and $1,500, depending on the quality of the lace. That was in 1864. I quickly found a site on the internet that could convert those amounts into today's dollars and I had to catch my breath. That gown today would cost between $17,000 and $26,000!

I ran my finger down the column of information and found the listing for the gown I'd found at the bottom of the trunk. It was described as *almost nun-like* in its simplicity, for a fraction of the cost of the ornate gowns.

Why did Emma have two wedding gowns? She was only married once.

I needed to walk to clear my head. I pulled on a sweater and went out the kitchen door. It was as chilly outside as my thoughts were chilling. I looked at the Lone Oak across the creek, its warm golden autumn leaves had long fallen to the ground. It still attracted the eye but in a different way. The intricate pattern of limbs grew off the trunk divided into branches and twigs. It was a breathtaking natural design obscured by the leaves in spring, summer, and fall. A magical place for two hearts to find each other, where their love could blossom under its sheltering arms. That was their special place. Where Emma and Daniel spent hours together spinning their dreams into a wonderful tapestry.

A tapestry that was never meant to be. An unfinished tapestry with a few loose threads that were tugged and pulled by a conniving family from the next plantation until it unraveled. The son of that family was willing to do anything in his power to ensure that his father's plan to take over Waterwood worked. Anything.

I did not want to imagine the outpouring of feelings when Emma was told that Daniel would never return to Waterwood. Thinking of her pain was almost more than I could bear, even a century and a half later. I paced the patio, rubbing my arms against the cool air. The sweater wasn't helping much.

Then I stopped, looked at the Lone Oak, and realized, with a single tear making its way down my cheek, that I knew the secret of the two wedding gowns.

Emma had made the lace gown on the dress form. She had altered and redesigned her mother's gown with the embroidered *B&E*. I felt certain that she'd made the cascades of lace that adorned it. She kept it on the form to preserve its beauty and perhaps in the enduring hope that her father was wrong. That her love would return someday. Even after her marriage to Joshua, she kept the gown on the dress form as a monument to their dreams.

When it came time to marry Joshua and join his plantation to Waterwood, she picked a *nun-like* simple gown. There was no joy in its selection. After the wedding, she'd be expected to keep it. She couldn't very well toss it out or use it for something else. People would not approve. Joshua might fly into a rage. So, Emma consigned it to the bottom of her trunk in her secret attic room where no one would find it… until now.

CHAPTER THIRTY-ONE

"In taking revenge a man is but even with his enemy; in passing it over, he is his superior."

— From *Godey's Lady's Book* 1864

I couldn't put it off any longer. It was time for me to finish reading about Sally's confession. I picked up the diary and found the rest of Emma's entry.

Dear Diary,

I write these words with anger and heartbreak. Sally told me the truth about my baby girl. The one I lost.

X, as I call him because he does not deserve a name, forced Sally to smuggle the baby out of Waterwood House to an old slave cabin. There, she tended to her so that she would live. Joshua would not have the baby's death on his

219

conscience. Even though he told everyone she was dead. Was that any way for a father to act?

He held a funeral for a mound of rags that others believed was my baby. In the dark of night, he bundled Sally and my living child into a carriage and drove north like a demon.

Sally said *X* yelled that the infant did not belong under his roof. In his drunkenness, he told her I had been unfaithful, and the baby was a love child!

Never! I hold sacred the vows of marriage. I would never give myself to another man. I am not like *X*.

Sally told me how the baby cried and cried. *X* threatened to pitch her out of the carriage if Sally couldn't quiet her. She was already dead to the family so what did it matter. But he could not follow through. His conscience would not allow him to actually kill a baby.

They traveled to a big city where they entered a large city home through the back entrance. There, Sally had to hand over my child to strangers. The men retired to another room for a brandy. Sally thought the woman who took the baby was the mistress of the house and had a kind face. She saw that Sally was distraught and offered reassurance. She explained she could not have a child. This was her only chance. The lady promised she would raise her and love her as if the baby was her own. Sally wanted to know her name, but the men returned. *X* stifled any more conversation and demanded they return to Waterwood.

As he took his leave of the woman's husband, X₀ patted the pocket of his greatcoat. It jingled. He had sold my baby.

I want to confront X₀. Yell and scream at him. Go at him with a knife.

But I hear Sally whispering to me from heaven. "Care not for the man, Miz Emma. Find your baby girl."

She is right. I send my gratitude to the woman who cared for me and loved me all my life.

Her confession confirms what I always felt was truth. My baby girl did not die the day she was born. I would have known in my heart and I did not feel that final sorrow.

I know where she is, or at least was, when she was a baby learning to walk and talk. My baby girl was in Annapolis, just on the other side of the Bay.

I had to stop reading. I could not fathom the cruelty of such a person. My hands shook so much, it was difficult to read Emma's words. I laid the diary on the table and walked outside through the kitchen door. It was one of those nights that was more winter than fall. The air made me shiver, but I didn't care. I wanted to stand there and stare at the Lone Oak. I thought about the selfish and destructive acts of Emma's descendants Josh and Stephani that had taken place under that tree. Now, I was learning about the actions of their ancestor, Joshua. Part of me wanted to pack up all the diaries and return them to the attic, but the part of me that felt connected to Emma made me feel that I had a responsibility to read all she had written.

CHAPTER THIRTY-TWO

"No human hand can bind up her broken heart, no human voice can charm away her grief."

– *Godey's Lady's Book* 1863

I'd been to Safe Harbor Farm, where Lottie and her husband Henry made their home. The memory of what had happened to Belle still gave me the shivers. I'd enjoyed the same view that Lottie had while she was reading the letters from her sister Minnie and her friend Emma. Minnie's letters were packed with words of displeasure and anger. Had Lottie found a way to ignore her sister's negative comments? Or had they poisoned her life and relationship with her husband? Remembering the remarkable view, I hoped she'd found a way to tune out the raging voices in her life and find solace.

I'd seen Safe Harbor House. What about Miles Bend House? I made a call and the librarian in St. Michaels gave me some good information. First, she found a record of its location though she wasn't sure if the house still existed. She suggested I go and at least get a feel for the area. The librarian also suggested I go online to a website called FindAGrave.com and type in Minnie's legal name. It might lead me to the family graveyard near the house.

I followed her advice and found Minnie's grave including the plot number on the website. I was thrilled to discover that I knew exactly where to find it and it wasn't on the family's property. Now, I wanted to see it for myself.

That afternoon, I bribed Maria to take me to St. Michaels to do a little reconnaissance. First, we took a public road outside of town, down toward the Miles River. There, following the librarian's instructions, we turned on a side road and stopped. This was once the location of the Miles Bend Farm according to the County land records. There was a beautiful view of the river. A few stately trees had survived the ravages of time and may have shaded Minnie and her family, but the house was gone. Someone had divvied up the land and populated it with custom homes. Still, the land, water, and sky were the same and it helped me make at least a small connection back to that time. The view was very similar to what Charlotte enjoyed from the opposite side of the river. I wondered about something and got out of Maria's car.

As I walked along the road, I peered through and around the trees and buildings. Fortunately, most of the trees had lost their leaves so I had clear glimpses of the far shore, but I couldn't see what I was looking for. I kept walking. When I heard the low hum of Maria's car engine, I couldn't imagine what she thought of my antics. I hoped she would be patient for a few more minutes.

Oh, this was getting frustrating. One homeowner had built a wide two-story house with a Widow's Walk that did an

SUSAN REISS

excellent job of blocking my view. Next door, someone had planted a grove of trees. I just needed…

The sun broke through the high clouds and there it was. Safe Harbor House. Minnie and her sister Lottie could have waved to one another across the river. I wondered if a small boat had ever ferried them from one house to the other? So close, and so divided… by war, by prejudice, by fear of change.

I got in the car with conflicting emotions. Standing up for one's beliefs was one thing, but life was too short to jeopardize relations with family. And then I thought of my own sister and could relate to the problems created by differing opinions. When all this crazy business settled down, I made myself a promise that I'd think about her and our relationship.

Maria turned the car around and we headed to St. Michaels. She parked the car and we headed off in different directions, agreeing to meet at a shop down the street. I entered the cemetery surrounding the Christ Church, carrying some chrysanthemums cut from the Cottage's garden, a garden gone wild. It was something else I needed to tackle at some point.

Headstones dotted most of the land surrounding the historic stone church hemmed in by town streets. Many of the stones dated back a hundred years or more. According to the graves website, this is where I'd find Minnie's last resting place. I walked around with a picture of her headstone. I'd stepped from an active sidewalk of St. Michaels into another world. Trees soared overhead maybe seventy-five feet or more and the church bells chimed the melodic line of a Psalm I recognized. Humming the tune, I walked among the rows of graves. It wasn't a ghoulish place. It was an island of calm and serenity in the middle of the bustling village. The stones were well kept, but some had lost their battle with time. Some of the carvings had worn down to nothing so the information inscribed there was lost.

Then I saw it. It was one of the taller markers in the cemetery, white with a rounded top set on a pedestal. The words read:

IN MEMORY OF
MARY TOWNSEND
Wife of William Townsend
Died
February 28, 1886
Now with the Saints in Glory

The rest of the inscription was gone. It showed that someone thought kindly of her at the end. The marker next to hers was identical, marking the grave of her husband William Townsend. My eyes strayed to the gravestone on the other side. The carving read

Charlotte Graham.

Lottie. On the far side of her grave was her husband Henry Graham. I guess they had glimpsed the future that someday ownership of their properties might move out of the family and a family graveyard might not survive. This way, they rested in sacred ground, together. They had found a way to set aside their political differences and let family love prevail. I split the bouquet of chrysanthemums and placed some on each of the sister's graves. It felt good to acknowledge the journey they had given me.

With a smile of satisfaction, I headed out of the cemetery and down the sidewalk to Jo-Jo's Cupcakes and Ice Cream Shop. Yes, I had uncovered Marie's weakness: rich, locally baked cupcakes. When I was feeling low during rehab, she had brought me the best Red Velvet cupcake ever from this shop. It was truly decadent and wonderful. Now, I was going to return the favor.

When I got back to the Cottage, my light mood, generated by the discovery that Minnie and Lottie had resolved their issues and fueled by an obscenely delicious cupcake, carried me back to the dining room and Emma's diary. She'd made notes about the battles she waged with sickness. She'd nursed someone back to health with homemade remedies. But not every illness had a good outcome. Sickness often came on suddenly and could become a crisis quickly. The mistress of the plantation was called upon to diagnose and tend the sick. Yes, a doctor might be summoned, but by the time word reached him, and he had driven to the plantation with his instruments and patent medicines the mistress didn't have, the patient was often too far gone or on the road to recovery. Notes showed that Emma was training her eldest son's wife in this work along with many other details and responsibilities. I found it interesting that Emma referred to her son as Jay in the diary rather than using his given name, Joshua. This family was traditional, almost fanatically conscious of the name given to the first-born son in every generation. This tradition continued to the present day. Stephani's brother was named Josh though it would be a long time before he got out of prison to sire a child who would carry his name.

My interest in Emma's life led me down a dark path when I continued reading.

There is not much to say about this day. Only that it has finally come to pass that my husband knows that I know. I know that all was not right about the burial of my dear sweet baby girl. He saw no tears, suffered no outbursts. I suppose I should thank him for giving me a way to submerge my grief. Unknowingly, he has given me a way to exchange it for anger and hatred.

This evening, Anna Grace sat by my side in the parlor while I showed her how to create a rosebud stitch. Before I knew what she was doing, Anna Grace took the baby dress out of my hands and held it up for her father to see what we are making. His words were controlled and unconcerned, but I've known this brute far too long. His bloodless lips tightened into a thin line. His beady eyes narrowed, but not before I saw a spark there. The spark of recognition. I looked down at my needlework to prepare myself for this moment that I prayed would come. I raised my eyes slowly and stared at him. The look on his face was vicious.

I know he never loved me. He loved only my father's money and the lands of Waterwood. Our marriage was expedient. Both of our fathers needed something. His needed relief from debt. My dear Papa needed someone in place to watch over the two things he loved most in the world—me and Waterwood— before the sickness took him

I was young and naïve when we married. I wondered at the time why we couldn't build a life together? But now I must ask myself why did I let him hurt me, first in small ways then in ways most monstrous? When Anna Grace found the baby's day dress, I resolved he would not hurt me again. He had done his worst using our sweet babe as a weapon against me. Yes, he had fathered the child. But not out of love.

It is true that I do not know all the facts of what happened after my baby girl was born. There is no reason for me to ask him. He would never tell me the truth. He would only belittle me for seeking answers.

But now, finally, he knows that I know what he did not do. He did not bury her as he should. And I shall never forget or forgive him.

CHAPTER THIRTY-THREE

Some men seem to get on as if success were a matter of course with them. People call them "lucky" but don't you see that luck was the result of work, the improvement of time, and the application of energy?

– Farmer's Almanac 1863

Again, my phone yanked me back to the present with the notification of a text from TJ.

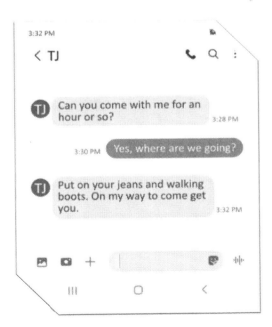

TJ was almost never spontaneous, so I was intrigued. After sprinting upstairs to change, I was sitting on the bottom step, lacing up my boots when he drove up. I met him outside, full of questions.

"Come on, we can walk from here, okay?" he said, smiling with a secret.

My curiosity was driving me crazy.

He stopped and gave me a sidelong look. "You were doing something else, right?"

I nodded, like a little girl, my blonde hair bouncing on my shoulders.

"Is it more important than coming with me this one time?"

He was offering me a way to return to the Cottage, to doing what was important to me. I looked at his hazel eyes, flecked with gold, sparkling with excitement. This was a man who knew what was important to him and was willing to do what was needed to protect it. A man who wasn't willing to take a shortcut just because it might be easier. One example of the way he did things was he wore a clean Oxford-cloth shirt with a button-down collar every day instead of a tee shirt. He didn't think it was necessary to look like a slob just because he worked with the land. If he wanted me to follow him, there was nothing more important for me to do.

"I'm with you," I declared.

I walked down my gravel drive to the main road. There, in the corner of the cornfield, stood a huge piece of farm equipment.

"What are we doing?" I asked, my steps slowing.

"You're always asking me about what I do. I still have to harvest my own corn. So, I thought that you, Miss City Girl, would like to come combine with me." He pronounced the word with the accent on the first syllable: **com**-bine. Not com-**bine**.

I stopped. "What exactly does that mean… combine?" I pronounced it the same way he did.

"It means that we drive the combine up and down the field and let it do most of the work. It cuts the cornstalks, strips the ears of the kernels then shoots the corn in the tank. When the tank is full, the kernels are dumped into the truck that hauls them away to the silo."

"And what do we do?" I wasn't sure I was up to this.

"Oh, sit back and watch. I need to keep the combine going straight and monitor things on the computer. That's about it. I'd like the company. I brought a thermos of coffee," he said as an enticement.

I took a deep breath, hoping it would help me find my courage. I didn't like machines that were so much bigger than me. It was probably a leftover feeling from the accident. I followed him and we had to do a little improvising so I could get up the ladder to the cab. I was relieved to fall into what he called the buddy seat. I was wondering if the sound of the machine would damage my hearing, but when he closed the door to the cab and started her up, there was only a gentle hum.

TJ set some buttons and turned some knobs. "Ready? Here we go!" He sounded like a little boy with his favorite toy.

I grabbed for something to brace myself, but I didn't need to hang on. It was a little bumpy but a surprisingly smooth ride. I surveyed the cornfield from about ten feet above the ground. There was so much to see. In front of us were cornstalks standing tall. Behind us, beyond the trailer, was a swath of stalks cut off near ground level that TJ called stubble. TJ was watching a computer monitor that showed him the moisture content of the crop. Having the right dryness affected the price he was offered. I marveled that farming was so much more than clear a patch, plant a seed, and later harvest the crop.

Something caught my eye. "What are those things back there?" Little golden bits were fluttering around the stream of corn coming out of the pipe. "Are they insects?" I said, my nose curling in disgust at the thought.

TJ turned to look and chuckled. "Those are called *bee's wings*. Extra chaff blowing away. A sign that the crop is drying out. That's a good thing, a sign the corn is ready."

We rumbled through the field to the low toe-tapping strains of modern country music coming out of the built-in speakers. I was a little disappointed when we'd finished the field in less than two hours. The time flew. It was exciting and fun. When TJ lifted me off the lowest rung of the ladder and spun me around, it felt like both my body and soul were flying.

When he set me back on the ground, we both were a little shy with one another. In the brief time we'd known each other, we'd gone through a lot, shared a lot, but this was something new.

He found a way to gently break the spell. "I've got to go," he said, pointing to the truck we'd just filled with corn.

"Yes." I said with a smile. "No!" If I didn't ask him now, I'd lose my nerve. I was always pushing my way into his settled and well-organized life. And I was about to do it again. "There is something I need to ask you."

"What's up?" He walked back to me.

I told him about Cookie's tearful admission at the library about her wedding.

"That's too bad. But she's right. There's no way she can have the wedding at Safe Harbor House. Not after everything that's happened there. I'd wager that the whole idea has been driven clear out of Nicky's head."

Looking down at my shoes deep in the stubble, I said, "Yes, I think you're right. That's why I thought—"

He jumped right in to head me off. "Oh no, there's no way you can have it here at the Cottage. You've barely moved in and gotten back on your feet, literally. No, don't even think about it." And with the confidence that the subject was closed, he brushed his hands together.

"What about having it at Waterwood House?" I asked.

TJ started coughing.

I hurried on before he could object. "It could be held outside. Easy. She has made all the arrangements for food and flowers and things. You wouldn't have to do much of anything."

"Only clean up the landscaping and do something about the grass. It's a mess of weeds and mud. And what if it rains? You'd want to move it inside. When is this supposed to happen anyway?" He didn't wait for an answer. "Soon, it will be too cold to eat and drink outside. No, no, I'm sorry, it won't work."

I hadn't thought of that. "TJ, what if it was held inside." He started to sputter, but I wouldn't let him speak, not yet. "Wait, hear me out. It's going to be a small wedding. We'd need only the front parlor, the dining room for the refreshments and cake, and the main foyer."

"That's all? And what about a room for the bride to get ready so she can make her grand entrance?"

Oops, I hadn't thought of that.

He leaned against the combine. "And I suppose the caterer would need the kitchen." He raised his shoulders in a huge shrug. "Only logical."

He was probably right about that, too.

"Okay, okay, you're right, but how do you know all about this?"

He hooked his thumbs in his belt and straightened up a little. "You don't give this farmer boy much credit." I opened my mouth to protest but he went on. "I needed a job when I was in college, so I went to work as a waiter at one of the sorority houses. It was close to my room, required only limited chunks of time out of the day, and they fed me really good food. Then my buddies learned that a caterer in town was looking for waiters to serve at faculty dinners, fundraising events ... and *weddings!*"

It all made sense now. There was no way I could con him into hosting Cookie's wedding. Then he surprised me.

"I feel a little ambushed, Emma. I'm not a bad guy. Give me a little time to think about it, but there are certain conditions." I nodded. "First, you don't spend one moment thinking you can have the wedding at the Cottage. You don't have the room to do anything like this. Second, you don't say a word to anyone about your harebrained idea. Not anyone. Especially not Cookie." I nodded in agreement. "Let me think about it." He pointed to the truck again. "I have to go." He started to walk away then turned back. "Dinner tonight?"

"Pizza at my place?"

He looked up at the sky as if checking the weather. "No, I think a restaurant in Oxford. Pick you up about 5:30?"

I was so surprised I didn't know what to say. Sure, we'd had lunch and dinner and even breakfast together, but he'd never made arrangements, asked me, like this. Was this a date?

"5:30?" he repeated.

"Um, yes. I'll be ready."

As he walked away, for real this time, he called back over his shoulder. "And find out how many people she's inviting." His hand raised over his head waving good-bye as he jogged away.

CHAPTER THIRTY-FOUR

"...the love, respect, and confidence of my children was the sweetest reward I could receive for my efforts to be the woman I would have them copy."

— Louisa May Alcott, *Little Women*

I think I skipped all the way back to the Cottage. I hadn't felt this light and carefree for a long time. Getting to know Emma through her diaries and Daniel's eyes, I was impressed by her purity of heart. Getting to know TJ, I was becoming convinced it was a trait that ran in the family.

There was time for me to check out another diary entry before I had to get ready for dinner so, I washed my hands, put on the white cotton gloves, and found the next undamaged entry.

It took ten days before Emma wrote again. I wondered if she didn't trust herself to write. Dealing with her innermost thoughts might have stoked her anger against her husband. Knowing what little I did about him, my impression was that it would not be a good idea to rile him. I read the next entry with great interest.

Dear Diary,

X is finally gone from Waterwood on one of his business trips. I must admit I have no idea what business he conducts while he is away. No matter. As long as the children and I are safe and Waterwood is well, I do not care. Everyone here seems so much more relaxed when he is gone. I am, too. It is a delight to see the children playing freely on the front lawn.

Thanks to Sally, I now know why X carved out that square of land across from Lone Oak. He thought I was untrue and that was where I met my lover.

Absurd.

It has always been my favorite place. Daniel and I played there as children and where we often met to be alone.

In a way, X was right to think I was untrue, only because I am loyal to a memory and always shall be.

I don't know how, but I will get my land back.

I was upset. More than upset. I wasn't sure how I could read her next entry. How did Emma feel when she first heard Sally's confession or when she wrote those words in her diary? Revulsion and anger ran through me. How could this husband, this man, do such things?

I wondered for a moment if he'd ever hit her. No, no, he didn't have to. What he did – giving away her baby then carving her favorite place out of Waterwood and hanging the land plat by the staircase – was worse than a superficial slap that stung the skin. It stung her heart, every day.

Tears began to burn my eyes. Angry tears of frustration. There was nothing I could do to soothe or support Emma, to help her as she learned the truth. No woman should have to endure such treatment. At least she could pour out her thoughts and emotions on the pages of her diary.

As I returned the diary to the table, I remember a friend saying that writing in a diary or journal was like writing a letter to yourself. I wondered if she ever considered revenge.

Me? I would have shot him.

CHAPTER THIRTY-FIVE

"It's amazing how lovely common things become, if one only knows how to look at them."

— Louisa May Alcott, *Marjorie's Three Gifts*

I was determined not to upset TJ by telling him what I'd read. It was obvious that I hadn't misjudged Emma and a strong sense of loyalty ran in their family. I scooted upstairs and put some effort into how I looked for our dinner. And when I heard TJ's truck pull up and saw the man get out, I was glad I did. He was all cleaned up, wearing a fresh, signature button-down shirt and slacks, not jeans. He was a farmer who never hesitated to get his hands dirty to do a job, but he rarely had dirt under his fingernails for very long. His ruddy face showed the signs of the long hot summer days he'd spent in the sun and the freshening winds of fall. Ghost hung his head out a window and I half expected to see him wearing a bow tie. As TJ walked to my door,

I realized something was different. I could see his sun-streaked brown hair. He wasn't wearing his ball cap.

He tapped on the door, opened it a little, and called out. "It's me. Can I come in?"

"Sure, I'm in the dining room. You look nice," I said when he walked into the room

"Thank you and so do you." He ran his eyes around the room, over the books, drying journals, papers, notes, computer, pens and more cluttering up the room. "Dining room? This looks more like a war room."

I wanted to laugh, but I felt a little defensive. If Daniel had never left that letter addressed to Emma on the plantation desk that used to occupy a space in my den, I probably wouldn't care about TJ's ancestors and who had lived on this land so long ago. But Daniel had made it personal. I felt connect to him and to his Emma. Learning about their lives and the lifestyle at Waterwood Plantation had become a mission.

I locked up the Cottage—yes, city-girl ways were slow to die—and we walked out to his truck together. He held the door open for me, but this time it wasn't because I was injured. He made me feel like a lady.

As we drove down the road, I leaned my head back against the seat rest. "This is nice. I needed to get out and do something fun." I watched the landscape pass by the window. It was constantly changing. First, a thick forest of pine trees that cozied right up to the line of utility poles that connected us to civilized services like telephone and electricity. Then I got a glimpse of water glinting in the distance. Then more trees… that stopped suddenly to border a farm field sleeping now until it was time for spring planting. We made our way through St. Michaels, the tourist traffic thin, the shops interior lights holding off the growing darkness of the last days of Daylight Savings Time.

Soon, with the time change, it would be dark before they locked their doors for the day.

Then we were back in the countryside. On the left, trees had been cleared for crop fields which allowed passersby see one of the old historical houses situated down by the water. The click-click of the turn signal got my attention.

"Where are we going?"

"Thought we'd take the ferry over to Oxford then drive the long way back through Easton after dinner."

I nodded and settled back. Something new. Something distracting.

There were more houses close to the road in this direction. Modern homes. Comfortable with warm lights inside as families made dinner. The speed limit sign forced us to slow down as we came around a bend and I perked up in my seat.

"Look at that!" There were two buildings, one on each side of the road with vast collections of things spread out.

"*That*," TJ said with emphasis, "is a landmark business here on the Bay Hundred. I don't know how long Oak Creek Sales has been in business, but I think it's been forever."

"What do they sell?"

"Anything and everything. Shopping there is like going on a treasure hunt. You never know what you'll find. And if you don't find what you want today, come back soon. That shop is always full of surprises. And it's an honest operation. Not out to scalp anybody. Probably why it's been in operation so long."

He made a turn, and, in that brief moment, I realized we had traveled through the downtown of Royal Oak and were on the road to the ferry. Fields opened up around us with modern houses dotting the farmland. The road ahead twisted through a pine forest. I opened my window a little to breathe in its clean, invigorating smell. After turns this way and another that way, we rumbled onto the ferry.

"Great timing!" I said to congratulate him.

"I'm glad. I'm so hungry, I might have ended up gnawing on the dashboard if we'd had to wait for the ferry to travel back to this side of the river."

We both got out of the truck, but Ghost stayed in the back seat. TJ lowered the window so he could enjoy the sights and smells of the crossing then he went to talk to the ferry operators. I stood by the rail taking in the beauty of this river and its shoreline in the fading light.

The engine revved up to a deep thrum and, laden with cars, pickup trucks, and people with their bicycles, it began to move. The water lapped against the hull as the ferry cut through the natural flow of the river currents. The gentle vibration was almost like a soothing massage. I turned to the west so the breeze off the Bay brushed against my skin and through my hair. The ferry's propellers churned up the smell of salt in the water. Close to the shoreline, maple leaves curling up along the edges floated along like little rafts pushed along by the currents and breeze.

Safe on the other shore, TJ drove us to the restaurant on the water. We gave our selections to the server and enjoyed a delicious dinner. I took out the leftover piece of TJ's steak. We both passed on dessert and opted to linger over coffee.

TJ opened the conversation. "I saw Nicky this morning.

I felt both relief and surprise. "Thank goodness! Then he's home. How is he?

"He's having a rough time as you might expect."

"Did he…" What was I trying to ask? Did the man confess to murdering Belle and hitting Dee in the head with a brick? How stupid was that? I just closed my mouth.

"He's not home, Emma. I saw him at the jail. They brought him back in. And they are—" TJ made air quotes. "detaining him."

"Why? I can't believe he would hurt either of the twins."

"They told him he has *striking physical characteristics.*" He put his elbows on the table and leaned closer to me. "They want to keep an eye on him while they wait for DNA results."

"DNA?" My surprise rang out to the tables around us and people looked our way. Now it was my turn to lean closer to TJ and I lowered my voice. "Why do they want DNA results?"

"The police are still trying to work out if it was an accident or...or you know. They want to check Belle's clothes..." His voice trailed off.

"To determine if he pushed her," I said in a tone just above a whisper.

"And they have the brick used to hurt Dee."

I gave a little start of surprise. "They can pull DNA off a brick?" I frowned, not sure I believed it.

"You should watch more crime shows. I guess they can pull DNA off just about anything."

"Did you learn anything else?"

"Nicky told me what he told the police. He didn't hurt either of the girls."

Oh, if we could only believe he was telling the truth. "Then did he see who did it? Why was he there? What—"

TJ held up one hand. "Whoa there, I'm in no position to answer your questions. He did say I can tell you what he told me in case we can figure out what happened, because he's at a loss."

The server refilled our coffee mugs and left us. I was wondering if I would need a drink instead.

"First, it's destroying him that he can't see Dee, can't take care of her, give her a place stay so she can recuperate from both the attack and the loss of Belle. It's cutting him up in little pieces. The fact that he is suspected of hurting them both, especially Dee, makes him so angry he wants to hurt someone. He told me that he thought of the girls as his family." TJ looked across the water for a few minutes as if looking for an answer to make sense of this crazy situation.

He looked back to me. "I didn't realize that Nicky and Dee were about to make it official. They were about to announce that they were going to get married and soon."

"Cookie said something—" TJ interrupted me as if lost on his own wavelength.

"Yeah, it was the real thing for them. Nicky is kind of practical and I guess Dee is too. They decided not to spend money on a diamond engagement ring."

"That was probably smart. With her work in construction and house rehab, the ring would sit in her jewel box most of the time."

"That's what he said. So, they decided to buy a house as their engagement/wedding present. They've been quietly looking for a house to rehab together."

"That's right, Nicky is a carpenter. I'd forgotten." It was all falling into place for me now.

"They kept it quiet. I guess that's what you do when you're looking for a specific kind of property." TJ shrugged in a slow, dramatic way. "This has all happened at the worst possible time."

"Why do you say that?" I asked.

"Because they found the house they wanted. Well, Nicky did. It seems that Dee saw it several years ago and fell in love with it, but it was too expensive, too big, too much land and all. But she loved the house. He found a way to buy the property and he was going to propose to her, down on one knee, holding a key ring with the front door key to the house."

The thought of such a romantic, personalized marriage proposal took my breath away until he continued.

SUSAN REISS

"What did she say?" I sat up a little straighter, desperate for some good news. "She must have been thrilled. Maybe it will help—"

"It was supposed to happen that day, that awful day at the farm…" His voice trailed off.

He was at the ice house to propose. I slowly sagged in my chair. The day that was supposed to be one of her happiest memories. But it was the day when Dee had lost a part of her. Her sister. Her twin.

"But why was he running away, TJ?"

"He said he was trying to call 911, but couldn't get a signal. He did what you did, went searching for a connection."

"Oh, TJ." I breathed.

His hand covered mine and squeezed. His hazel eyes shone blue as they lingered on my face. His caring gave me comfort. I wanted to give him some consolation in return, but I didn't have it in me. I dropped my eyes down to the downy-white table linen and thought back to the lovely dinner we'd shared, now only a wisp of a memory. Just as the plans Nicky and Dee were now.

"We're leaving," TJ said firmly. "We're leaving right now. You go to the truck while I pay the check." He handed me a little plastic box. "Take the doggie bag to Ghost. He'll be even happier to see you. And Emma," he called after me. "Don't give him the whole box at once. Bit by bit or he might choke. He's not the most gracious eater when it comes to treats like this."

Outside, trying to figure out how to give Ghost the leftovers of our dinner certainly consumed my attention. I didn't have time for tears. I had to remember the commands I'd seen TJ issue to the dog when he was giving him a treat. The first step was to let Ghost jump down from his place in the truck. I was so worried that he'd run off into traffic or in the restaurant looking for TJ, or who knew where he would go. What a delightful surprise it was to see him jump down to the ground,

244

shake, and then sit at my feet. He did survey the area looking for TJ but didn't leave on a reconnaissance mission. I talked to him the same way I'd talk to a person, just as I'd seen TJ do so many times.

"Okay, Big Guy, I've brought you some treats. You have to be a good boy, slow and gentle."

He started panting a little in anticipation. He knew what was coming. If I could catch a whiff of those heavenly aromas, he must have been getting a noseful. I wanted to put the open box down on the parking gravel, but hesitated, remembering TJ's warning.

I sat down on the running board of the truck and opened the box. "Let's see what we have." Ghost shifted so he sat at my feet directly in front of me, his wagging tail creating a swirling dust cloud. I picked up a piece of veal. It was big. I wished I had a knife to cut it in pieces. I was going to tell Ghost we had to wait when I looked up and saw his liquid brown eyes wide with anticipation. I was tempted to put the meat on the ground, but who wants a treat coated in dirt? "Okay, but don't choke. Gentle." I held the piece out to him. I squinted my eyes and tensed for the grab that I hoped would leave my fingers intact.

With the sensation of a slight breeze and a puff of hot breath, the meat disappeared.

"What a good boy!" I leaned over to rub his ears and almost upset the box in my lap. Ghost cocked his head to the side in that cute-puppy way as if asking if we could postpone the praise until he had finished the goodies. Without hesitation now, I fed him the rest of the bits, one by one, then put the box on the ground so he could lap up the leftover gravy.

"I see you have found your way into Ghost's heart," TJ laughed as he picked up a perfectly clean leftovers box and we got into the truck.

"It was easy to do with all those goodies. I can't believe how well-trained he is."

TJ shot me a look of disbelief. "Why are you surprised? You've spent time with him. You've seen him act right."

"Yes, but it was always in response to your commands. He was so good with me."

"He knows you're our important friend," he laughed. "Part of our pack."

Ghost sat in the back seat with his head between us, sharing his steak breath all the way home.

CHAPTER THIRTY-SIX

"I wish I had no heart, it aches so..."

— Louisa May Alcott, *Little Women*

When TJ took the turn onto the Waterwood road that led to his house with a turn-off to the Cottage, I let out a deep sigh of relief. Safe and home. TJ drove slowly to help reduce the amount of dust the vehicle kicked up. It hadn't been that long since we'd had rain, but for some reason, this stretch of road always dried out quickly.

I scratched Ghost behind an ear. The whole cab reeked of onion and garlic now, but I didn't care. I hoped TJ wouldn't mind in the morning. The surprise dinner invitation was just what I needed. What a lovely break from my merry-go-round of activities. Getting out and enjoying the ferry ride reminded me what a beautiful and soothing corner of this world it is. The story of how Nicky planned to propose was heartwarming and so heart-wrenching all at the same time.

"Nicky was going to propose to Dee with a key ring?" A little smile touched my lips. "That is so romantic."

"What?" TJ was caught off-guard, probably lost in his own thoughts. "Oh, yes. That's what he'd planned to do. Even went to one of the local jewelers for a silver key ring to make it extra special. He wanted to do it with Belle right there. She knew how much her sister loved the house. He said it was like a thank-you for all she'd done to make it happen."

I sat up, interested in the details. "Like what?"

"You can imagine that Safe Harbor once had a lot of land, a plantation that was almost self-sufficient. Over the years bits and pieces were given to family members to establish their own farms or sold off to raise cash. That's what happened to Waterwood. It's hard when you're land rich and cash poor. Even with all the divvying up, Safe Harbor Farm is still a substantial property, more than Nicky and Dee could afford. Enter the clever real estate agent." He paused for a moment. I was sure he too was remembering that she was gone now.

When he resumed his story, his voice was softer. "Belle knew just what to do. She sat down with the present owner of the big property, an old curmudgeon if ever there was one. He told her how disappointed he was that no one in the family wanted any part of the Eastern Shore." He shrugged. "I don't understand it, but it happens, even in my own family. The old guy didn't care that much about the farmland, but he wanted the main house to go to somebody who would restore it, live in it as a home. He hated the idea of it being used as a senior center, torn down to rubble, replaced with million-dollar houses on the water was more than he could handle."

I felt a spark of excitement. "He wanted to sell to someone like Dee and Nicky?"

"Yes, but they couldn't buy the whole thing, house and farmland. The old man was overwhelmed by what he'd have to do to divide it up. He figured he'd die there and let someone else figure it out. Instead, Belle went to work, proposed a plan, and the old guy approved it. She followed through, got everything done. I'm not exactly sure what she did, but it involved creating building lots away from the main house to protect its setting. I have no idea of the details she had to manage. Those lots will bring a nice price so the old man was happy and, no question that Belle would end up with a nice commission." A smile crept over TJ's lips. "The old man liked Nicky but wanted to meet Dee. Belle got Dee out to the house to repair something so he could talk to her. Even showed her around, told her some of his family stories. She loved it and never guessed what was in the works for her and Nicky. It was obvious to the old man that she loved the house as much as he did. That was the final trigger that set the whole plan in motion."

A feeling of dread began to creep over my skin like a chilly fog. "There must have been a lot of details to handle." It was more of a question than a statement.

"From what Nicky said, there were a mountain of details. Belle could handle a lot of it on her own once the original agreement was in place, but those pesky details kept popping up."

"And Belle had to consult with Nicky about them? And keep him up to date on progress." Again, not really questions. Statements. The chill was seeping into my bones. It was the chill of realizing the truth.

TJ stopped the truck in front of the Cottage and turned to me. "Yes, I guess so. What's with the questions?" When I didn't respond immediately, he pushed. "Emma?"

"I think I've done something terrible."

He dismissed my serious tone with a little laugh. "What could you have done that was terrible? You didn't know what was going on."

"I ran into Dee at the library one day. We'd both skipped lunch and were starving. We went to the Pub to grab something to eat."

"So?" He was frowning now.

"So, we saw Belle and Nicky sitting at a table in a corner."

"And did you go over and say hi?"

"No," I said with deep regret. "They were talking and laughing and having a great time. I remember how Dee had stiffened. It must have brought back memories of when they were girls and Belle would zoom in on boys Dee liked and draw them away. Just because she could. Belle was more outgoing. Flirty. Prettier."

"How is that possible? They look exactly alike," TJ insisted.

"It was possible because Belle used makeup to accentuate her features. She must have been a very tempting package for teenage boys."

"And when Dee saw Belle having a good time with Nicky, she must have thought it was déjà vu all over again," TJ said in a flat tone.

"Yes. I tried to get her to go over to their table, to find out if she was right. You know, kind of confront them."

TJ shook his head slightly. "But Dee, being Dee, shy and non-confrontational, refused."

I nodded.

We sat staring out at the dark landscape surrounding the truck. Only the stars winking between thin clouds offered any light.

"Now that I think about it, there were papers all over the tabletop. They must have been going over the plans for dividing up the farm and separating the main house with the land Nicky wanted to keep." I jammed my fist on my thigh in frustration. "I should have made her go over to their table. I should have made her face them. Instead, I stood there like a dolt while she ran out the front door of the restaurant."

"For what it's worth," he said weakly. "If she had found out the truth that day, it would have spoiled the surprise."

"Wouldn't that have been better than what happened? It's better to *know* than live a false reality," I declared, my voice becoming shrill. "Believe me, I've been there." I crossed my arms, giving myself a hug to keep myself from falling apart. My memories of what I should have done were piling up. It was a horrible feeling.

Ghost let out a little growl and I gave into his warning. "I'm sorry, TJ. I feel so responsible."

TJ was quiet. His right hand hung on to the steering wheel like it was a lifeline. He didn't move. He didn't speak.

I was about to put my hand on his and apologize again for my outburst but what happened next almost broke my heart.

He spoke in a voice so soft, I could barely make out his words. "Sometimes a person doesn't want to know."

My outburst hadn't offended him. It had ripped a scab off a deep wound he kept hidden.

CHAPTER THIRTY-SEVEN

"To be strong, and beautiful, and go round making music all the time. Yes, she could do that."

— Louisa May Alcott, *An Old-Fashioned Girl*

For once in my life, I didn't say a word. I sat silently and waited. TJ wasn't a kindergarten boy who had to be coaxed to tell me something. He was a man who'd had life experiences, experiences he could share or keep private. It felt like an age until he spoke again.

"Her name was Rita. I thought she was *the* one. We met while I was waiting tables at her sorority house. She'd sneak into the kitchen at the end of my shift. We'd talk for hours and nibble on leftovers. I didn't have the money to do much else. When she told me about her dreams and plans, she was incandescent. She had chosen me. She told *me* her innermost thoughts. I can't tell you what that felt like. She made me part of her life. I always wanted to be in her glow.

"Then my cousin came to visit me on campus. The cousin who was supposed to inherit Waterwood. The one who didn't want to be a farmer. When he came, I introduced him to Rita, my love."

Oh no, I didn't want to hear that his cousin, stole his girl.

I was too caught up in my reaction, so sure of where this story was going, that I didn't notice TJ looking at me, reading that reaction on my face.

"No, no, it wasn't like that," he said. "We spent hours together at dinner one night. My cousin made the effort to get to know the woman I hoped to marry. She opened up to him." He chuckled softly at the memory. "I'm sure the wine and shots loosened her tongue."

Then his face darkened again. "The next morning, after I sobered up and treated my hangover, he took me out for breakfast and some straight talk. He was honest with me, brutally honest. He said I could marry her, but I'd lose myself. 'Did you notice,'" he said changing his voice to mimic his cousin. "When she was spinning out her plans and dreams, she never said *We?* It was all about her, in a big city like New York, doing I-don't-know-what.' He told me he knew I was smart and cultured enough to enjoy the shows and shops and museums in New York, but I...me... TJ would die if I stayed with her. He reminded me that my heart was with the land. My lifeblood was Waterwood. And Rita wouldn't last here for a New York minute." His lips twitched with a little smile at his joke. "My cousin was right. I knew it. I just didn't want to hear it. So, I rejected what he said. Almost broke our friendship. I wanted to prove him wrong. I talked to her more about Waterwood and agribusiness. For the rest of our senior year, we bumped along, sitting in the kitchen, but she wasn't available as much. Said she had to study.

"I'll never forget the day I came out of the kitchen during dinner carrying a tray of desserts to see Rita standing in the middle of the dining room with girls clustered around her. They were admiring a rock of an engagement ring. And I remember the way she looked at me. Happiness. Surprise. Maybe a little regret. But then she settled on pity. That's what she truly thought. I was a loser."

My hand tightened on his. He sighed and looked at our hands together on the steering wheel.

"I dropped the tray. Made an awful mess. Walked out. Never went back." He raised his shoulders and let them drop. "So, you see, sometimes there really isn't anything you can do. Sometimes the hurt's got to come in its own way."

We moved our hands apart. "What did you do after that?" I asked.

"What could I do? I knew who I was inside. I had my own dreams. I finished my degree and got on with things."

Almost afraid to ask, I said, "What about your cousin?"

He chuckled. "Not too long after that dinner disaster, I made a special trip to D.C. I needed to make amends in person. I had to search him out, but I finally found him studying in the law library. He was surprised to see me. We talked and put things right. We're closer than ever now, as close as brothers should be." TJ cracked a bright smile. "It was the best thing I ever did."

I felt myself smiling now, too. "Because you're good friends now?"

"That and because of what he said just before I left him that day. "Pops wants to talk to you.'

"Pops?"

"My uncle who owned Waterwood at the time. That's when I found out he wanted me to take over what was left of Waterwood."

"So, it all worked out." I sat with my hands in my lap looking out at the darkness, not wanting to meet TJ's eyes.

"For me, it did. And it will for Dee. We don't know how, but it will."

I didn't react.

"Emma? What is it?"

"I didn't leave well enough alone like your cousin did. I told Craig what happened at the Pub," I admitted.

"So...?"

"I threw suspicion squarely on Dee. Suspicion that Dee might have hurt Belle."

TJ guffawed with a loud, boisterous laugh that split the silence of the night. "That's absurd. Dee might have pushed Belle. Or maybe Belle stumbled and fell. But you forget. Dee was hit on the head. Almost killed her. She didn't do that to herself. Maybe Belle got mad at the accusations... if Dee accused her of coming on to Nicky but...."

"I heard angry voices," I reminded him.

"Belle might have resented the criticism and lashed out. She was known for having a temper if you pressed her."

Picking up the thread of his idea, I added, "Maybe Belle got mad, grabbed whatever was near at hand..."

"Like a brick."

"Like a brick," I repeated, "to scare off Dee and stop the accusations."

"Somehow it connected with Dee's head and in the process, Belle lost her balance and fell down the ice pit."

We sat quietly, each with our own thoughts. Finally, TJ spoke. "It could have happened that way." I nodded my agreement. "A series of tragic accidents and misunderstandings."

We both heaved a deep sigh.

I opened my door, and the dome light revealed the sadness on his face that I'd heard in his voice. My heart was breaking. First, Emma's admission in her diary that there was no love in that marriage, only cruelty and resentment. And now this, a love match and a sister's deep love and caring all distorted by misunderstandings

Slowly, I moved out of the truck until my feet touched the ground. "Thank you for a nice dinner. I really enjoyed the ferry ride," I said trying to salvage some of the good feelings of the evening. I could tell from the strained look on his face that the weight of what happened to the twins would color everything else, at least for now. I closed the door and he drove off.

The dark night surrounded me except for the pool of light from the electric lantern by the front door. "Good night, Ghost." I whispered. I could have used the comfort of that big, loving dog right then.

CHAPTER THIRTY-EIGHT

"...marriage, they say, halves one's rights and doubles one's duties."

— Louisa May Alcott, *Little Women*

After TJ dropped me off at the Cottage, my mind was too overwhelmed by what I'd learned that evening to settle down to sleep. I walked past the dining room, lecturing myself that I'd had enough of *everything* for one day. I went upstairs and changed into PJ's and a robe. I looked at my bed, gave up, and went back downstairs. I ignored the dining room even though Emma's diaries were calling my name. I made some warm milk, sipped it at the kitchen window, and watched the starlight play over the Lone Oak. By the time I'd put my mug in the dishwasher, I knew it was a losing battle. I went back to the dining room and picked up Emma's last diary from the damp table in her secret room:

This is the last entry I shall make in this diary and then I shall leave it here in my secret room. I do not think I shall have the strength soon to make the climb to the top of the house. Weakness is now a constant companion. But I shall not stop making entries. I have one more diary and I shall use it.

Writing those words does not make me sad though I do have one living regret. Of course, there is the regret of not spending my life with Daniel, my best friend, my confidant, my one and only love. With him gone, I began my diary journals so I could capture my deepest thoughts since I have no one else to talk to, no one else I trust.

My one living regret is that the search for my long-lost daughter has failed. I shall not give up as long as I have breath in the body that gave her life in 1871.

I shall write no more in this diary about what I've learned. It shall begin a new journal for mine eyes alone in the secret place made for me in my room by Jedidiah, a former slave, and a loyal friend. He stayed on at Waterwood because he said someone had to watch over me. He will tell no one of my special place. It will be hard to find because he is an excellent carpenter. I shall place that journal in my secret place where I stand in this room to watch the morning sun rise.

I carefully turned pages to find that Emma wrote about the Waterwood operations, visitors, who she met in town, but nothing more about Joshua and Sally. It was time to find Emma's other secret hiding place. That meant, I had to go to Waterwood House.

CHAPTER THIRTY-NINE

"I can't help seeing that you are very lonely, and sometimes there is a hungry look in your eyes that goes to my heart."

— Louisa May Alcott, *Little Women*

I left the bedroom curtains open so the sun's rays would wake me. I wanted to catch TJ before he headed out to work in a field so, I sent him a text that everything was okay, but I would be coming to Waterwood House soon. Because that was where Emma's last diary was hidden.

TJ was at the door when I appeared. I brushed past him and headed up the stairs. "I just need to go upstairs. I discovered something."

He was quick on my heels. On the second floor, I veered away from the staircase and went down the hall.

"Hey," TJ said, trying to keep up with me. "The stairway to the attic is this way."

"I know," I said, without stopping. "I need to go to the east side of the house. I passed one closed door after another. "Which one of these rooms was Emma's bedroom?"

"The last one on the right." He must have answered without thinking because he then exclaimed, "HEY! You can't go in there. That's my bedroom."

Too late. I was already through the door.

"Emma, really!" He rubbed the back of his neck. "I wish you'd—"

"Don't worry about it." I wasn't interested in an unmade bed or a pile of laundry. "I just want to look at the east windows. Nothing else. Please." I needed to act fast before he booted me out as was his right. I skittered to a stop. I was faced with another puzzle. I fingered the tiny brass key I'd put in my pocket. One key. TWO windows facing east.?

"Please," I said softly.

He must have heard my desperation. He came to stand next to me, looking at the two windows. Confused, he asked, "What are we looking at?"

I pursed my lips then said, "Emma wrote that she hid her final diary in a secret place in this room where she would stand to watch the morning sun rise. She didn't say there were *two* windows. And how could she hide a journal in a window anyway? Was there ever an armoire or dresser here? Maybe it was moved."

"It's been a long time since Emma slept in this room," TJ pointed out.

"You're right. She wouldn't have hidden the diary in a piece of furniture that could be moved out." Then I remembered her last line. "She wrote, *the diary is safe with Waterwood House*. No, that diary and its secrets are here."

I walked over to the corner of the east wall and started examining it, running my hands over the wallpaper.

"What are you looking for?" TJ asked. "Maybe I can help?"

I stepped back for a moment, fearing that our efforts would be in vain, but determined to try. "I'm looking for something irregular or maybe there's a safe, a hole in the wall, someplace she could put a small book"

"I'm sorry to disappoint you. I think that wall, along with many others on this floor, was rehabbed when my uncle lived here. He said the outside walls needed insulation and he had the work done. It's more likely she hid the diary in or around the fireplace." He pointed to the north wall. "Isn't that a favorite hiding place in the movies?" He headed toward the mantle and marble surround to investigate.

I turned back to the east wall. Emma was specific in her second letter to me. If she had meant the fireplace, I felt certain she would have said so.

"Did your uncle have them replace the windows?" I asked.

"No, my uncle liked the old glass. He left them as they were originally built."

The windows. It has to be in one of the windows, but how.

Each of the east-facing windows was tall and surrounded with formal wood molding. They were large, heavy pieces, like crown molding at the top and bottom. The wood along the sides was relatively narrow.

I pointed. "Can you bring that chair over here please?"

The look on TJ's face went from surprise to disapproval. "You are not going to climb up on a chair with that leg of yours. You can't—"

"I just need to see what's up there."

With a deep sigh, he dragged the simple wooden side chair over to the window and climbed up. "Okay, what am I looking for?"

"A keyhole."

SUSAN REISS

He looked down at me in disbelief. "You want me to find a keyhole up here? What do you think it's going to open?"

"I have no idea. Just look please."

I forced myself to stand quietly though I wanted to pull him down off that chair and look for myself.

"Nothing," he reported. "There are no holes or indentations of any kind." He jumped down. "Do you want me to check the other window?"

"No, that was wrong." I narrowed my eyes. "Emma would never have a hiding place way over her head. She was short, like other women of that period. She would never have been able to reach up there, even standing on a chair." My eyes focused on the bottom sill of the windows. "It has to be down here." I stepped forward and inspected one. "There's nothing to suggest there is a hiding place here." I shifted my attention to the other window. "Nothing."

"That's what I tried to tell you." He started to walk to his bedroom door. "Now, can we—" He stopped when he noticed I wasn't paying attention. "Emma?"

Caught up in my search, I'd walked back to the first window and laid down on the floor. The key was tiny. It would have to be a little keyhole. A place that no one would ever think to look. A safe place to hide her secrets. My fingers moved smoothly along the painted surface until my index finger dipped into a small depression then continued up along the straight surface again. I went back. Yes, there was something here.

My fingers moved smoothly along the painted surface until my index finger dipped into a small depression then continued up along the straight surface again. I went back. Yes, there was something here.

"TJ, I think I found..." I jammed a fingernail into the depression and picked at it. A little paint came loose. "Yes, there is something here." My voice was ragged since I was twisted

262

around in an uncomfortable position and couldn't take a deep breath. I shimmied around to get a better view. "Yes, it's here, underneath the sill."

TJ's words were coiled tightly like a spring. "What is *it*, Emma?"

Thank goodness he wasn't the type of man to push me aside, all macho. He gave me the time and space to do what I needed to do.

"Let me get a closer look." I brushed away some tiny paint fragments. "It's a keyhole, I think. I found a keyhole."

I scooted my body along the floor, away from the wall so I could stretch out straight.

"Now, what are you doing?" he asked, barely keeping his excitement contained, but just barely.

I dug around in my pants pocket to find the tiny key that I'd found tied to the skeleton key in Aunt Louisa's box. We'd come a long way since that first day in the Waterwood dining room. I should have kept the ribbon tied to it so I could find it easily. My fingers wiggled through the folds of the pocket. *Please, don't be lost.* Finally. At the bottom. In the lint.

"Got it!"

My hand slid out of the pocket. Sunshine glinted off the piece of brass held tightly between my thumb and index finger.

I held it up for TJ to see. His smile was worth all the trouble.

"And now?" he said, raising his chin slightly toward the window sill.

I wiggled back into position under the sill. With a silent prayer on my lips, I slipped the key into place and turned it. The lock resisted but only for a moment. After all, it had been a long time since it had last been worked by Emma.

There was a click. The lower part of the sill popped away from the wall about an inch.

Gently, I moved the wood to reveal a small compartment. It was dark. I couldn't see inside clearly. Not wanting to wait for a flashlight, I cringed and reached into the opening, hoping there were no spiders lurking in there. Instead, my fingers touched something manmade. I gripped it and pulled out a small book. Seeing it, TJ gasped.

It was Emma's last diary, about eight inches high with a black cover. Just like all of Emma's other diaries.

"Are you sure it's her diary?" TJ asked.

I wanted to laugh. "Who else would hide a book in a window frame?" And there was that sweet scent again. I knew, for sure.

We sat on the floor, side by side, with our backs against the wall and I opened the cover. The decorative endpaper was a complicated design of flowers intertwined with leaves printed in a sage green that matched the color of TJ's eyes. I turned the page and there, in elegantly flowing handwriting were the words,

Last Diary
of
Emma Elizabeth Ross Collins

This was it. Her secret diary that she didn't want anyone to stumble across and read. And now, it was in my shaking hand, shaking with excitement.

TJ stood up. "Job well done, Emma. You've worked hard on this project." He took a few steps toward the door. "I'll leave you with your treasure."

"Don't you want to read—"

He smiled. "Thanks, but no. This is your find. You deserve to read it on your own. After all, you're probably the first person to read that diary since Emma wrote it. Enjoy."

He walked out of the room to leave me alone with Emma's last diary then walked back in the room again.

He stood for a moment looking down at the floor. "Um, could I ask one thing?"

"Sure, anything."

"Could you read her diary someplace other than my bedroom?" A little flush of pink appeared at his collar.

I scrambled up off the floor. "I'll take it back to the Cottage, if that's okay." It was the least I could do after he'd let me invade his most private space. I followed him out of the room but couldn't stop myself from taking a quick glance at his bedroom and had to stifle a giggle. Typical male. Oh, not the furniture. It was definitely antique, maybe even dating back to Emma's time or even earlier. Some clothes were on the floor in the corner. I had to give him credit for not strewing them all around the room the way my ex-husband did. Drove me crazy. TJ had straightened the bed sheets and comforter, sort of. At least he was trying. When he got up this morning, I'm sure he didn't expect an invasion of his privacy. Ready to give him his privacy again, I went downstairs and out the front door with Emma's diary clutched in my hand.

CHAPTER FORTY

"Our actions are in our own hands, but the consequences of them are not. Remember that, my dear, and think twice before you do anything."

— Louisa May Alcott, *Jack and Jill*

I opted to walk back to the Cottage though TJ offered to drive me. I had taken too much of his time already. He was busy harvesting crops for other farmers. This was the yield that would determine if they'd have a good year. Besides, it would be good to walk off some of the adrenaline rush of searching and finding Emma's last diary, now safely tucked under my arm.

It sounds trite, but it was a beautiful day. If the chilling puffs of wind were any indication, autumn was giving hints that winter was on its way. But the sun was strong and kept me warm. Or maybe it was my burning curiosity to know what Emma had written that she couldn't record in her regular diary. I hadn't finished reading the diaries drying out in my dining room, but I suspected there was nothing more about her feelings toward her husband X, as she referred to him. Why did she have to create a final diary?

I walked a little faster in anticipation then stopped. *Honk, honk* sounded above my head. A large flock of Canada geese was flying southward, another sign that winter was approaching. They preferred cold weather but escaped to the Chesapeake Bay area to avoid the brutal weather of their homeland. Our temperatures here must have seemed moderate, even balmy to them.

I watched as they flew in a VEE formation. I'd read somewhere that it helped reduce wind resistance for the rest of the birds. In that formation, they could fly farther before they had to stop and rest. It was hard work for the one in front, so they changed positions often. It was sort of like race car drafting in the sky.

The geese had flown on their way, and I quickened my steps to the Cottage to find out more.

Dear Diary,

My mind is consumed with thoughts of X as we wait for the recovery of his body. The men say that the warmer temperatures will help in their efforts. I do not want details. There is enough on my mind and pictures in my nightmares. I hope this waiting will soon be over so we can have a funeral and get on with our lives.

In the meantime, there is something I must confess. My hand may shake a little as I sit in my slipper chair and consign my innermost thoughts to your pages.

I have often thought of how I would make a brew from the seeds, stem, and beautiful pink flowers of the foxglove plant in my garden and give it to X for a final, fatal drink.

At those times, I felt it was just punishment for how he has treated me all these years and how he broke my heart by stealing away my baby girl. I still cannot fathom how he would think I had been with another man and that she was a love child. Never would I have done such a thing. He has spirited away his own child and cast her adrift in a callous world.

But murder was never the answer. What if I was caught? My boys would have been left without a mother and a father. Even now, they are not quite ready to take over all the responsibilities of Waterwood. I must complete their education and continue the search for my baby girl who I was going to give my name, Emma.

I closed the diary with great care and placed it on the table. I rocked back in my chair, the dining chair with arms. The one that the movers had used to carry me into the woods that first day when we discovered the garage. The day we pulled the blue tarp off the plantation desk. The day my adventure began with Daniel and Emma. Two people I'd grown to respect and yes, love.

Now, as I looked at Emma's most private diary, I was rocked by what she had written. She had kept her feelings and sorrows buried deep inside for the benefit of her family. That was expected of women more than a century ago, but women still did it today. I thought about the geese flying in their Vee formation. *What we do for our families, even birds.*

Emma had sacrificed to care and protect her family and Waterwood. Now, I wanted to put her first.

CHAPTER FORTY-ONE

"Then why cannot you tell me your secret? Why do you not trust
me? What is it that is to divides us?"

— From *Godey's Lady's Book* 1861

The knock on my front door made me jump. It opened and
TJ called out. "Hello?" I could hear him walk in and close
the door. "Emma, it's me."

"In the dining room," I replied as I shuffled the diaries away.
I didn't think I could deal with TJ's reaction on top of mine. And
why was he here anyway?

"Are you about ready?" he asked.

"Ah, for what?"

He stopped moving and looked at me with one raised
eyebrow. "To pick up Dee from the hospital and bring her here
to the Cottage." He phrased it like a question. "Did you forget?"

I closed my eyes. Yes, I had forgotten.

"You don't have to do this, Emma. You have a lot going on." The sweep of his arm took in all of Emma's things spread over my table meant for hosting dinners, not research. "She can take a bedroom at Waterwood House. Maybe I can get Maria to come in this afternoon and make up a bed and—"

"Don't be silly. Maria has her room ready upstairs and fresh towels in the hallway bathroom. She even left dinner for us in the fridge." I groaned. "I'm sorry. I was supposed to invite you to come. She made extra just so you couldn't say no." I dropped my eyes, a little mad at myself. I wanted to make Dee feel welcome and I was botching it already. Thank goodness Maria was on top of everything. "I hope you can come. It would make it easier I think," I admitted.

"Yes, I'll be here. Just tell me when." He looked at his watch. "And speaking of time, we'd better get a move on."

As we made our way up Route 33 to Easton, TJ cleared his throat and spoke. "I'm glad we have some time to talk without interruption."

That sounded ominous. I turned toward him as far as my seat belt would allow. "What's up?"

"I've been thinking about your idea of having Cookie's wedding at Waterwood."

Thank goodness. A topic far away from murder and betrayal.

"Good, you've been thinking about it. Did you come to a decision?" Mentally, I crossed my fingers.

"I think I have, but I wanted to talk to you first."

"Okay, shoot." I relaxed into my seat now that I knew I didn't have to brace myself for something terrible.

"I want to talk about the details, but there is one big important question." When he turned to me, I nodded in encouragement. "Okay, I'm worried that you're taking on too much."

I started to respond, but he said, "Let me finish?" I nodded again. "You're barely out of rehab from the car accidents. I will admit you are doing really well. But are you ready to take on a full schedule of responsibilities? You applied to become a substitute teacher in Talbot County. You've made the commitment at least to yourself to work on a writing project. You're doing all this research work on Emma and Waterwood. You've invited Dee to stay with you until she figures out where to live. And now you want to help Cookie with her wedding. I'm exhausted just thinking about it all."

"When you put it like that, it does sound like a lot. Let's take it one step at a time. I submitted all my paperwork to the county, that's true. It's going to take them a while to do the background check and process everything. I'm not expected to do anything else to make that happen. Now, I wait. Yes, I've committed myself to a writing project, but, as Maureen has pointed out, I don't just sit down at the computer and start typing. I have a lot of thinking to do and she wants me to do quite a bit of reading about the writing process. So, the writing project will be more of an ongoing thing. My research about Emma is more of a hobby. It engages my mind and my imagination. It's better than watching TV. The important thing is that there is no deadline. As far as Dee is concerned, she needs a place to stay. Someplace where she can be calm and quiet. Maria is willing to help and take on the heavy lifting of cooking and cleaning. I think Dee needs some alone time to process everything that's happened. That leaves me time and energy to help Cookie. It's really the only thing that has a hard and fast deadline. The most difficult part will be keeping the wedding preparations away from Dee.

After what Nicky told you about his plan to propose, Dee should be planning her own wedding now instead of mourning."

"So, you really think you can handle it?"

He wanted to hear a simple declaration. "Yes, I do, and it will be a nice distraction from all the sadness."

TJ shrugged. "Okay then, assuming we can work out the details, Cookie can get married at Waterwood House."

I clapped my hands like a little girl. I hadn't realized how much I wanted this to happen.

TJ gave me a dubious look. "I wouldn't get so excited yet. You haven't heard about the details and my concerns."

"Okay, let's have them."

"First and foremost, I only work with you. I don't have the time or desire to go through the minute details that are always so important to a bride. That would drive me around the bend in about fifteen minutes."

I nodded. "I can understand that. You're a guy. I'll deal with the bride, figure out what's important, and translate those things to you. How does that sound?"

"Perfect. Now, you're not going to expect me to paint walls and things, are you?"

I patted TJ's arm. "We'll keep the requests to a minimum. The main rooms aren't that bad. Besides, Waterwood House is historic. One should expect to see a crack or two in the wall. It's part of the charm. TJ, you're so kind to let us use Waterwood House. The event should be fun for you, too, not a burden. What else?"

He was quiet for the longest time then he said, "Well, if that's your attitude, I think we can move forward. I have some more caveats like no wandering all over the house, but we can deal with things as we go along and shouldn't have a problem."

"Thank you!" This time, I didn't clap my hands. I settled back looked out the passenger window but couldn't hide my grin.

When we arrived at the hospital, we found a woman eager to be released. She still had a small bandage on her head where the doctor had stitched up the wound made by the brick. I shuddered thinking about it and what could have happened. I took charge of the short stack of discharge instructions we'd have to follow. Dee was still taking some prescription drugs for pain and such. We had them call the orders into Pemberton Pharmacy so we could pick them up as we drove through St. Michaels. Then we had to do a terribly tough thing.

We had to go to Belle's condo. Dee needed some clothes and personal items there. When Dee had sold her little house, she'd moved in with Belle for the time being.

When we pulled up in front, I was starting to get out of TJ's truck when Dee stopped me. "Where are you going?"

"I was going to go inside with you. I thought maybe you'd like company. You know…"

"I'm fine." Her voice was flat, empty of emotion.

TJ countered the idea. "You're still not super steady on your feet, Dee."

"That's why I have this stupid cane."

"But what about…" I began gently.

"Going inside my dead sister's apartment?" she barked.

I was struck by her harsh attitude.

Dee hung her head. "I'm sorry. Please don't try to stop me. I've been wanting to do this, needing to do this. I still don't remember what happened in that ice house. The doctors say my memory may come back. Maybe it won't. I need to know what happened. I need to clear Nicky. He'd never hurt us. It must have been someone else." Her shoulders sagged. Such a long statement sapped her energy.

"Dee, I think—"

She held up her hand for me to stop. "No." She took a deep breath. "I appreciate you trying to help and when we get to the Cottage, you can help all you want." She dropped her hand in her lap. "But right now, I need to do this, and I need to do it on my own." She glanced from me to TJ then declared, "I think being in our home might trigger my memory, get my mind working again. Seeing her things, remembering how we'd have coffee together in the morning—me in my jeans, ready to fly out the door, Belle in her robe, ready for her endless routine of taking a shower, doing her makeup, picking out her outfit for the day, spending what felt like hours mulling over which shoes to wear..." Her gaze traveled out through the windshield to the naked trees outside. "I think being there will help. I have to do this alone. But knowing that you two are out here waiting, that helps." She opened the passenger door. "I won't be long. And Ghost..." TJ's dog perked up next to me in the back seat. "Don't let them fret. I'll be fine." She slipped out of the truck and slowly made her way inside.

TJ and I looked at each other, not sure what to say. Then Ghost broke the nervous silence with a sharp bark. We both laughed.

TJ looked at his watch. "We'll give her fifteen minutes. If she's not back by then, you'll go in and get her."

"Me?" It felt good to tease him rather than focus on the situation. "Why do I—"

"Because you're a woman. You're nurturing. You'd know what to say and do." He reached in the back seat and picked up a leash off the floor. "For now, Ghost and I are going for a walk around the block." In a flash, TJ was out of the truck, opening the back door and attaching the leash to Ghost's collar. "Sorry, boy. We're in the big city of Easton. These people don't know how to deal with a big, scary dog like you. It's for your own safety. We'll be back." And they were off down the street.

I sat in the truck with only my thoughts for company. First, there was the discovery of Emma's final diary then my brain bounced to Dee inside her sister's place all alone hoping that the missing truth would emerge. It was almost too much to handle. I felt a wave of relief when I saw the big white dog pulling his owner back to the truck as Dee came out of the front door of the building carrying a suitcase.

I restrained myself from blurting out the question that I knew was also on TJ's mind. Instead, we all settled back in our places and TJ maneuvered his truck into traffic.

"Next stop, the pharmacy then home?" TJ announced.

Dee and I agreed, and we drove a few blocks in silence.

"I'm so fortunate to have such good friends." Dee choked back the tears in her voice.

I touched her shoulder, and she patted my hand.

"You're so kind not to push me. But you deserve to know …" she took a breath. "Nothing happened. Nothing came back to me. No great revelations. Nothing."

Dee and I had a quiet dinner with TJ. Maria had prepared a variety of foods hoping Dee would be enticed to eat. Our conversation avoided upsetting topics. TJ's stories about Ghost's antics had us in stitches. After he left, we went to bed early.

All was peaceful, until about three o'clock in the morning. A murmur that sounded like people arguing pulled me out of a deep sleep. Had Dee invited someone to the house in the middle of the night? I tiptoed to my bedroom door and listened. The sounds were louder. But it was only one voice. I opened my door and listened. The poor girl was having a nightmare. The light was on in the hall. I went into her room and spoke softly, but my words didn't reach her. I sat down next to her bed and gently rubbed her arm, speaking to her.

"Dee, it's Emma. You're at my house, the Cottage. You remember the Cottage. You've been here before. You're safe here and—"

She sat up in bed with a muffled scream.

"Belle? Belle?" She called out, desperate. She looked around. "Where am I?" She turned and stared at me. "Y-You're not Belle." And she started to cry.

CHAPTER FORTY-TWO

"ICE: frozen water, a crystalline solid. Often transparent, but may be made cloudy by impurities. Brittle if thin."

– Definition

I knew if I went back to my room, I would stay awake listening in case Dee had another nightmare. Instead, I put some pillows and a blanket on the floor, brought some herbal tea and Emma's final diary upstairs, and settled in to read the next page without fear of water stains stealing her thoughts.

Dear Diary,

This afternoon, Jedidiah rode up the drive to Waterwood House like he was fired from a canon bringing us the sad news that X died while ice boat racing on the Miles River.

At first, there was great wailing among the slaves though I did not feel it was an honest reaction. I had them to hush up because they were upsetting the children more than they ought. Everyone is shocked this has happened, but Diary, I am not surprised. X₆ was always eager for a thrill and new adventures. He was never content to stay at Waterwood, to enjoy the life it gives us. He thought he was entitled to spend money to travel and buy things we did not need. His attitude has long been an object of my resentment.

Today, he was bound and determined to beat some boat from Dorchester County. I think there was some money riding on the outcome though he said it was a matter of honor. The racing marks were set up on the Miles River. The boats were meant to round them as fast and in any way they could. The first boat to cross the finish line won.

It seems a squall left some snow on the ice that would slow down a boat. Arrogant as always, X₆ went wide to what looked like clear ice. But it was thin. X₆ and the boat crashed through to the icy waters. They say he struggled, thrashed around for something to keep him above the surface. There was nothing. The men and slaves watched as he sank before they could reach him. They hope to bring his body home, but the recovery work is fraught with danger.

Dearest diary, the Lord works in mysterious ways. X₆'s reckless behavior may teach my son Jay to curtail such tendencies I fear he has inherited from his father.

As I stood at my window tonight and watched the moon cast a glow off the ice, I must confess I felt only relief in my heart. I am finally free of this bully.

Of course, I shall assume the role of grieving widow. I have dutifully changed into a black gown and a black scarf covers my hair. I shall comfort my children. I shall make sure that Waterwood is safe. Soon, our Waterwood family will see our life improve. Papa taught me how Waterwood should be managed. All these years under X's control, we have all suffered. Now, I no longer need his permission to do what is right.

There was another entry written on the same date.

Dear Diary,
I must share the deepest thoughts of my heart.
I know it is not Christian, but I am glad he is gone. Thanks be to the angels. The Lord has done what is right.
I, the dutiful wife, will rectify his wrongs as I had done so many times before. Not by giving him a lethal drink, but by caring for our family. Our sons need not suffer his bullying and reckless ways any longer. My sweet Anna Grace escaped his brutal treatment years ago when she was carried off by the measles. How I remember her desire to hold a baby in her arms. It is the same ache I feel. Oh, to put my arms around my baby daughter now a young woman. That is why I am driven to find her.

CHAPTER FORTY-THREE

"Nothing is impossible to a determined woman."
> — Louisa May Alcott, *Behind a Mask:
> The Unknown Thrillers of Louisa May Alcott*

I stayed in the hallway until sunrise, then wandered back to my own bed. We both slept in until Maria made a rather noisy entrance downstairs. I'm glad I raced downstairs and found her in the dining room as she was plugging in the vacuum cleaner.

"Oh, please don't. Dee is still asleep," I said, as a big yawn caught up with me.

"And good morning to you, too," Maria said. "Oh, I should say good day, since it's almost time for lunch." She put her hands on her hips and looked around. "This room is in desperate need of a cleaning. Look at the dust."

"Maybe you can do it later." I looked at the diaries and notes spread out and changed my mind. "Maybe you can leave it like this for now."

"But—"

"I know. It offends your sense of organization, but my project involves things that are more than 150 years old." She started to sputter, but I kept talking. "The good news is that I'm almost done. Then I'll package up everything and you can do what you'd like to the room." That plan pacified her.

"And how is she doing?" She raised her chin to gesture upstairs where Dee was sleeping.

I sighed. "We were up most of the night. She is having a rough time." I said barely above a whisper.

Maria leaned toward me. "This is a good thing you're doing for her. Yes, it is a good thing." She brightened. "Yes, I think I'll make something special for the two of you to have for lunch." She headed toward the kitchen with a click of her heels on the floor. She stopped in the doorway and turned. "No, think of it as a special brunch and I know just what I'm going to make if I can…" And another of her endless sentences followed her into the kitchen.

As I climbed the stairs, I was relieved to hear the shower running. Dee was awake and starting her day.

Later that afternoon, I was working at the dining room table when I had a random thought: what would Uncle Jack think of the way I was repurposing the rooms of the Cottage? I hoped he would be pleased since this whole adventure was his fault in a way. If he hadn't hidden the plantation desk in the old garage without a word of explanation, none of this would have happened. And now it was time to finish it. There were only a few more written pages in this, Emma's last diary.

Dear Diary,

X is gone forever. May the angels rejoice. My life of freedom began today at the reading of the will. My son Jay was surprised that the ownership of Waterwood came to me and not him. Not yet. It was part of the original arrangement before we married. My dear Papa insisted on it. With the vagaries of time, disease, and war, he wanted the assurance that if my husband preceded me in death, I would control Waterwood. He wanted it to be my decision who would inherit after me.

My sons need not fret about their futures. They each will come into their own when they are ready.

I dearly love my first-born son. He has grown into a fine man. He earned the love of a good woman and is raising a robust family here at Waterwood, where they belong. My only wish is that he did not carry his father's first name. That is why I call him Jay.

I am not worried about my second son though he is still too young to marry. If he lives up to his grandfather's name, Benjamin, my own dear papa, the world shall be as he wishes.

I have chosen not to marry again. I have written my will so that Jay inherits with accommodations for his younger brother. Sadly, those are the only two babies who survived to become adults.

I have been free to do as I pleased.

Once it was clear that Waterwood was mine, I tried to buy back the section of land that X sold to strangers. My efforts were not fruitful. The property is still owned by a middle-aged couple who look forward to spending their final years there peacefully.

I was able to accomplish one thing. We have agreed to rescind the caveat that X_6 attached to the deed. The present owner thought it was an outrageous restriction. In his mind, the property should never have been carved out of Waterwood. He was grateful that it was so he and his wife could enjoy it. Since I was the owner who would enforce that requirement, we engaged an appropriate attorney and had it removed legally. Now, I have an open invitation to walk in my favorite place in the world anytime I wish.

I saw something out of the corner of my eye and jumped. It wasn't Uncle Jack. Dee had walked in wearing silent suede moccasins.

"Oh! You startled me." Understandable since I'm working with ghosts, but I didn't say anything about that. Though it was funny that I felt more on edge with Dee in the house than I did while corresponding with a ghost.

Maria walked in and held her hands at the waist of her apron, flashing a big smile at Dee. "I thought I heard voices. You're back from your walk. Good. I just took something special out of the oven. Come along." She turned and marched into the kitchen, but Dee didn't move.

"Emma, do you think I could ask her to pick up something for me the next time she goes to the grocery store?" She held out a piece of paper to me. "Do you think she'd mind? I'll pay for it." These last words were urgent and came out in a rush.

I glanced at the paper, saw the word beer, and waved it away. "Give it to Maria. She'll be glad to help make you feel more comfortable."

"Coming Miss Dee?" Maria called from the kitchen.

I smiled. The poor girl was going to gain a ton of weight under Maria's care as I had. Dee soon went upstairs to nap which was good for her and for me. No matter what I'd said to TJ, I had a lot to do.

CHAPTER FORTY-FOUR

"The engagement ring should be worn on the fourth finger of the right hand (counting the thumb as a finger); the wedding ring is worn on the fourth finger of the left hand."

– *Godey's Lady's Book* March 1864

When I'd called Cookie about TJ's decision to have the wedding at Waterwood House, we set a time to meet. We only had weeks to get ready. TJ had confirmed that Cookie and I could come that afternoon.

At the appointed time, I rushed outside, lightly closing my front door so I wouldn't wake Dee. Then the bride and I headed to Waterwood House.

Cookie's hands flew to her mouth in surprise when she saw the front of the house and the view. "It's like a fairy tale."

"Keeping in mind that TJ has final approval, I thought we might have the ceremony outside on the lawn, if the weather cooperates. If not, we could have it inside." I led her through the front door, and I prattled on with ideas. I hadn't forgotten my first moment of awe when TJ had opened his front door to me, seeing the large area, the magnificent staircase, and the crystal chandelier overhead. But, after all that, Cookie was drawn to the silent portrait of Emma, the one painted in the years following her husband's death.

"Oh, she is beautiful," Cookie said, barely catching her breath. "Who was she?"

The painting in an ornate wooden frame still had the same effect on me. Emma wore a soft blush-pink gown, its sleeves were full at the shoulder then drawn in tightly at the elbow. Her eyes were the color of the deep blue waters of the Chesapeake on a sunny day. Her flaxen hair was drawn up softly under a straw hat that gave her flawless pale skin a little protection from the sun. A soft smile touched her lips.

While Cookie gushed about how beautiful she was, I hoped she never saw the other painting, the family portrait TJ had tucked away. In it, Emma looked worn and unhappy. We'd all experienced enough sadness for now. It was time to plan a happy occasion.

We sat in the dining room and Cookie briefed me on the plans that were already in place. I felt a sigh of relief. The caterer for the food and cake would only need to shift the event address. I told her about TJ's offer of his family's silver punch bowl set with the caveat that someone had to polish the bowl and all the little cups that went with it. I thought Cookie would swoon right out of her chair. She volunteered as long as I showed her how to do it. I made a note to gather up the silver and take it to the Cottage then remembered my houseguest. Maybe TJ would let us do the polishing here in his kitchen. I added a note to have the crystal chandeliers cleaned. Cookie quickly took some shots of the new venue for the lady doing the flowers and added a floral consultation to her To Do list.

I was tickled to see a photo of Cookie's wedding gown. It was not a modern off-the-shoulder, body-hugging design. The simple bodice and long sleeves were accented with lace and small pearls. The full skirt, adorned with lace at the hem, was not as wide as the gowns in the 1860s Godey's Lady's Book illustrations. I thought Emma would approve.

As we left, Cookie looked back at Waterwood House. Tears sprang to her eyes.

"Oh no, what's wrong?" I asked with great concern.

"Nothing, nothing is wrong. It's so perfect!" She threw her arms around me and almost knocked us both to the ground. "How can I ever thank you?"

It warmed my heart that I could do something to make someone happy.

Later, I texted TJ about our progress. I filled him in about polishing the silver and cleaning the chandeliers along with the assurance that I would supervise so he wouldn't have to worry about the house. His response made me smile. He wrote: *I trust you.* He agreed to everything except the idea of using the kitchen when the butler's pantry was designed for such work.

A butler's pantry! Why didn't I think of that? I thought with a laugh.

When I got back to the Cottage, Dee was still napping, and it was too early to heat the dinner Maria had left for us. Both my brain and body were tired from the day's activities. I opted to start a little fire in the living room fireplace and read. I must have fallen asleep, because I awakened to the crackle of a log to find Dee kneeling by the fire.

"I'm sorry, I didn't mean to wake you," she said. "The fire had almost gone out."

"It's no problem at all," I said. The grandfather clock chimed. "It's time for dinner. I hope you're hungry. Maria has probably put together another feast."

"I think I could eat. No offense to Maria, but anything has to be better than hospital food." We laughed in agreement. "In fact, I think I'll check the fridge to see if she was able to pick up…"

As she got up, Dee had to grab on to the mantle to keep from falling.

"Steady." I moved to help but she shook me off.

"No, I'm okay. Really. Just moved a little too fast. Now, to the fridge."

As she walked out of the living room, each step looked solid, so I didn't follow her. I watched tendrils of flames grow as the fire found fuel and strength. Dee soon appeared carrying two glasses.

"What do you have there?" I asked as she handed me a glass half-full.

She settled in a chair on the far side of the fire. "RAR Hefeweizen. It's an excellent local craft beer. I like it with an orange slice. I thought you'd like to try it. You've been so kind to me. I wanted to share one of my favorite things."

Though I preferred wine over beer, I took a sniff and found it pleasant. I followed Dee's example and gave the orange slice a little squeeze before I dropped it into the glass.

"When I'm out with the guys after working at a site, I drink beer," she said. She shook her head and took a long sip. "That's good. They think I drink it to be *one of the gang*, but I'll let you in on a little secret. I drink this beer because I like it and it's brewed right in my hometown of Cambridge."

We chatted for a bit then headed to the kitchen where we had to eat because I had commandeered the dining room as a research library. We pulled out all the dishes Maria had prepared, and both ate too much. Afterward, we slipped on our coats and took a little walk under the stars.

Away from the light pollution from the Cottage, the stars leapt into view as if someone had plugged them into an electrical socket. Even the moon couldn't drown out their fire, but it was still strong enough to cast our shadows on the fall leaves spread everywhere on the ground. I remembered begging my mother when I was a young teen to let me go to the beach on the nights of a full moon with all the other girls so we could get our *moontans*. Some people talked about a starry night sky making them feel small. I always felt like it made me feel part of something bigger.

Dee and I walked along the path in silence when a swooshing noise and an unearthly sound split the quiet. *KKKEEEEE-RRRCK!*

Dee threw her arms around her head in terror and crouched down. "What was that?"

I patted her arm. "Not to worry. It's only a blue heron, making himself known."

The swooshing of wings passed over our heads. "He's gone now. Guess we disturbed him."

"Sorry." Dee stepped back. "I've never heard such an unearthly sound. And from such a beautiful bird. Are you sure…?"

"Yes, I remember the first time he launched himself out of a pine tree, chastising me for coming too close. I guess the angels ran out of beautiful bird songs when they got to the heron and made up for it with a graceful form and unique shades of blue."

Dee stopped and looked at me. "That's something that Belle would have said. She always thought that angels played a big part in our lives." She glanced with a sigh in the direction where the bird had disappeared.

When we returned to the Cottage, we both headed up to bed. Fresh air and good food would do that to a person.

I fell into a peaceful sleep until I heard crying from down the hall.

"No, no..." Dee kept repeating.

Another nightmare. What was bothering her mind?

Once Dee slipped into a quiet sleep, I climbed back into my own bed. But all I did was toss and turn. The question of what was bothering Dee kept poking at my mind. Finally, I gave up and went downstairs. I didn't want to make a cup of coffee. My nerves were already jangling. I found a hot chocolate mix on a kitchen shelf and silently thanked Marie as I heated a cup of milk.

With my cuppa, I wandered into the dining room and sat down in the dining chair with arms. The one the movers had used to carry me to the garage in the woods where we pulled the blue tarp off the plantation desk. It was how my adventure with Daniel and Emma began. Two people I'd grown to respect and yes, love. I gazed at all the things on the table. Emma's things. The fine pieces of lace. The issues of Godey's Lady's Book. Even the pink ribbon was significant as it tied the two keys together. From the outside, one might think Emma had everything to live a happy life: a handsome husband, lovely children, a beautiful home, a successful plantation. She kept the truth locked away in her secret room, in her diaries, and in her heart.

My body ached for rest, but my racing thoughts wouldn't allow sleep. In the living room, I awakened the fire and wrapped myself in an afghan on the sofa. I thought about the things locked away in her secret room for so long. I suspected it was the only place she could be herself without fear. Her imagination flew away while reading adventure books. The delicate christening set that I now assumed was for the little girl who was stolen and sold. And there was her mother's wedding gown remade with hopes and dreams joined together in new pieces of lace.

Finally, my eyes grew heavy, and I slept.

I awoke to a day filled with planned wedding activities. Fortunately, I didn't have a lot of work to do for the event. Cookie had taken charge of notifying the guests of the change of venue, finding cleaners for the chandeliers, and updating the florist and caterer. I could see why Belle trusted her to handle the details of her transactions.

Today, we'd planned to deal with the silver and the heavy cleaning, Cookie arrived with young men equipped with ladders, heaps of cloths, and gallons of glass cleaner to clean the chandeliers. She set up the butler's pantry for silver polishing.

Everything was going according to plan when TJ appeared. "Oh, I thought you'd left."

"Don't worry," he said with a broad smile. "I'm on my way out, but first…" He opened a door of a mammoth piece of furniture in the dining room. "This is the silver cabinet. Start with the punch bowl set. I understand there used to be a lot more family silver, but…" He winked at me. "As we know, someone buried it in a place unknown. But you'll find everything you need here, I think. Good luck." And he was out the door.

When I uncovered the bowl, my breath caught. It was huge and covered with an ornate three-dimensional pattern of roses and leaves, all hammered out of the silver. Fortunately, there was little tarnish except in the deepest recesses of the design which emphasized its detail. I lifted another cover to find a multitude of small punch cups. Each handle curved up to the edge of the cup ending in a single rose surrounded with leaves. Thirty-four cups. We'd have to ask the caterer to bring more cups--glass, not plastic. The punch ladle also featured the Rose Stieff repoussé.

On another shelf, there was a note on top of the cover.

Found this knife and
server ... to cut the cake? TJ

What a thoughtful man, in so many ways.

Hours later, the chandeliers were done and so were we. Gleaming silver pieces were set on the dining room table where I'd first worked with Aunt Louisa's box. Emma and I had come so far.

Cookie giggled and gave me a big hug. "It's really happening, isn't it?"

A voice behind us said, "Yes, it is. You've done a great job. I'm impressed." TJ flipped on the light switch for each chandelier and drew in a big breath. "WOW! I've never seen them look like that." He flipped off the lights and turned to Cookie. "Would you like to see the bride's room where you'll get dressed?"

Cookie's eyes sparkled as she bounced up the steps of the main staircase and to a room furnished with a mirrored vanity, chair, and a full-length cheval mirror.

Adjusting it, he said, "I found it in a room upstairs." He smiled, knowing that I recognized it from Emma's secret room in the attic.

Cookie's eyes were glistening. 'It's perfect. Thank you, TJ."

And it was. I turned toward the door to head downstairs, when I realized that I was the only one who'd moved.

Cookie had locked eyes with TJ. In a serious tone, she spoke. "Thank you for everything you've done, that you're doing for me." TJ started to speak, but Cookie wasn't finished. "And I'd like to ask one more favor."

TJ's eyes slipped over to me. I gave him a slight shake of my head. I had no idea what was coming.

"Oh, Emma doesn't know what I'm going to ask and, if she did, she'd probably tell me to be quiet.' Cookie took a deep breath. "As you know, Nicky was going to host the wedding at Safe Harbor Farm, but that wasn't all." She took another breath and closed her eyes. "He was going to walk me down the aisle." Her whole body tensed as she squeezed her eyes tight. "Would you do me that honor now, please?"

My jaw dropped. TJ flipped his gaze back my way in surprise. Then I saw his face relax. He didn't need my help.

"Young lady, you have to open your eyes," he instructed.

Slowly, her shoulders relaxed and peered at him through her lashes.

"That's better," TJ said softly. "You don't have a father, brother, cousin, or friend to walk you down the aisle?"

She cast her eyes downward. "No?" A slight shake of her head.

TJ turned to me and put his hands on his hips. "Emma, this is a problem."

I braced myself. TJ hadn't signed up for this.

"We can't have this young woman take her last steps as a single woman all alone." He turned back to Cookie. "I would be honored to walk with you."

I hoped he was ready for Cookie's normal exuberant response, but he wasn't. She almost knocked him over when she threw her arms around him. We huddled up and laughed.

CHAPTER FORTY-FIVE

"...for it is the small temptations which undermine integrity unless we watch and pray and never think them too trivial to be resisted."

– Louisa May Alcott

The next day, the detective and I were in the kitchen, brewing some coffee. Craig had called earlier, suggesting a conversation about the confusing aspects of this case might be helpful. When I heard the tires of TJ's truck crunching the gravel, I popped in his favorite flavor and went to the front door.

When he came up the steps with Ghost and stopped at the door, he leaned forward and whispered, "Is this a good idea? We could go up to Waterwood House if you want."

I was confused. Then it hit me. He was worried about Dee overhearing our conversation about Belle's death in the ice house. "No, it's fine. Dee has a doctor's appointment and Cookie drove her."

He relaxed and came inside. With our hot cuppas in hand, we opted to sit on the patio to enjoy the warm Indian Summer day.

"I'm glad Dee is at the doctor's so we can talk freely," I said. "She hasn't been sleeping well."

Craig wanted details. "Sometimes nightmares are a sign of a guilty conscience."

"What are you saying?" TJ almost demanded.

Craig pursed his lips and shrugged. "I'm just saying her relationship with Belle might not have been as rosy as we think. I've been doing some reading about twins. They can look alike but have unique personalities. They are often competitive and need their own space. Dee confirmed that in one of our conversations. She said she stopped trying to compete with Belle after they graduated from high school. Instead of reading fashion magazines, Dee found she loved working with her hands."

"Yes," I said. "She told me how she earned all kinds of certifications in the building trade." A little laugh escaped my lips. "I can just imagine Belle's face when she first saw Dee doing a welding job."

Craig added. "Dee said she stopped using makeup and trying to walk in high heels. I don't think you'll find any of those three to four-inch heels with the red soles in Dee's closet." Craig gave me a quick nod in gratitude for the information I'd given him. "I talked to Cookie about the shoes. You were right, Emma. The shoes she was wearing at the library were in fact Belle's. She insisted that Belle had encouraged her to practice walking in them, but only around the office. Cookie admitted, with a lot of tears, that she didn't have permission to wear those incredibly high heels outside."

"Did you find the other shoe?" I asked, remembering that Belle was found in the ice pit wearing only one shoe.

"Yes, but it wasn't easy. A petite and agile female crime scene investigator came down from Baltimore. It cost me a lunch, but she got the other shoe from the pit. She is a seasoned professional, but she admitted that slipping down into that pit unnerved her."

A shiver ran through me. "I can understand. It looked so dark and..."

"Actually, that wasn't the reason. She got spooked when she had to grab hold of the crossbeams. That's what killed Belle, falling on those beams. She was alive when she went into the pit. Again, no clearcut evidence of murder. There is nothing simple or straightforward about this case."

I couldn't agree more. The idea of writing a book seemed so much easier than unraveling this situation.

Craig continued. "She also brought additional information."

"Like what?

"Belle wasn't pregnant which blew apart my easy assumption that Belle was having an affair with Nicky." He sipped his coffee. "And I checked out Cookie's alibi. It held up. She was in the real estate office working on Belle's deals when it happened."

TJ looked across the creek at the Lone Oak and asked the question that was on all our minds. "Who is your best suspect?"

With no enthusiasm, Craig said in a flat voice, "I have two."

"Two?" My body shuddered at the thought. "Does that mean you're still looking at Nicky?" I wasn't willing to believe he could have hurt the sisters.

"And who else?" TJ asked. "A stranger?"

Craig shifted his eyes to me. "There was only one other person there."

Slowly, I straightened, my spine coming off the chair's back cushion. "Me?" My voice rose in disbelief. "You mean me?"

TJ jumped to his feet. "You can't accuse Emma."

"She was there," Craig reminded him calmly.

"She didn't do anything," TJ shot back.

Craig leaned back and looked up at TJ towering over him. "And how do you know that?"

"I-I-I know because I believe what she said. She wasn't in the ice house when it all went down." TJ was taking in gulps of air. He seemed desperate for something else to say. Finally, he flung an arm out in my direction. "Ask her!"

Craig let out a short breath. "Relax, that isn't necessary. I believe her, too. She was an innocent bystander at the wrong place at the wrong time. Emma doesn't fit the description of a psychopath and she has never exhibited any signs of guilt."

"Like what?" I demanded to know.

Craig threw up his hands. "Now, she wants to know everything I've learned in years of training classes and interrogations." He crossed his muscular arms across his chest. "Okay, start with this…you never lost empathy with the victim or her twin. I never caught a hint of a smile when we've talked about the incident. And at the scene and that evening, you never wanted to lie down to sleep. It's a sign of guilt, you know. After the rush of adrenaline when someone commits murder, the body wants to rest. Satisfied? You both need to get a grip. I'm not accusing anybody here of anything."

I rested back in my chair then his words sank into my muddled brain. "Not accusing anybody here," I repeated slowly. "But you still think Dee is responsible for Belle's death?" I popped up out of my chair and started to pace around my small patio. "You don't know what you're talking about. I thought we agreed that a right-handed person couldn't hit herself on the left side of her head and do that kind of damage." I started to head down to the creek, muttering, "I don't know, I just don't—" But TJ's next words stopped me. I called back. "What did you say?"

"I said," TJ repeated, "I think Dee is left-handed."

"No, that's not possible. I've seen her using tools with her right hand."

I needed TJ to confirm Dee's innocence, but he looked down at the stones of the patio. "Most tools are made for people who are right-handed. That's the dominant side. They make tools for left-handed people, but they're usually expensive, if you can even find them."

"What about a hammer? A screwdriver?"

"You're right," TJ shot back. "Some tools work for either hand, but have you ever tried to cut something with your left hand using a regular pair of scissors? There's the pocket knife, a corkscrew, even the tool belt you wear around your waist, they're all made for right-handed people."

TJ motioned me back to my chair. "Take the measuring tape. When a lefty uses it to mark a piece of wood, her hand would cover up the numbers. It would be easier for her to learn to use her right hand for certain things." He sighed. "And when she was at my place, she made notes and wrote out the estimate with her left hand."

Slowly, I turned to Craig. "So, where do you go from here?"

"I have to figure out if it was Nicky or Dee. Remember the scene you described to me at the Pub when Dee saw Belle with Nicky?"

"Yes, but—"

"I think Dee hurt Belle. I'm not sure how, but I think Dee is responsible for Belle falling into the ice pit and breaking her back—severing her spinal cord, breaking her neck—whatever the medical examiner declares as the cause of death."

"But they are sisters," I insisted. "There must be another explanation…" My words trailed off as I looked at Craig's face but it had turned to stone. I knew that nothing I said would change his mind.

I looked back at the Lone Oak and thought of my own big sister. We were born years apart. She always treated me like a child, even after I graduated from college. We never had much in common. I was wrapped up in playground rivalries while she was worried about college entrance exams. Sure, she made me mad, but I never wanted to kill her, not really.

There was a knock at my front door. Grateful for the interruption, I went and found Cookie standing there.

"Hi, Emma." She held out a violet-blue hoodie. "Dee left it in my car."

"Isn't she with you?" Madly, I looked around.

"No, I dropped her off a little while ago. I wasn't very far up the road when I noticed she'd left it in the car."

I took the hoodie and nodded blankly as Cookie left. As I closed the door, Dee was coming down the steps. She said nothing but the expression on her face let me know that she had overheard our conversation on the patio. That we believed she was a killer. Or, equally devastating, that it was Nicky.

That evening, Dee and I had a delicious dinner together again, thanks to Maria. We danced around the subject that sat in the middle of the table.

I wanted to ask Dee a mountain of questions. Had she overheard our conversation on the patio? Had she hurt her sister, Belle? Had she seen Nicky hurt Belle? Had he come at them both?

But I kept the conversation light when we talked at all.

Finally, as I rinsed the last dish to put it in the dishwasher, Dee blurted out, "You think I did it. You think I murdered my sister."

I was so stunned that I almost dropped the plate. "Um, I never said that."

"You think I did it!" Her voice was rising. "Y'all do."

"Who?"

"TJ, the detective, and YOU!" That declaration cut like a knife. "I know. Don't lie. I heard y'all out on the patio talkin' 'bout me. Everybody is talkin' 'bout me. I'll never be able to work in this county again. Everybody will think I'm a murderer."

I realized how upset she was as her Southern accent got heavier. Carefully, I put down the plate. We didn't need any broken china to add to the drama.

"Now, let's take a deep breath. We can talk about—"

She cut me off. "You think I'm pretending that I don't remember. You probably can't send a murderer to prison if she can't remember a thing. So, I'm either the crazy one or a liar."

"I don't think you're crazy. And if you're acting, you're in the wrong business. You should go to Hollywood because you're very convincing."

Dee's gaze dropped slowly to the floor as if all the energy had leaked out of her. She slumped into a kitchen chair and stared at nothing.

I pulled out the other chair and sat down. "I'm sorry you overheard our conversation."

She pulled her eyes up to meet mine. They were ablaze with anger. "Why? 'Cause you got caught talkin' behind my back?"

"No," I said slowly. "If we could come up with a logical possibility, it might help you remember."

Dee opened her mouth to fight back, but my words must have sunk in. She closed it again.

"No one is trying to put you in jail," I said softly.

"The detective is," she shot back.

"No, he's trying to find the truth." I sat back, groping for something to say that would calm her. "You've heard that old cliché, *The truth will set you free?*"

She gave a little nod. "I think so. I wasn't that good in school."

"It doesn't matter. I think it applies in this situation. If or when we can figure out the truth of what happened, you will be free of all this doubt and paranoia that people are out to get you. They don't know what to believe so they're grasping at straws." I chuckled a little. "Sorry, I guess this is my night for clichés."

It was the right joke to make. A small smile touched her lips.

"When you put it that way, I can see your point. Not remembering is drivin' me crazy. Nasty thing not knowin' if you killed your twin sister." She took in a deep breath and let it out slowly.

"Maybe an early night is what you need, Dee. A good night's sleep can solve a lot of problems."

"You're right. I don't think I've been sleeping well."

I didn't dare tell her how she'd awakened me with screams and crying in the night and how I'd gone to her room to help. Each time, I found she was still asleep. It didn't seem to be a good idea to wake her suddenly. Instead, I said, "Do you need anything?"

She shook her head. "No, everything is fine, thank you." She looked down at her hands. "I think I'm having nightmares."

"About what?" I asked gently, hoping she could break through the barrier blocking her memory.

She shrugged. "I don't know. I can never remember."

I plastered a smile on my face. "Maybe tonight you'll get the sleep you need."

A low rumble in the distance made us both turn quickly to the window. It was an announcement of an incoming storm.

"I think we're in for some more rain. They say the pitter-patter of raindrops can help you sleep," I said lightly. "You go on upstairs. I'll finish up here."

As the storm electrified the air outside, the air between us relaxed as we said good night.

CHAPTER FORTY-SIX

"Good-night, good-night, to the sad and weary,
Whose hearts are filled with grief."

— Godey's Lady's Book 1863

The storm broke over the Cottage before I made my way upstairs. The low rumble had turned into an almost constant competition between the growls of thunder caused by crackling bolts of lightning and the constant drumming of fat raindrops. I tried to check the weather app on my phone, but I couldn't bring up anything on the internet. That wasn't a good sign. Maybe a tower had been hit. I went to a window. There was lightning above us and off in the distance. This storm must be huge. I hoped there were no red cells on the weather radar that could mean a potential tornado. It wouldn't matter anyway. I didn't have any service on my cell phone. No bars at all.

Then the landline rang, splitting a calm moment in the cacophony outside. Who would be calling at this hour? I picked up the receiver. My greeting of hello was met with a recorded message warning of a severe thunderstorm and the precautions I should take. No, I thought as I hung up, I wasn't planning to go for a stroll. Nothing would pull me from the Cottage tonight.

The call was a little late in coming as the storm banged overhead, but somehow, it was comforting to know there was someone or something watching out for me. I walked around the Cottage as quickly as I could to make sure all the windows were closed against the storm and locked all the doors.

I was halfway up the stairs when a clap of thunder rolled through the whole house. With my feet on the steps and my hand firmly on the banister, vibrations rumbled through my body. Mother Nature had reached inside the Cottage, my sanctuary, and awakened my childhood fears of storms. Mom always told me I was safe. Nothing could harm me. Her reassuring words didn't quell my fears then and they weren't helping now.

The storm was here, vibrating my body, making the hairs on my arm stand up, blinding me with its bright-hot light. The safety of my bed seemed miles away. I only had to raise my foot a few inches to the next step. But first, I had to relax my muscles that were locked up tight.

Then Dee screamed!

I rushed up the remaining steps and down the hall to her room.

Dee sat bolt upright in bed, her hands clamped over her ears. Her eyes were so big, I thought they might pop right out of her head. And she was screaming. This was no nightmare. Dee was wide awake.

I hit the light switch. I always felt safer with the lights on.

Nothing. No surprise. The power was out.

Lightning flashed at the window. Mother Nature mocking our modern conveniences. But in that flash, I could see well enough to make my way to Dee's bed and put my arms around her. I could feel the sweat from her face on mine. This wasn't fear. It was terror.

At first, she fought my hug. I had to speak up, so she'd hear my soothing words. I held her so tight I could feel the waves of gut-wrenching panic roll through her the way the thunder rolled over the land outside. I rocked her gently and finally felt her body droop a little. It helped that the central violence of the storm had moved over to someone else's part of the world.

"Dee, it's okay. You're safe. The storm is almost over." I repeated those words over and over.

Without warning, she broke my hold and leaned away. "No, it's not over. It will never be over."

I was confused. Lack of sleep and the storm had clouded my mind. "Of course, it will be over. It's moving off now. You're safe."

She jumped up and madly paced around the small bedroom. "Not the storm... what I did. It will never be over. Why... why...why..." She marched back and forth. She kept repeating that one word: *Why? Not the storm... what I did.*

What did she do? Was her memory coming back? Was she remembering what happened in the ice house? Did she kill her sister?

I shook the thought right out of my head. This storm had unsettled me, too.

Dee's steps slowed. Her mumblings quieted. I reached out. She stopped in front of me and she let me take hold of her hand.

"Dee, it's okay. The storm upset you, that's all." I could hear only distant rumblings. "It's going away now. Do you want to crawl back in bed?" I patted the pillow.

She shook her head like tiny shudders. Her lovely strawberry blonde hair fell across her face. It was so like Belle's.

"Then let's go downstairs and make some warm milk with honey. Guaranteed to do the trick when you can't sleep, okay?"

This time, she nodded gently. I pulled my phone from my pocket, turned on the flashlight app, and led the way downstairs, keeping her hand in mine.

In the kitchen, I dug out some candles and lit up the room. I turned off my app, not knowing how long it would be before I could charge the battery again and tucked it into my pocket. I pulled out a pan and was about to put it on the stove, but it ran on electricity. So much for the idea of warm milk.

"I'll be right back." I grabbed a candlestick and made my way to Uncle Jack's den. In the bottom of a cabinet, I found the bottle of brandy he kept *for medicinal purposes.* I smiled at the memory. It was a rite of passage when he poured my first small glass of the fiery potion. I'd escaped to the Cottage during a stressful college term. The ritual did wonders for me. I hoped it would have a similar effect on Dee.

I prepared two small glasses of milk and poured some brandy in each, though I put more in Dee's glass. Then I added Uncle Jack's secret ingredient: a little sugar. I sat down at the table and she joined me. We clinked our glasses without a toast. I sipped, but Dee was unsure. She sniffed the concoction, then took a tentative sip. Liking it, she drank some more.

"Better?" I asked.

She put the glass down and nodded. Slowly, her eyes traveled around the kitchen, looking for a place to rest. Seeing the glass again, she raised it to her lips and tipped it back until all the milk was gone.

I was surprised, but thankful she was calming down.

"A little more?" I suggested.

She nodded and I made another of Uncle Jack's medicinal drinks. After a good sip, she raised her eyes to meet mine, then looked away.

"I'm sorry. I'm sorry I'm so much trouble," she said in a small voice.

I reached out and covered her hand with mine. "Don't be silly. This is what friends are for."

She looked down at our hands. "I never really had a friend before. Except Nicky, but he's different. I guess you could say I never needed a friend before. I have...had Belle. My other half."

My attention was tugged away from what Dee said. What was striking the windows, like fingernails tapping impatiently on the glass? Was it sleet that often heralded a tornado?

"When we were kids, we played together," Dee continued, oblivious to the sounds from outside. "We never needed anyone else." She paused then added quickly, "Sure, we needed Mom to make our meals, wash our clothes and stuff. But friends? We had each other."

"That must have been a special way to grow up," I said with only part of my mind focused on what she was saying. Now that I was noticing the sounds outside, I thought I heard some thudding on the roof.

Rain, I assured myself. *It's only rain.*

Dee went on, not noticing me. "It was a great way to grow up. I'm embarrassed to say if we didn't agree with something Mom wanted to do, we ganged up on her. What could she do? It was two against one, and she didn't know which was which."

I shot a glance at the kitchen windows facing the creek. The storm must have been coming from that direction. Fat raindrops were throwing themselves against the glass.

"It was great until we were old enough to notice boys," she said. The tightness in Dee's voice drew my attention away from the window and the storm. The words were getting caught in her throat, choking off her breath.

I hesitated, but it might help to ask, "When you were teenagers? What happened then?"

I watched as her face contorted. She bit her lower lip. She frowned. Her eyes closed. All in rapid succession. Memories must have been galloping across her mind.

Realizing that the question must have opened the floodgates of times past, I tried to put them in perspective. "You were teenagers. I think that's part of growing up. It even happens to best friends who aren't related. It was bound to happen with twins. You girls must have been attracted to the same kind of boys. It's natural—"

She sat there as if carved from granite, not hearing a word I said. What should I do? Was I making things worse?

I heard tapping on the door. TJ checking on us. Relieved I opened it.

But it wasn't TJ. A torrent of rain was blasting away at the Cottage. I muscled the door closed and went to Dee, but she hadn't noticed a thing.

Dee murmured, "Nicky. Nicky is different. She can't have him…"

The storm slung pelts at the Cottage. Mother Nature was angry. A flash of lightning lit Dee in a garish light. She leapt up, her chair crashing to the floor.

"Dee?"

Her eyes weren't focused. She declared, "I hurt her." Then she pronounced the verdict. "I have to pay."

Dee ran to the kitchen door and flung it open. Rain and wind roared into the room.

"Dee, you can't go out there," I yelled. But she was gone.

I couldn't leave her out there alone. If I took the time to call TJ or get a raincoat, I'd never find her in the blackness of this turbulent night. Rain slapped my face before I made it outside. I pushed forward, calling out her name.

The only answer that came back in the pitch blackness were the sounds of the storm's fury. Tree limbs flailed. Leaves swirled around me, flying against my exposed skin like dull knives. Dirt pelted my face.

"Dee? Dee! Come back." The howling wind swallowed my words.

I moved forward. My bare feet left the stone patio and sank into the mud. It squeezed between my toes. There wasn't time to find shoes. There was no time to go back.

Out here in the open, the ground had had enough with rainstorms and wouldn't, couldn't absorb any more water. Sloshing through deep puddles, my slacks were soaked from the bottom up. My shirt and sweater were drenched from the sheets of rain bombarding me. A chill shriveled my wet skin.

"DEE!"

"Go away!" she screamed.

At last, an answer. I had a direction. "Dee, you have to come back. The storm—"

But my words were lost in the crack of lightning hitting a tree across the creek. I only hoped it hadn't hit the Lone Oak.

"Leave me alone," she yelled back at me. "I deserve this. I deserve to be punished,"

She had headed toward the water. If she got to the creek and fell in, there would be nothing I could do to save her. It was too deep, too wide…

"Dee!"

"Go away!" She screamed.

I could see in a lightning flash that she'd stopped and turned toward me. I moved faster, splashing through the darkness, hoping I wouldn't hurt my leg or fall.

"Dee, stay right there. I'm coming."

"There's nothing you can do to stop her."

"Who?" Was someone else out here in this storm?

"She's punishing me." Dee was calm. "I deserve it," she added bluntly. "I was wrong. I'm sorry," she screamed at the storm.

I kept heading toward her, barely registering what she was saying. Was she confessing to the murder of her sister?

FLASH! Thunder over my head. I couldn't leave her to the elements.

Three more running steps and I was on her. I grabbed Dee by the shoulders and got in her face.

"We have to go back to the Cottage. We can talk there." I pulled her a little to get her walking in the right direction.

She raised her arms and broke out of my grasp. "NO!" And she pushed me away.

It was so sudden. I couldn't steady myself. I tripped… and screamed. And went down in the muck.

When I opened my eyes, Dee was leaning over me. Rain, no, they were tears streaming down her face. "I'm sorry, I'm so sorry. I'm so sorry, Belle."

CHAPTER FORTY-SEVEN

"Many an April shower and gusty thunderstorm had swept the heath, driving away all the horrors of war, and leaving only the sweetness of pure nature behind."

–From "The Last Plantagenet" by Mrs. Ann S. Stephens
Peterson's Magazine 1865

B ELLE?

Dee thought I was her sister.

"I'm so sorry, Belle," she wailed. "I didn't mean to push you."

Dee pushed her sister into the ice pit?

"But you shouldn't have done that. Y'all shouldn't have pushed me first. That was very wrong. We're not kids anymore. We shouldn't fight like kids."

They had a fight. A shoving match?

"We're sisters, twins. You're part of me. I'm part of you." Dee threw herself on top of my body and whispered through her tears, "I'm sorry, Belle. I love you."

With the weight of the young woman's body, I felt like I was sinking into the mud, never to rise again. It helped that the storm was easing. I needed help. I put one arm around Dee, an instinct to offer comfort and to keep her from running off again. With my other hand, I felt in my pocket. With a grateful sigh, my fingertips touched my phone. With a little luck, it hadn't been destroyed by the rain or our tussle in the mud. And that service was back.

With one hand, I patted Dee on the back to help ease her sobs. With the other, I hit speed dial for TJ. He answered in a gruff voice. I must have awakened him but how anyone could sleep through that storm was beyond me.

I had to fight back tears of relief. I wasn't alone anymore. "TJ, I'm all right, but I need you."

He was clear and alert immediately. "What's wrong? Where are you? Why are you whispering?"

I lowered my voice even more. "We," I said with emphasis, "are on the path to the cabin or close to it. I think Ghost can find us. Hurry. And tell Craig."

Dee's tears were subsiding. She let out a moan.

"Hurry!" I slipped my phone back in my pocket with a sigh. *TJ is coming.*

I rubbed Dee's back, more to comfort myself than her. She started to stir. Since I didn't know what could happen next, I put my other arm around her. "It's all right, dear sister. I'll take care of you. Rest now." I felt her body relax.

We both might have dropped off for a few minutes from all the emotion.

Soon, I felt an explosion of warm breath on my face. When I opened my eyes, I was looking at the liquid brown eyes of Ghost filled with caring. His nose was working fast, taking in every scrap of scent. Then his wet pink tongue washed my face. And I laughed a little.

TJ skidded to a halt in the mud and dropped to his knees next to me. "Emma, what—"

"Sh-h-h, I think she's asleep. Be gentle, TJ," I whispered. "Her memory is back, and she is having trouble dealing with it. Is Craig coming?"

He nodded.

"Go tell him what's happened and that she needs some special psychological help now. Right now. Please, she's fragile. If we're not careful, we might lose her."

As he began to rise, he stopped and leaned close to my ear. "Did she…"

I barely shook my head. Then I whispered the word, *accident*.

When the enormity of the truth hit him, his chin dropped to his chest. "What a waste. Got to save her." He pulled himself up, gave Ghost his hand signal to stay, and headed back to the Cottage.

Now that the storm from the heavens and the one from Dee's imagination had petered out, the driving rain subsided into a misting drizzle that felt more like a caress. I used one hand to scratch Ghost behind the ear and soak up his calm. It wasn't long before I heard people coming down the path, speaking in hushed tones. Columns of light from flashlights were leading the way. Thankfully, they didn't shine their brightness on us, but moved around in the glow when aimed off to the side.

A young man in a dark uniform knelt down next to me. "My name is Thomas. Are you hurt?"

I shook my head.

"Is she?"

When I shrugged, Dee stirred.

"Try and wake her. Be gentle. Tell her I'm here for her." He gave me a slight nod of encouragement.

"Dee? It's time to wake up." She stirred a little. "I want you to meet a friend. His name is Thomas."

Dee moved. "Who?"

The man leaned forward a little. "Hello, I'm a friend. My name is Thomas. I'm glad to meet you."

Dee turned her head his way and inspected him. "Hello," she said tentatively. She started to turn her face to me, but Thomas spoke quickly.

"Here, look at me, Dee. Give me your hand and I'll help you up." He kept her attention focused on him by giving little instructions and she followed them carefully. Without a glance back at me, he and his unit had Dee taking her first steps back to the Cottage toward the help she needed.

Free of her weight, I looked up at the storm clouds now parting to reveal a few twinkling stars. As if he knew I needed the consolation and support, Ghost took to licking my face again.

"Hey, Big Guy, that's enough. Let the girl breathe." TJ and I laughed a little. "Emma, there's an EMT here ready to check—"

"No," I tried to pull up my shoulders, but the sucking mud held them in place. "Just help me up. Please."

It took both men to coax my body out of the mud, that's how strong its grip was on me. They half-carried me back to the Cottage so my feet barely touched the ground. In the kitchen, Craig announced that we needed to talk. Dangling in the hands of the two men, I insisted he'd have to wait until I had a hot shower. In response, he pointed at the coffee machine, and I nodded. Without hesitation, they whisked me up the stairs and into the master bathroom.

"Okay, gentlemen. That's as far as you go. I can take it from here."

"Emma, are you sure?" TJ's face was lined with concern.

"Yes," I said, my hands shooing them out. "I'm perfectly fine. Now, *out!* I'll meet you downstairs when I run out of hot water."

And I swear I must have used almost every drop. When I stepped out of the tub, I felt a pang of guilt leaving a muddy mess behind. I'd make it up to Maria somehow. Comfy in a pair of deep green fleece pants and a hoodie, I went downstairs to face Craig and all his questions.

CHAPTER FORTY-EIGHT

"Love is the only thing that we can carry with us when we go, and it makes the end so easy."

— Louisa May Alcott, *Good Wives*

The next day, I paid the price for staying up most of the night talking to Craig and TJ. I started yawning and fighting the urge to nap. Despite my loud protests, TJ insisted I see the doctor to make sure I was okay. I gave in because it was the only way to get him to relax. It was with a little smile of triumph when I climbed back in the truck and reported I was truly fine

As we drove away, Ghost assumed his new favorite position. He stretched his neck from the back seat of the cab and laid his head on my shoulder. Whenever he did this, it was the most comforting feeling. It gave me the strength to face the one thing we planned to do before going back to Waterwood: a meeting with Craig.

We settled in a small conference room that I suspected was really for interrogations. I went over everything again that happened the night before. Everything seemed to support Craig's opinion that Dee had assaulted Belle and could be charged with manslaughter.

I grabbed TJ's hand in desperation. "She didn't do it on purpose. She didn't kill her sister on purpose. If you could have seen her, heard what she said, how she said it…"

Craig slowly shook his head from side to side. "The facts fit what the law requires. It's manslaughter."

"But it can't be," I screamed at him.

"Unless…" Craig glanced down at the empty tabletop.

"Unless what?" I knew I was reaching for anything, but I was sure Dee was innocent.

In the grip of a new idea, he hunched over the table toward me. "Unless you can tell me." He paused and began again. "Tell me what you heard that day outside the ice house… exactly."

I clasped my hands in my lap and concentrated on them. This was it. I had to get this right. "I was walking toward the ice house to meet Dee. I remember hearing loud voices. I waited. I didn't want to walk into an argument. I think they were pushing each other."

Craig jumped on what I said. "How do you know that?"

"It's what Dee said last night, that they were pushing each other like children."

He sat back in his chair. "No, that doesn't help."

"Why not?" TJ wanted to know.

"Because it would be assault. They would both be guilty of assault and, if someone died as a result, it would be murder or manslaughter, depending."

TJ turned to me, his eyes filled with pleading. "Is there anything else you remember?"

"Anything at all?" Craig was really trying to help.

"I remember someone saying 'Y'all better stop that. Don't you do that again.'"

Craig leaned forward again. "Who said that? Which woman said that?"

I shook my head gently and looked down at my hands again, feeling drained. "I don't know. They were twins. They sounded the same to me."

Craig fell back in his chair again. His frustration added to mine and made my stomach hurt.

Then my body straightened up slowly. I felt my eyes growing wide as I realized something else. I drew in a deep breath. "There was one other thing." Both men moved toward me. "Yes, they sounded the same, angry. But it was the words that might tell us who said what." I looked from Craig to TJ and saw only blank expressions. Someone said, 'Y'all better stop that. Don't you do that again.'" I looked at them again and added. "You hear the Southern accent? *Y'all better* stop that. It was Dee who yelled that out. Belle was coming at Dee, coming at her again! Dee must have pushed her away and…"

Craig was shaking his head again. "I don't know."

"But I do," said TJ. "Belle worked really hard to get rid of her Southern accent. She once told me she thought it made her seem uneducated and unsophisticated. Believe me, no matter how mad she got, she'd never utter the words *Y'all better…*"

Craig looked from TJ to me and back to him. "Would you both be willing to talk to the DA?" We both nodded. "You may have to testify in court."

We exchanged looks and shrugged. "Sure."

"Okay, I may be able to work with this along with the testimony of the doctor about what Dee remembers now." He pushed back his chair and was out the door without a good-bye.

We rode in silence on our way home, but my mind was racing with thoughts about the complicated relationships sisters created for themselves.

Long ago, Minnie bombarded her sister Lottie at Safe Harbor House with accusations just short of insults, all because the loyalties of the sisters were on opposite sides of the war. It might not have been that neat and simple, but it showed how much damage sisters could do when they didn't listen to each other. Minnie was very clear about what divided them and, as a result, must have caused great stress and hurt. After the war, the sisters, must have found common ground again so they could lie together in the churchyard for all eternity.

If only that could have happened with Belle and Dee. If only they could have been honest with one another, talked to each other before things got out of hand, before tragedy could strike. Tears welled up when I thought about how one life was cut short and the other was marred forever... by a misunderstanding.

But there was hope. Days later, Craig told us the DA had listened to his perspective on the case and was reviewing the evidence and reports with an eye to declaring it an accident. If that happened, maybe with Nicky's help, Dee could find a way to live her life to the fullest.

I'd heard that Nicky and Dee had decided to hold on to Safe Harbor House. They felt a commitment to the old man who had agreed to the sale. They couldn't turn their back on all the thought, creativity, and effort Belle had put into making the property transfer happen for them.

Nicky didn't hesitate in dealing with the ice house. He had it plowed down and the hole filled in. That whole area would be landscaped with dwarf maple trees and many varieties of roses intermingled with daisies. It was to honor both twins who had been named after their mother's favorite flowers. This was not the time to remember how much both girls disliked those names. The design of the garden featured a place in the center for a sculpture. Not just any garden sculpture. Dee and Nicky wanted to put a stone angel in the middle because Belle had loved angels.

Dee remembered something Belle used to say, *You should believe in something. I believe in angels.*

So, an angel it would be. They would pick it out together after Dee finished her hospital/rehab stay and felt stronger to face her new reality. I only hoped she could forgive herself for what was a horrible accident and never again punish herself as she had with the brick. Until then, the roses, daisies and trees would send out their roots and establish themselves to stand strong... and beautiful.

CHAPTER FORTY-NINE

"Wouldn't it be fun if all the castles in the air which we make could come true and we could live in them?"

— Louisa May Alcott, *Little Women*

The day had finally come. Cookie's wedding day.

I'd walked to Waterwood House early to breathe in the fresh air with a tang of salt, drink in the view of the landscape usually blocked by the high cornstalks, and feel the kiss of the sun's warmth on my skin. This was probably the last remnant of warmth as we had crossed the threshold into November.

Would this fine weather hold throughout the day? If it did, we could move the ceremony outside. When we'd discussed the possibility, it was more of a whim, but the day had dawned with perfect weather for a wedding. I'd check the electronic sources for weather information later. Right now, I wanted to enjoy what was right in front of me and predict the weather the way the early English tobacco growers did. The way Emma would have searched for hints about the weather. The way TJ, the farmer, had taught me.

I searched the bright azure blue sky above my head. I looked to the western horizon. That was usually the direction to watch for incoming weather. Clear, not a wisp of a cloud. I turned south. The wettest weather usually came from that direction after scooping up humid air from the Gulf of Mexico. Whenever there was a winter forecast for snow, knowing the direction was important. Sure, the white stuff could come from the west, but if the storm was coming from the south, it was time to go to the grocery store and buy flashlight batteries and toilet paper. Today, there was nothing to the south but blue sky.

As I approached Waterwood House, I was relieved to see the Swan Cove Florist van with its door open and people hustling about. That was a good start. Had she started decorating the main parlor for the ceremony? That would make any thought of having it outdoors impossible. I quickened my step.

No, I'd arrived just in time. If I'd had one more cup of coffee, I would have been too late. After quick consultations with Debbie, the bride, and TJ who I found hiding in the kitchen, we decided to tempt the fates and move the ceremony outside. But we weren't brave enough to move the reception, so the staff was able to work on the dining room. I smiled when the florist showed me a small arrangement.

"It's for the bride's dressing room," Debbie said, her sunny smile matched the morning.

"Oh, did we order that?" I asked, a little confused.

"No, it's my treat. She's been through so much, I thought it would add to her joy today."

It added to my joy to know that someone would do something special *just because.*

I heard a truck drive up to the back of the house and found the caterer coming into the kitchen. TJ poured a fresh cup and escaped upstairs.

Cookie's friend who was overseeing the final arrangements appeared right on time. Cookie had already briefed her about the move outside. Again, I could see why Belle liked the way Cookie handled the big and little details. Since there was nothing more for me to do, I walked slowly back to the Cottage.

The cornstalks had left what TJ called stubble over the field. He'd take care of that when he planted the winter cover crop. I checked my watch. It was too early to dress so I thought it was appropriate to read the last pages of Emma's diary.

Dear Diary,

I have had five glorious years of freedom, but it's all about to come to an end. There is a growth in my breast that is stealing my energy and sucking out my life. I am growing weaker every day. A draught made from that lovely Foxglove flower in the garden would bring relief. The pain would be gone. I would be with Daniel. That is my dearest wish. The waiting has brought indescribable sadness. It is time for joy.

But no, I must stay because tomorrow may bring word of the one who will always be known in my heart as Emma, my lost daughter.

May the Lord deliver her to me before he calls me home.

Emma Elizabeth Ross Collins

And thus, Emma's story ended.

I went into the dining room and looked at all the things—her things—that led me to this moment. There was the sampler of childish stitches that showed her growing confidence to make the delicate stitches on the christening gown and elegant work on the wedding gown she never wore. The pieces of lace, even the practice pieces, were exquisite and told a story all their own. The books. The magazines. And more. But above all, there were the diaries. Without them, I would never have known her story beyond the name and dates on her gravestone. In my heart, I thanked her for her guidance in my search. I added my gratitude for Aunt Louisa's work in gathering things. And TJ. Without his support and trust, none of these things would be in my dining room.

My phone drew me out of my revelry. TJ was calling. "Are you dressed and ready for me to pick you up?" he asked.

Pick me up?

"Earth to Emma…"

"OH! The wedding!" I looked at the time and bolted out of my chair.

"Yes! The bride just called. She'll be here in a half-hour. You need to be here. Are you ready?"

"Um, yes, come in 20 minutes, okay?" I barely heard his response as I scooted upstairs to my bedroom.

Thank goodness I had laid everything out and my hair just needed a little curling iron touchup. When I heard TJ honk, I headed down the stairs, but not to the front door. Not yet. I picked up a piece of tissue and checked to see that a piece of Emma's lace was still cradled inside. TJ had approved the idea to give Cookie one of the small loose pieces of lace that Emma had made while living at Waterwood House. It certainly qualified as *Something Old* for the bride.

We arrived moments before the bride and her maid of honor. Cookie was calm and composed. The florist had placed the wedding arch in a picturesque spot on the front lawn. Everything looked as if we'd always planned to have the ceremony outside.

As we walked up the front steps of the house, Cookie pulled me aside. "Everything is perfect. Thank you so much."

"I wish your mom could have been here."

"No, the trip would have been terrible for her. Emphysema is a horrible disease. Don't worry, I'll send her lots of pictures. She'll love that. Everyone else who is important to me is here...almost." A tear threatened to slide down her cheek. "I wish Belle and Dee and Nicky could be here."

I gently tapped her chin. "No more tears. In a way they'll be here. Belle has made a permanent impression on you. Now that I've seen you in action, I can see what a capable young woman you are. Belle would be proud. And Dee is still a friend who is getting the help she needs. And Nicky, you understand he couldn't handle attending a wedding right now. He sent his best wishes to you both. And now, it's time for you to go upstairs and put on that beautiful gown of yours." I pulled out the piece of tissue and gently pulled back the corners. "And this is for you to take as your *Something Old.*"

When Cookie saw the piece of lace, she drew in a breath. "It's ...it's...."

"It was made by TJ's several greats-grandmother. He wants you to have it as a memento of your wedding here at Waterwood House." Her tears threatened to tumble down her cheeks. "Okay, young lady, it's time for you to get ready for your wedding."

The photographer caught all the lovely moments of preparation in the room upstairs that TJ had prepared for Cookie. The florist brought in her bridal bouquet.

There was Emma's scent again. "Wait! What flower is that?" I stuck my nose close to the snowy-white blooms.

Cookie's eyebrows shot up in surprise. "You mean the gardenias?"

"Yes, that's it!" *Emma's scent!*

"Yes, the gardenia has always been my favorite flower," Cookie said as the photographer gently positioned her for yet another picture.

It was time. TJ and I went down to the bottom of the staircase where we waited until the bride appeared. She would take his arm for that walk to the flower arch and her groom.

"You've done a beautiful thing here today, TJ," I spoke in a soft voice. I tilted my head in the direction of the portrait hanging in the hallway by the front door. "Emma would be proud of you."

He stared at the painting for a moment then leaned closer to me. "Maybe, in some way, it helps balance out the wedding she never had and the wedding she suffered through. I hope so."

We heard a sharp intake of breath from people around us and we turned to see a vision in white coming down the steps. Cookie was transformed. Her sweet smile spread happiness to us all as she took TJ's arm.

As I watched them make their way down the grassy aisle, I realized that even though I'd been burned once, I still liked the idea of marriage, having someone to share life with, someone I could depend on. But I wondered if I'd ever have the courage to try it again.

As the couple exchanged vows, I sent up a prayer that all the unhappiness was now behind them, and that Cookie and her David would have only small bumps in their life together.

White rose petals flew in the air as the couple made their way back to the house for a reception of refreshments and cake. I lingered by the door, not quite ready to go inside.

Thoughts of Emma filled my mind. This was the home she'd loved so much. Where she'd dared to have dreams and saw them shattered time and again.

A small flock of graceful white swans flew overhead, their wings sending a strange whistling sound through the air. Two settled in the water nearby. A stately blue heron stood almost motionless on the shore's edge, eyeing the water and what swam beneath the surface.

So many elements of what made the Eastern Shore special had gathered here. This was the place and the kind of wedding Emma should have had so many years ago. I could almost imagine her in the wedding dress of her dreams, standing with Daniel in his formal suit, there in the afternoon's golden sunlight. That's the way it should have been. I whisked away a tear from my lashes before my mascara ran.

The last guests made their way inside leaving me alone on the front lawn of this beautiful place, Waterwood. I looked out over the land and the light glinting off the water. A question seemed to be whispered by the breeze. It was the last question of her life:

Did Emma ever find her daughter?

AUTHOR'S NOTE

Thanks to Christine Jones and Jim Wolff of Historic House Parts, Rochester, N.Y. It is wonderful to have knowledgeable people get excited when I ask, "If Emma goes into the attic, what does she find?"

St. John's Chapel mentioned in this story truly exists and can be seen from the road and bridge as described. I find its history interesting as it shows how life evolves in a neighborhood. If you visit, do not go poking around the site. The area is fenced off because it is unstable. I would hate to lose a reader. Please appreciate it from afar.

The book, *Talbot County: A History* by Dickson J. Preston is a wonderful resource for those with an interest in the historical background of an area of the Eastern Shore.

Beth and Keith Shortall of Shortall Farm have patiently answered my questions about TJ's activities, especially about custom farming. Their experience and fascinating details add to the story.

When I started thinking about the wedding scene, I thought of Debbie of Swan Cove Florists, an institution here in St. Michaels. Always calm, creative, and happy with the freshest of flowers. I just couldn't do a wedding without her.

Cookie's real estate commission disaster happened to me when I first got my real estate license many years ago. My "Belle" was my broker and mentor. My sales contract was worth more than $3,000 to me. She offered me a check for $500 or the door. It was a special day of sweet revenge when I hit a million dollars in sales… because I took my license and left. Funny how real-life creeps into novels.

A very special thanks to Jeff Sanders, my computer guru! He saved the day when my computer froze and gave me the message, *Cannot Repair.* He revived my terrified psyche, secured a new computer, set it up in hours and pulled this book down from cloud in its entirety. Thank goodness he knew that I needed an automatic backup system.

Thanks to my writing buddies, friends, and wonderful readers who are so encouraging and supportive.

And as always, thanks to my family for your love and support always. Barry, Erin, Zoe, Matt, Maggie and our newest addition, Joey, I love you to the moon and back!

Susan Reiss
St. Michaels, Maryland

ST. MICHAELS
SILVER MYSTERIES

ST. MICHAELS
HISTORICAL NOVELLAS

AVAILABLE NOW   COMING 2022

IN TIME SERIES

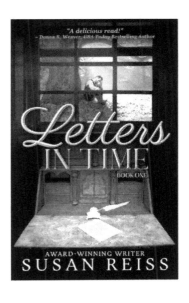

Made in the USA
Middletown, DE
29 October 2023

41463886R00205